AN ITHACA
AFFAIR

Jess William Esposito

ISBN: 153497847X
ISBN 13: 9781534978478
Library of Congress Control Number: 2016910688
CreateSpace Independent Publishing Platform
North Charleston, South Carolina

This book is dedicated to the people of Ithaca.
For it is this community that I will always cherish
and hold dear to my heart.

1

THE DECISION

"**I**thaca is gorgeous," I said to my wife, Allison, as we looked out across Beebe Lake. The sun was just starting to set on a beautiful and flawless summer day, and we were taking full advantage as we soaked up all the natural beauty that surrounded us. We were sitting together on the granite bridge, which was on the east side of the lake. It was our favorite place to rest and relax for a few minutes during our weekend walks and just enjoy the most serene lake in the world. At least that was how Allison and I felt about this little lake, which was a short walk from our house on Fall Creek Drive and adjacent to the north side of the Cornell University campus in Ithaca, New York. Most every weekend involved taking our golden retriever, Rosie, for a walk around the lake. It was a great way to start Saturday, and Rosie looked forward to it more than anyone.

"It certainly is," said Allison as she took a deep breath, smiled, and squeezed my hand. "Do you remember the first time we saw the bumper sticker?" she asked me. She was referring to the Ithaca Is Gorges logo, which was a play on words and made reference to the awesome and picturesque scenery of all the gorges and waterfalls in Ithaca.

I thought for a moment, and it came to my mind quite easily. "Yes, I sure do," I replied with a snicker. "The old Volvo station wagon—right?" I continued as I kept looking out across the lake. I was referring to the time we decided to move our family to town over fifteen years ago, and I remembered it so clearly, as it was an uncertain and tentative time that would ultimately change our lives forever.

Allison and I met at Cornell University, during our sophomore year. I was in the Applied Economics School, and she was studying mechanical engineering. And just like most kids, we met at a party, after a long week of classes. I remember trying to drum up enough courage to go over and talk to her. I also remember how unbelievably cute she was as she stood with her girlfriends, off to one side of the room. After a couple of beers and some prodding from my buddies, I made it across the room, walked up to her, and introduced myself. I don't quite remember what I said, but she laughed, and we spent the rest of the night together. I fell in love with Allison that night and will always remember it as the night I met my best friend.

Allison and I graduated together, and both of us accepted job offers with firms on Long Island. She accepted a position as an aerospace engineer at a major employer on Long Island, Drummond Aerospace, and I entered a financial advisor training program with Stanford James. We enjoyed a nice little life on Long Island and wound up buying a house on the north shore, in the little hamlet of Huntington. Allison had grown up in Charlotte, North Carolina, and her parents were still down there enjoying their retirement. I had grown up in Pleasant Beach, which was a small coastal town on the south shore of Long Island. It was nice to go back and forth from Huntington, make our way to the beach every weekend, and spend time with my parents and siblings. We had a great life. Pleasant Beach had the most wonderful stretch of wide beach, and it was so pleasurable to walk along the shoreline and enjoy the scenery and watch the break of the waves as the sandpipers scurried back and forth and seagulls flew over our heads.

I remember getting the big news one Saturday morning. I had gotten up early to go for a run around the neighborhood, and then I came back to the house to find Al still in bed. She had this big, sweet grin on her face, and a sense of calm was in the room.

"Are you okay, Al?" I asked her.

She smiled back at me, paused for a moment, and then told me her secret.

"I'm pregnant," she said softly.

I remember the instant joy of that moment. I sat on the bed next to her, leaned over and stroked her hair, and kissed her. We held each other for a long time that morning. It was the start of the next phase of our lives, and we were both ready to take that step.

Allison worked right up to her eighth month of pregnancy and then took time off and stayed at home. I was always so proud of her because she was such a hardworking person, but she also put her career on hold to stay at home. Our first daughter, Liz, was born in the middle of a cold January night, at Huntington Hospital. I was there for the delivery, and I remember the doctor telling me to sit down, as he was bringing Liz into this world. He said that I looked queasy and told me that redheads always seemed to faint a lot during birth. Allison still has a lot of fun reminding me, and everyone around us, about how the doctor had to pay more attention to me than to her during the birth of our first child.

As I said, Allison stayed home and took care of Liz as I went in each morning and worked on my licensing and trained every day at Stanford James. It was hard to leave them every morning, but I was so happy that Allison was the one watching our child and giving her a great start in life. A year and a half went by, and then Gracie came into this world to make us a family of four. Allison had to work a little harder to give birth, but everything came out great in the end. This time it was a beautiful summer evening, and I remained in the waiting room the whole time of the birthing process. Apparently, word gets around when you're a squeamish guy, and the doctors have enough to deal with during the delivery and don't want any distractions, especially someone like me, who could faint during the procedure. I remember going into the room to see Allison and Gracie, giving them a kiss, and looking at them in amazement. The doctor came back into the room to check on everyone and had a little bit of a laugh at my expense.

"Sorry I made you stay in the waiting room. It's always the big, tough-looking ones who seem to faint and drop the hardest on the floor during deliveries," he said, looking squarely at me with a slight smile on this face. He was a great guy and terrific doctor, and he gave Al every bit of his time during her stay at the hospital.

And so for the next four years of our lives, we lived on Long Island, and Allison put her career on hold and raised the girls while I went to work each day and did my training and studied for all the tests that were necessary to fulfill my licensing requirements for the financial industry. It was a great start to our lives, and we had a lot of fun bringing the girls back and forth to my parents' house on the weekends and going to the beach with them. Allison did such a wonderful job with the girls and was so gracious and unselfish to stay home with them every day, but after four years, I knew she was ready to get back to work. When the girls were napping, she spent a lot of time searching job openings on her computer. She no longer had any emotional ties to her old company and was open to anything at this stage of the game. We sat down to the dinner table one evening, and she asked me the question that would, ultimately, change our lives for years to come.

"What do you think about living in Ithaca?" she asked me as she tended to the girls dinner plates. She then looked up at me for my reaction as she dispersed vegetables to Liz's and Gracie's plates, much to their dismay. That question caught me off guard, and I looked back at her to see if she was being serious with her request.

"Ithaca? What do you mean?" I replied in a confused state.

Allison kept helping the girls. She poured each of them some more milk and explained her thoughts. "Well, I've been searching for openings on the computer, and there was one that came up at Cornell that looked perfect. It's an administrative position in the Biophysical Engineering Department. It's more of an entry-level management position…and I think it would be a great fit for me."

It totally caught me by surprise that she would consider moving back to upstate New York, right smack in the middle of snow country, but I didn't answer right away. I just started to think about all the great times we had had in Ithaca. Since we had both gone to Cornell, there was always a special place in our hearts for Ithaca. I started to think about the hockey games and pizza at the Nines. I started to think about hanging out with all our friends at parties all over the campus and spending time on Cayuga Lake. I remembered having so much fun in that college town and going to homecoming for football games. We worked our butts off at school, but we certainly had a great time when we put the books away. I'll be the first to admit, sometimes we had too good of a time. I thought for another moment or so and then looked over to Allison. She had given so much of herself to put her career on hold and raise the girls, and I could see how much this meant to her.

"Al, do you really want to move back there? Are you sure?" I asked as I looked to her and waited for a genuine response.

"Yes...I do. I think it would be a nice little life. I think the girls would love it. I know they are totally having a great time here. They love the beach, and we would miss your parents. But we would only be four hours away, and I would love to work on campus. The houses are a lot cheaper there, too," she said.

I clasped my hands together, brought them up to my chin, and rested my elbows on the table. I took a moment to digest her proposal. I would miss the beach, all right, but wouldn't miss the traffic. I would miss my mom and dad. Sometimes it was so cold up there that the snow squeaked when you walked on it. As I saw the look in Al's face, I realized that this was something she really wanted to do. I also knew, deep down in my heart, that she deserved this chance, should the opportunity present itself.

"Al, if you really want to give it a go in Ithaca, I'm all for it," I said with a firm nod coupled with enthusiasm.

"I was hoping you'd say that, Jack. I'm so happy you're willing to give it a shot. I think the girls will love it up there," she said with joy as she came over and gave me a hug. I knew I had said the right thing the moment she kissed me.

"Actually, to be perfectly honest, I've already reached out and had a long conversation about the position with Human Resources at Cornell. They thought I would have a real good chance to get the position, since my engineering background and experience gave me a little edge above the rest of the candidates. With that said, I have an interview next week for the job. I hope you're not mad at me. I thought we could all go up together and check the area out," she suggested. Allison was always one step ahead of me. She made me think that I was in control of the household and she pretended it was a democratic vote, but she knew exactly how to lure me in all the time. Ever since we had started dating in college, she had had the power to control me with her beautiful eyes and easy smile. I was always helpless in her grasp—and unbelievably in love with her, too.

And so I gave her a wry smile to acknowledge her victory and talent in the current negotiation.

The following week, we started our journey to upstate New York. It had been a while since Allison and I had graduated from college and a few years since we had been in Ithaca. The drive itself brought back a lot of fond memories of the road trip from Long Island to Ithaca. Every time I crossed over the Tappan Zee Bridge, my stress level and heart rate went down. The same thing happened this time. I always felt so at ease once I got through the Bronx and over all the bridges. That was really when the world opened up to me. I loved the drive along Route 17 and liked staring at all the small towns along the way. The Catskill Mountains were just a beautiful backdrop for a trip back to the town I held so close to my heart. The last leg of the journey was the half-hour ride down Route 79, which brought us into Ithaca. After passing through a bunch of small country hamlets, we turned right onto Pine Tree road, which brought us onto the Cornell campus. As we came to our first stoplight, we sat behind an old seventies Volvo station wagon. It was plastered with an array of bumper stickers, but one stood out more than the others. "Ithaca is Gorges" was what it said. We both must have read the sticker at the same time, because at the same moment, we just turned and looked at each other and smiled. It looked as if some college kid was making his way back to school, and it was quite ironic that we were driving a brand-new Volvo station wagon and had two little girls sleeping away in the backseat.

After we pulled onto campus and found a place to park over by Barton Hall, we woke the girls up and showed them a little of the campus. We took them over to the football field and told them about homecoming games and how much fun it was to play our rival schools. Then we went over to the hockey rink, walked inside, and showed them the arena. We thought it was a must to show them the most feared rink in college hockey. I always felt that the other teams must have thought they were being thrown to the lions in that place. The atmosphere during a game was unbelievable, and the students were a huge part of the show. Believe it or not, the biggest part of the venue was the band that got the kids super excited and enticed them into a frenzied state to do their cheers. You have to attend a game to know exactly what I'm talking about here. It was a lot of fun to wander around the campus and show the girls where we went to school. Liz and Gracie were only three and four years old, but they walked right along beside us and loved this little adventure.

"Well, it's time for my interview, guys. It's going to be about two hours," said Allison as she looked down at the girls and then up at me. She was checking to see if I could handle the girls for a couple of hours.

"I got this, Al. The girls and I are going to have some fun together and explore the town," I said in a positive and upbeat manner.

And with that said, Al bent over, kissed the two girls, and took off for the engineering quad for her appointment. I grabbed Liz and Gracie by the hand, and we headed back to our car. I got them buckled in their car seats, and we started our drive off campus, down the hill to the middle of town.

"Are you girls hungry?" I asked as I checked the rear-view mirror for their reaction. That was a silly question because these two were always hungry and could eat constantly throughout the day. It was a good thing they were extremely active outside the house and ran around a lot to burn off all the food.

"Yes, Daddy. We're starving," they said together.

So we drove down Buffalo Street, parked the car, and walked to my favorite lunch spot, Collegetown Bagels. I ordered my favorite sandwich, the Octopus, which I was glad to see still on the menu. I then ordered the girls two peanut-butter-and-jelly sandwiches on white bread. I might as well get them what they like, I thought. We grabbed the food and headed back to the car. I thought we could check out the town, or Commons, as it was referred to, after we picked up Allison later in the afternoon. It was such a nice summer day that I wanted to be near some water.

"Girls, Daddy is going to take you to one of my favorite spots for a picnic. It's a little slice of heaven, and I think you'll really like it," I announced buoyantly as I looked over my shoulder.

"Where are we going to have lunch, Daddy?" said Gracie, hoping that it wasn't going to be too far away.

"We're heading over to Robert Treman Park. There are plenty of picnic tables, and there's also a waterfall that comes down into the swimming area. I think you girls will love it. It was one of our favorite places to hang out on the weekends when we came up to visit in the summertime."

The girls' eyes got big as I told them about the waterfall. And they were even more astonished when we walked in through the gates and the waterfall and swimming area came into clear view.

"Wow, Daddy, it's amazing," said Gracie as her sister nodded.

I held their hands, and they just looked all over the park and at the swimming area, which had a bunch of people braving the temperature of the water. It came right down from the mountains, and I don't think it got warmer than sixty-five degrees. All the locals loved the place. It was a little sanctuary to most of the Ithacans, and the park always drew a big crowd on the weekends. The girls wanted to stay right in the action, so we picked a place on the grass, put out a few towels, sat down, and had lunch. Thank goodness for Allison, because she had packed us up some towels, bathing suits, bottles of water, and snacks. We were all set for a glorious day in the park.

"Daddy, what is the big line over there?" asked Liz with a puzzled look on her face. She was referring to the line behind the diving board. It must have been about ten to fifteen kids deep, which was the usual number at all times.

"That line is for the diving board, Liz. Just keep watching the kids," I said.

All three of us kept our eyes glued on the little boy who was getting ready for his plunge. He looked at his friends, who were standing in line behind him, and then he ran and sprang off the board into the chilly water below. He resurfaced and shouted out to everyone by the board, letting them all know how cold the water was. And then he made his way to the waterfall. The girls watched every move he made and followed him with sheer curiosity. The boy swam over to the ledge that sat right below the falls and let the water just gush onto him like a humongous shower. A group of swimmers would usually collect underneath the falls, and it was quite the workout to hold your position on the ledge because of the force of the pounding water.

We sat and ate our lunch and watched everyone around us. The girls' eyes were all over the place as they took in all the sunbathers around us and watched all the people swimming and jumping off the diving board. We walked around the park a little, and I showed them a lot of the surroundings. Both Liz and Gracie were very active and would never sit still for too long anyhow. Then we went back to our towels, grabbed our bathing suits, and changed in the park's restrooms. I took the girls to the edge of the shallow end of the swimming area, and we sat and dangled our feet in the water.

"Wow, that water is cold," said Gracie as her sister looked at her with total agreement.

We had a great time sitting and watching everyone and everything around us. It certainly brought back fond memories as I thought of the many times that Al and I had taken the plunge into this frosty but refreshing pool.

"Did you and Mommy come here a lot?" asked Liz, as her sister looked up to see the answer on my face.

"Did you dive off the board, Daddy?" Liz continued.

"Yes, Mommy and I would come here in the summertime, when school was over, and just sit and relax and enjoy the day. And the water hasn't gotten any warmer, either. And yes, I did go off the board, and I remember clinging to the ledge and letting the water fall all over me. It was great fun. We would come with a lot of our friends and spend the afternoon here. Great times," I replied as I looked in the direction of the top of the falls.

"I'm going to jump off the board when I get older, Daddy. After I finish swimming lessons," said Liz in a buoyant manner.

"Me too, Daddy. When we finish swimming lessons, I want to go off the board too," added Gracie, not to be outdone.

Her sister looked over at her with squinted eyes and a puckered-up face. These two were always very competitive, and they were only three and four years old. I could only imagine our household when they got to be teenagers, I thought.

We walked around the park some more, and then we rested on our towels and just people watched the rest of the day. After a couple of hours of fun, Allison called, and it was time to leave our lunchtime oasis and go pick her up. We hopped back in the car, made our way onto campus again, and picked up Al, who was sitting on a bench right outside Hoy Field, where the Cornell baseball team played all their home games. It has always been a beautiful place to watch a baseball game, and I would often stop and watch a few innings when there was an afternoon game and I had some time between classes. It was an even better sight to see Allison sitting there with a big smile on her face. She always had a wonderful smile. I really lucked out the day I met her and gathered the courage to introduce myself.

"Hi, guys. How was your day?" she asked, first looking at the girls and then over to me.

"We had a great time, Mommy. Didn't we, Gracie?" Liz replied with a huge smile.

I knew they were mine and I was biased, but they were both very cute girls, especially when they were happy and getting along with each other. On the other hand, look out for yourself and batten down the hatches when they were squabbling and nose to nose.

The girls proceeded to tell Al about their fun-packed day down at Treman, and we drove around the campus a little more. Then we headed over the Thurston Avenue Bridge and made our way into Cayuga Heights. This was a quaint village of Ithaca with a lot of historic homes, and it was just off the campus. When we were students, we didn't pay too much attention to different towns or school districts, but since we had became parents, we had gotten a lot more accustomed to knowing and learning about different school districts and property values. The Ithaca area was unique, and very fortunate, in that there were plenty of nice surrounding towns with great schools. I was aware that our company had a small office in Community Corners, which was a small shopping area just about one mile from Cornell and adjacent to Cayuga Heights.

With that said, we made up our minds, before we came up to Ithaca, to concentrate on this area and check out the Cayuga Heights Elementary School. So we drove over to the school, parked the Volvo, and wandered around the outside of the grounds. The girls got a glimpse of the playground, ran over to the swings, and went right to work competing to see who could get the highest off the ground. Each girl rocked and swayed back and forth with all her might.

"Well, tell me about the interview, Allison. How'd everything go?" I asked her as we parked ourselves at a picnic table adjacent to the playground.

"Actually, Jack, it went great. I would be doing a lot more administrative work than engineering, but I think it would be a perfect fit for me. It's more of a management role, and they like my experience working with engineers. Since I have an engineering degree, there would not be much of a so-called language barrier between the professors in the Biophysical Engineering Department and me. I talked for a long time with the Dean of Engineering, who would be my boss, and then met most of the department professors. They took me for a tour of the building and some of the labs, and then I had a nice lunch with the Dean, Leslie Wilkins. Oh my goodness, Jack. This is hard to say, but, long story short, she offered me the position," Allison said as she looked at me with an entertaining look on her face that was both elated and hesitant.

I looked at her and smiled, and then I looked over at Liz and Gracie, who were chasing each other around the playground and heading over to the big slide at the far corner of the playground.

"Well Al, I think it's up to you. You took a lot of time off to raise our girls, and that was quite unselfish of you. You put your career on hold—and did an excellent job, I might say. And they're grateful to have a great mom, and I'm grateful to have a wonderful wife. You've given our family a great start, and now it's your turn. If this is what you really want, then I think we can make it work," I said as I grabbed her hand with both of mine and looked right into her eyes.

She leaned over, gave me a kiss, and moved closer to me. We both sat for a moment and watched the girls take turns going up and down the slide.

"Thank you, Jack. I told Leslie that I would talk to you first and then sleep on it, and then get back to her in the morning. She was real nice about everything and knows this is a big move for our family," Al said as she looked over the school grounds and out at the neighboring houses.

"You know, it could be a great life, Al. I heard this is a great elementary school, and it's so close to campus. The neighborhood looks wonderful too. You would be working at Cornell, and Stanford James has a small office right in Community Corners. It could be a nice little life for our family. I would miss my mom and dad, though, and I would definitely miss the beach. But, I think we could make it work if you really want this job. There is one other item. What do you think Liz and Gracie would think?" I asked.

Allison nodded to me, and we both looked over to them again.

"Well, let's think about this some more and talk today and tonight, and then we'll make a decision in the morning. I think I know a great place to take the girls, and then we can ask them how they feel about moving to Ithaca. Since we're staying at the Statler, we can have dinner there tonight and then walk around campus some more. But first, we have to show the kids the Commons and have a little snack. You know all three of us girls have a huge sweet tooth," said Al as she looked over to the girls. She called them over to us.

"I know what you're thinking, Al. That would be buttering them up a little, wouldn't it?" I said with a wry smile.

"Hey, girls, how about we go downtown and have cookies. We're going to go to the Home Dairy. They make the best half-moon cookies. They're huge cookies that have chocolate frosting on one half and vanilla frosting on the other. How does that sound?" asked Allison, enticing the youngsters as I shook my head.

"Yea! Thanks, Mommy!" they screamed in unison as they jumped up and down. Allison and I smiled at each other, and we had a nice family hug on the playground that day. Then we took off for downtown, had half-moon cookies, and let the kids play on the swings and run around the playground. They were having quite the day, and I knew they would sleep well that night.

But now it was time to call them over and ask about how they would feel about living in Ithaca. I called them over to where we were sitting, and then Al sprang the question on them.

"You guys look like you're having a great time out there. Did you have a great day?" asked Allison.

"Yes, Mom, it's been wonderful. I love Ithaca," said Gracie as she looked at us with a chocolate-stained New York Rangers T-shirt. It was impossible to keep her clean, no matter how hard we tried or how many napkins we gave her.

"Me too, Mom. They have swings all over the place in Ithaca. Can I have another one of those moon cookies?" said

Liz, with an excited look on her face. Liz was one year older, and, unlike Gracie, she was very neat and never needed to be told to use a napkin. Not that there is a huge difference between three and four years old, but Al and I knew each had her own little personality, and we loved that they were a little different.

Then Allison asked the big question with little bit of hesitation. "How would you guys like to live in Ithaca?"

"Really? That would be awesome!" said Gracie, nodding quickly, big eyes sending her answer loud and clear. Then she took off for the swings again.

"Wow, Mom. That would be great. The school looks great, and they have the park, and the best cookies, too. Does that mean you got the job, Mom?" asked Liz with excitement. Again, she was only four years old, but she was quick and right on top of things, as usual.

"I didn't accept it yet. But yes, I was offered the job," Al said as she looked over at me for reinforcement.

"We would love to move here. It would be amazing," Liz said enthusiastically, and then she ran over to play with her sister.

Al and I just looked at each other and laughed. We really hadn't known how the kids would react to a move upstate, but we were sure glad they had responded so happily. I think kids are just so open to change, especially at a younger age. We watched the kids on the playground and talked more about this possible change in our lives. Then we grabbed the girls, strolled around the Commons, and popped in and out of some local boutiques. Downtown Ithaca was such a unique place and really had a good combination of ways to entertain kids, with a few different play areas as well as nice shops and restaurants. The students from Cornell and Ithaca College always wound up down there with their families on parents' weekends, but the place took on a whole new meaning when it was just the students there. I remembered popping in and out of a few different establishments for beverages with a gang of friends and then finally making it home in the wee hours of the morning. Of course, we might stop by Manos Diner for a quick bite before we all went back to campus and hit the sack. It certainly kept bringing back memories as we strolled around the town.

Then we took the girls up to the Statler Hotel, which was located right on campus, and got situated in our room. Liz and Gracie were looking pretty exhausted, so we just ordered some pizza up to the room. It wasn't that long after we finished our dinner that we gave the girls a bath and put them both to bed. They went out like a light, and Allison and I stayed up and tried to give this idea a little extra thought. Actually, it wasn't long afterward that we each took a shower and hit the hay ourselves. It had been a long and tiresome day, but a fun one, for all of us, and we were certainly glad we had made the trip.

The next morning, we decided to get on the road early and head back to Long Island. I went out early and grabbed some bagels for the ride, and then we made our way off campus. It was another beautiful sunny day. The trip down Route 17 was exquisite, and it was quite enjoyable to talk with the girls as we showed them the different towns. They seemed to be mesmerized by the countryside and mountains as their eyes soaked up all the beautiful scenery. We got about halfway home, and the girls started their nap.

"Well, Al, do you want to go for it?" I asked.

She looked at me and then back toward the highway. She looked excited but reluctant, and then she answered my question. "I do. I really do. I think it would be wonderful."

I grabbed her by the hand and smiled. "Why don't we pull over, then, and you can make that call to the Dean," I suggested warmly.

So we found a little rest area along the way and pulled into a parking spot. Al got out with her cell phone while I watched the kids. A couple of minutes later, she got back in the car, looking like a kid on Christmas, and gave me the news.

"I accepted the position, Jack, and I'm slated to start in sixty days. They'll even help with our move and get us situated if our house isn't sold by that time.

"I hope you're happy, Jack. Thank you," she continued.

I was nervous about the move and about telling my parents, but I was also happy for our family, and I was definitely happy for Allison.

"Al, I'm very happy. I'm proud of you, and I love you," I told her.

She looked back at me with her beautiful smile, and then she leaned over and gave me a kiss, and then she looked back toward Gracie and Liz, who were still sound asleep in the backseat.

"I love you too," Al said as we pulled out of the rest area.

Everything went pretty quickly after we got back home and put the game plan together. We had a lovely house, and it sold inside a couple of weeks, and we spent a lot of time putting together boxes of all our belongings and making arrangements with the moving company. We contacted the girls' schools and made the necessary contacts for the Ithaca schools as well. They were both pretty excited to start at Cayuga Elementary

School, and it worked out that they would be there for the first day of classes, which was just after Labor Day. I had a few meetings and conference calls with my company leaders at Stanford James, and they prepared an office for me in the Community Corners branch. We also spent a lot of time with Grandma and Grandpa at the beach over those two months. I think we went there every weekend. We were certainly all going to miss being close to each other, but they were happy for us just the same, and we were really only about four hours away. That wouldn't be too far for some weekend visits, and I told them we would make it down as much as humanly possible. My mom and dad were always looking out for our best interests, so they understood everything and were very happy for us.

Allison spent a lot of time working with an Ithaca realtor and looking at houses online. She fell in love with an old colonial revival that was just off campus, in Cornell Heights. The realtor told her that these homes moved very fast because they were extremely desirable, due to their proximity to campus, and that a lot of professors tended to snatch them up rather quickly. Long story short, we wound up putting an offer on a house without even seeing it first. Allison loved all the old features with this house. It had a nice little yard, and the realtor said it had "good bones." I guess that's something they use to get the sales on these older homes, but she was certainly right about the sturdiness of the house.

And so, just before Labor Day, we closed on our house on Long Island, packed up the car, and made our way upstate to check out our new home. The moving van had come the day before and would meet us in Ithaca in two days. We had said our good-byes to my parents and all our friends, and everyone was looking forward to starting the next phase of our lives. The girls were extremely excited, but I could tell that Allison was the happiest of all.

The girls slept most of the way this time, and they woke up just after Whitney Point, which was about thirty minutes from campus. We stopped alongside the road on Route 79, picked them up ice cream cones, and then headed down the road again. We made the right onto Pine Tree Road and made our way through campus and across the Thurston Avenue Bridge. It was just a few blocks past the bridge that we took a left and found 502 Fall Creek Road. I pulled into the driveway, and everyone had huge smiles as we stepped out of the car. Allison and I stood together in the driveway as the girls ran to the back of the house and then back around to the front yard. Then they ran up to the front porch and checked out the view of the yard from up top as they bounced around with excitement.

"Mommy, can we go in?" shouted Gracie as she and her sister looked for approval.

"Yes; I believe it should be open," Al shouted back to them. It was a wonderful 1911 yellow colonial revival with white trim, and it had big black shutters that gave it quite the classic historic look. Both Allison and I loved the architecture of older homes and thought they were well designed and built better than a lot of the newer homes.

The girls opened the door and ran inside to check it out. Allison and I followed them in and shut the door behind us. It all happened so fast and furious, but that was how we began our lives in Ithaca.

"It all just seems so long ago, Al," I said whimsically as I looked around the lake.

"Time sure has flown by, hasn't it, Jack?" she replied as we both admired our surroundings. The stone bridge was such a nice place to rest during the walk. You had a great view in front of you and a great view of the lake behind you. Just before the start of the bridge, there was a walkway that took you back to a beautiful little waterfall. It had a little wooden bench overlooking the falls, and usually it was just Rosie and I who went up that way. I guess that was just one of our special places. She loved to look at the moving water as much as I did. Every once in a while, we saw some college kids diving or swimming around there, but not too much anymore. I guess there were just too many spots for them to cool off during the hot days.

As Al and I leaned on the ledge of the stone bridge, I glanced over to Rosie's area. There was a small overlook just past the bridge that had a big oak tree hanging over a long and bending stone bench. Rosie loved to lie down on the slate underneath the tree. She was pretty hairy, and this kept her nice and cool. I usually brought a water bowl in a backpack on our walks and poured some water for her, and she would take a break as we sat on the bench and rested for a few minutes. Now, Al was my first true love, and the girls I loved dearly, but Rosie was always my special love. She was just a sweet dog. I never had to chase her down, and she always listened to me and was just a great companion. She was slowing down a bit at twelve years old, but we took our time whenever we walked the lake.

"Ready, girl?" I asked Rosie as I leaned over and picked up her dish. She popped up, and we moved along to our next spot.

We headed down another hundred yards or so to what we considered the most romantic spot in the world. There was a larger overlook that had two small, round picnic tables with oval benches. Both of these tables provided a great view of the lake, but the one on the left had the only bench that faced the lake. This was our spot. Rosie knew right away to tuck down under the table, and we unloaded our small backpack. Al always packed us a lunch for our Saturday walks around the lake. She usually tucked in some sandwiches, a small container of white wine, and some water. We had a bite to eat and a glass of wine and watched the Canadian geese land on the water. There was a small marsh island in the middle of the lake, and there was usually a blue heron or family of ducks playing around this area too. It was just so peaceful and romantic at the same time. When lunch was done, we usually completed our stop with a kiss and then moved along the other side of the lake. There was an upper and a lower path around the lake. But the picnic area led to the upper path, so we usually completed our walk along the top of Beebe.

We made our way to the end of the lake, which had a small footbridge that crossed Triphammer Falls. We usually took another short break there and watched the falls for a bit. As we watched the water flow, Rosie would always get to say hi to a few passersby. People loved to stop and pet her as they moved by. I guess it was just a calmness that they sensed, so she was very approachable.

After a few minutes, we continued off the bridge and left Beebe Lake and made our way onto Thurston Avenue and headed home. The walk always made for a great start to the afternoon, and we all felt so lucky to be just a stone's throw away from such a romantic lake.

2

MOM AND THE GIRLS

Mom and Dad wound up moving to Ithaca about ten years ago. Dad had suffered his first heart attack, and my mom thought it would be better if they lived near us so they could spend their golden years with family. They bought a nice little ranch on Cayuga Heights Road and are only about a mile from our house on Fall Creek Road. It's been great having them so close and spending time with them through the years. They attended a lot of school and sporting events for the girls, and Al and I have gotten to spend a lot of quality time with them as well. Liz and Gracie wound up playing a lot of different sports growing up before settling into golf and hockey. There's a great girls' hockey association here in Ithaca, and my mom and dad made it to every home hockey game and golf tournament. The girls absolutely love seeing their grandparents in the stands or on the fairways watching and cheering for them.

It was about a year ago that we checked Dad into Bridges, an assisted living house in the middle of Cornell Heights, only a short walk from our home. It was a beautiful place, inside and out, and it had a bunch of wonderful people working there. This place was just amazing, and the staff provided an impeccable level of care to all its residents. They had everything you could imagine to make one's stay completely comfortable, as if you were living at home. There were plenty of licensed professionals on site, as well as a world-class chef and concierge. The three homes that made up Bridges were beautifully appointed turn-of-the-century mansions, and each was designed in its own distinct manner. They sat adjacent to each other, and Dad lived in a magnificent Tudor Revival. Just when you thought you were in awe of the exterior, you would walk inside and become completely taken aback. To just look around and see the huge French doors, which were originally from an Argentinean monastery, and the high ceilings and Persian rugs and cherry woodwork made you stand still and gaze at its beauty for a few moments. My parents were blessed to be able to afford this luxury, and, to this day, we feel that all the people who work at this grand establishment are an extension of our family.

My dad needed a little too much extra care, and the doctors suggested to Mom that he should be in a place that would provide him with twenty-four-hour care. He was getting more and more forgetful as time went by, and the physicians had diagnosed him to be in the early stages of Alzheimer's. After a few uncomfortable episodes that frightened my mom, we knew a tough decision had to be made. Also, he was on special medicines for his heart condition, and Mom wanted to make sure that he had trained nurses and caregivers close by. It was tough for all of us to have him live somewhere other than his own home, but everyone knew it was for the best.

Dad was eighty-eight years old, a very strong-willed and proud individual, so, needless to say, he didn't go without a fight. He has always been a great dad and has given a lot of love to all us kids. He spent a lot of his free time coaching all of us in various sports and really enjoyed having a lot of family time. We did a lot of camping when we were kids and went on a lot of family trips. It seemed that camping was the most affordable way for our family to take vacations, and we all looked forward to spending the week at Lake George or the Catskill Mountains. It was quite a lovely childhood for all of us. We all played sports year round and took family vacations in the summertime. As you would expect from an old military man, he taught us a lot about life from his personal experiences and travels around the world while he was in the service during the Korean War. He spent a lot of time teaching us about tools and showed us how to maintain and work on cars, too. We really learned a lot from our father and it was tough to see him in this fragile state, but I guess that's the circle of life. As I said, he's getting more and more forgetful, but we still have great conversations to this day. Mom walks over to our house every Sunday morning, and we have a cup of coffee and then walk over to see Dad, which has become part of our weekend routine.

"Well, good morning, Rosie," Mom said as she walked in through the back door and Rosie greeted her with a fast-wagging tail and big smile. Actually, Rosie greeted everyone who came to the house in the same manner, but I've never mentioned that to Mom.

"Good morning, Mom," I replied as I looked up from the dining room table.

"Hi, Mom," added Allison as she made her way into the dining room. "I see Rosie has already said hello," she continued with a little laugh.

"Come on in, Mom, and have a seat. I'll get you a cup of coffee," I said as I made my way over to the coffee pot and poured her a cup.

"Thank you, Jack," replied Mom as she pulled up a chair to the table. "Are the girls up yet?" she asked with a slight grin.

"It's only nine o'clock, Mom. We have another three hours before those two shake themselves out of bed and come downstairs," replied Allison. Mom was well aware that teenagers tended to stay up late and sleep late as well, especially on weekends and during the summer months.

"What have you been up to, Mom?" I asked as I took a sip of coffee.

"Well, I've been keeping quite busy. I've been playing a lot of golf down at Newman with the ladies' league, and I'm doing okay. But I need to keep working on my short game. The gals down there can really play, and in order for me to keep up with them, I need to be better at chipping and putting. I was hoping to get some more tips from Gracie and Liz. I'll call them later to see if we can set up a tee time to play later this week," she said as she took another sip of coffee. My mom was referring to the nine-hole municipal golf course that sits just off the inlet of Cayuga Lake and has always been held in high regard by a lot of the local golfing talent, especially Liz and Gracie, who have been playing down there since they were in elementary school.

"You know they love to play with you, Mom. Give them a call. In order for those two to wake up early, you need to set a tee time. That way they're up and out of the house on time," said Al as she chuckled.

"I will, Allison. Well, what do you say, Jack? Shall we get going to see your dad?" asked Mom. She finished most of her coffee and placed the cup on the table.

"Let's do it," I replied as I stood up from the table and grabbed the basket of cookies that Mom had prepared for Dad. I kissed Al and said good-bye, and we headed out the door and started our walk over to Bridges. Since we lived just off campus and the assisted living home was just a few blocks away, it was very convenient to stop by and check in on my dad and visit with him at a moment's notice. It was usually just my mom and I who walked over on Sunday mornings, and that little stroll gave us some personal time together to catch up with each other and talk about my dad.

"How's he been doing, Mom? Any changes lately?" I asked as we walked through the neighborhood.

She took a deep breath and then looked at me and grabbed my hand. "He's doing okay, Jack. Some days are better than others, but all in all, he's doing okay. I've been getting over there at least twice every day, and we sit together and watch TV. You know your dad. He can be stubborn as a mule sometimes. I think when these older macho guys, like your dad, start to slow down and can't do what they want to do and how and when they want to do it—and used to do it—it just seems harder for them to make the transition to old age. Especially into an assisted living situation with nurses and other people around you all the time. The staff is wonderful at this place, and they all like your dad. You know he can be quite the flirt and quite likeable when he wants to be," she said with a smile.

"He can be at that, Mom. He can be at that," I said as I squeezed her hand. It was always a special thing to walk the neighborhood and hold my mom's hand. We had such nice conversations, and it always made me feel good. I had nice talks with my dad throughout the years, but my mom was a great listener. She was really in tune to what I was saying, and it was just a little easier to talk to her most of the time. My dad and I talked a lot about work and sports and politics. He was a great educator, and he taught us all about all the fundamental necessities that one needs to know to make one's way through life. Mom and I just seemed to operate on a different wavelength. We talked a lot about the girls and their boyfriends and about my relationship with Al and our friends. I guess that just made it more of a personal conversation to me.

We strolled up the stone steps to the entrance of the home and went inside. This time of the morning, my dad would be finished with his breakfast, so we went right to his room on the second floor. We said hello to some of the nurses and other patrons on the way, and then we came to Dad's room and looked inside. He was sitting in his chair, to the left of his bed, watching TV. He usually had the news on the television, or a baseball game or golf during the summer.

"Hi, Dad," I said with a smile, and he turned and looked up to us. He had on a nice white polo shirt with a pair of khakis and his bedroom slippers. He was always a snappy dresser and just gravitated to wearing his slippers a lot when he sat around his room.

"Well, hello there, you two. Come on in," he said with a big smile. It took a moment for him to focus, but it sounded as if this was a good day for him. His memory had been going in and out and he was getting quite forgetful, but every once in a while he would surprise you and seem right on top of his game.

"Hi, Ben. How are you this morning, dear?" my mom asked. She walked over to him and gave him a kiss and rubbed his back. My parents have always been very devoted to each other, and they loved each other very much. It was hard on both of them to be apart.

"I'm doing good, Kate. I miss you," he said as he looked up at her and smiled. "I wish I didn't have to stay here, but I understand, I guess," he continued.

As I looked up to the television, I knew exactly what he was watching. The British Open was on, and he had gotten up early to watch it. Coverage started at 5:00 a.m., and this was one of our favorite professional golf events. Both of us liked to watch the best players in the world struggle against the elements of nature on the famous links course St. Andrews in Scotland. His favorite player was Jack Nicklaus, and mine was Tom Watson. Both of them had multiple wins at the Open Championship under their belt, and Tom had won the event an amazing five times. As I looked over at my dad, I remembered all the times we had gotten up early together to watch this tournament. My dad would wake me up when I was very young, and he would make us breakfast, and we would sit together on the sofa in the living room and watch the tournament together. I loved to do that with my dad. It got to a point that I was really excited the night before and found it hard to sleep. It was like Christmas in July for me. I also reminisced about the times he would wake me up at 4:00 a.m. to go play golf at Bethpage. This was another course that was nationally renowned, and golfers got up early and showed up at the gates to play because you couldn't make tee times. And to this day, diehard golfers still arrive at its gates in the middle of the night and wait in line to secure a coveted tee time. Yes, we certainly had some great experiences that revolved around early-morning golf.

"Hi, Pop. Who's on the leader board?" I asked as I walked over and gave him a smile and a hug and then looked up at the television. I could see there were tough conditions this morning; the flags were waving heavily back and forth with the wind, and it was raining pretty hard, and the players were in their rain gear and had winter hats on. I loved watching this event, and it made me chuckle to see these guys brave the elements. It was a pure test of mental strength and courage. I had stopped by to see Dad on Friday to see replays of the first two mornings of play, but I missed Saturday's coverage. With my work schedule and chasing the girls around with their sports, it was a lot harder these days to watch the entire event together, as we had done when I was a teenager.

"The Europeans are dominating the board now, Jack, but Phil and Tiger are right behind them," he said, and then he took another sip of his coffee.

"How you doing, Jack? How's...Al?" he continued as he looked up to me. He seemed to pause and ponder a moment to remember her name, but it finally clicked.

"Everyone is great, Dad. Allison is home getting some things done, and she sends her love. The girls were still sleeping when we left this morning. They're excited to be going to school soon. Golf and hockey practice start as soon as they arrive on campus. They'll be right into it, and I think they're just enjoying as much time as possible with their friends while they're home. They also seem to be sleeping in as much as possible. I guess they always did that whenever they didn't have a golf or hockey tournament, though."

"I miss those kids. Could you tell them to stop by later, Jack?" Dad asked, looking up with a kind smile. My dad spent a lot of time with the girls and treasured every moment.

"Of course, Dad. They would love to stop by, and as soon as I get back, I'll tell them to swing on over. You know how much they like the Open," I replied.

I then pulled up a chair and sat down next to my dad, and the three of us watched golf together for the next two hours. I loved talking sports with him, but we really connected with golf. As far as we were concerned, it didn't get any better than watching the British Open at St. Andrews in Scotland. And if you had some wind and rain thrown in there, well, that just made it the best golf in the world. My dad and my mom had been to St. Andrews, and that made it even more special. They would comment on the course or the town, and we could sit and talk and watch television for hours. Since my dad had played St. Andrews, he would be able to give me a little more inside information as we watched the professionals try to navigate the course on television. The pot bunkers were my favorite menacing feature to keep an eye on, and if one of the players wound up in one, well, it was just awesome to see how he would choose to recover and get himself back into position. As I watched television with my dad, my mom straightened up his room and got us some drinks from down the hall. She then came over and sat on the arm of my dad's chair and rubbed his back and kissed his forehead.

"I love you, Ben," she whispered to him as they looked into each other's eyes.

"I love you too," he replied as he grasped her hand.

After we watched a little more, we all got up and sat at Dad's small table and had some cookies and drinks and talked some more as the golf played in the background.

"How's Liz been hitting the ball? Is she excited to get back to school and have another good year?" Dad asked as he took another bite from one of Mom's homemade cookies.

"She's been hitting it real nice, Pop. Short game is on, too. Her chipping and putting are awesome. I think she's going to have a great second year. She's gotten a lot of nice practice in down at Newman. You know how the girls love that course. She always seems to get down there for the skins games on Saturday mornings to take all those old guys' money, too. She was always a hustler," I responded with a slight grin.

"That's my girl," Dad said proudly with an even bigger grin.

"That Liz takes right after her grandfather," said Mom as she shook her head. She didn't like Liz playing in the skins game, but she knew the competition made her a better golfer. There were always a lot of pretty good players involved on Saturday mornings, and even some retired local professionals would show up from time to time to get in on some of the fun. It was mostly for bragging rights, and the players just enjoyed the competition and the good old-fashioned needling that went along with the matches.

"How's Gracie doing?" asked Dad.

"She's doing great, Pop. She's very excited to get up to Clarkson. She says the team will be stacked this year, and as a freshman, she has her work cut out for her. But she's big and tough, and that comes in handy for a defenseman. She also sees the ice well and has a knack for moving the puck out of the zone and to an open forward," I replied.

"That girl has always had soft hands. It certainly comes in handy for a hockey player. And she always plays really physical.

I think she'll get up there and do great. I told her to knock a few players down hard during practice, and she'll get time," said Dad in a boastful manner.

"Honey, that's not necessary," my mom chimed in. She loved sports but was always a little partial to golf. On the other hand, my dad loved to watch the girls play all sports, especially hockey. He would cheer really loud whenever Gracie or Liz knocked another player down on the ice during a game. That always made my mom uncomfortable, and the other player's parents would stare at him in the stands. But he wasn't fazed one bit. He's always been very competitive and loves the physical play of hockey. I guess that's the reason Gracie has grown up into such a rough-and-tumble hockey player.

"That's how the game needs to be played, Kate. If Gracie wants to make the team as a freshman, she needs to knock some other players on their butts," retorted Dad in proud fashion.

"I guess you're right, dear...just that it's a penalty to do that, you know," said Mom as she got up and started to straighten out Dad's room a bit more. She always tried to add a woman's touch to his room and straighten out his bed and make sure all his clothes were in order in his dresser. Mom loved Dad, and she missed him at home. A piece of her was missing when he was not around. But, she knew he needed a little more professional care, just in case he had any more episodes that would put him in danger and she wasn't around to watch him. It was for the best, and we realized that it was a necessary precaution, and we all knew he was safer with highly trained people around him at all times.

"You don't have to worry about Gracie at all, Dad. She's made plenty of good teams by her physical play, so she's used to that, for sure," I added with a smile. It felt great to visit with my dad. It always did. Just to sit with my parents and talk about the girls and watch television together made me feel good inside. It had a different feel to it, because it was in an assisted living facility and not my parents' home, but it felt good just the same. Some of my fondest memories are of the three of us huddled around the television and watching golf. It just makes for an easy and relaxing day.

After a couple of hours, I felt it best to let my mom and dad have some time to themselves. This was when my mom could inquire about any tests or results or any other personal issues that involved my dad. She felt he opened up a little more when they were alone.

"Well, you guys, I'd better get back to the house and check on the girls. I need to make sure they do a couple of chores around the house and help Al. I'll have them stop over later, Pop," I said as I stood up. I then gave my mom a kiss and hug and bent over and kissed my dad on the head and told them good-bye. As I kissed my dad on the head, he looked up at me with loving eyes. He was a real tough guy with a big heart. As he looked at me, I could always see that he loved me. I could always sense that it was tough for him to see me leave his room. And he was right. I missed him, and he missed me.

I left the room and walked down the hall and smiled at the staff on my way out. The sun was shining, and it was quite warm for this part of the day. I stood on the steps and looked up toward the sky. I felt blessed and sad at the same time. I walked over to a bench that was under a massive mulberry tree on the front corner of the property and sat down. I began to reminisce about my dad, when he was a younger man. He was so big and tough and compassionate at the same time.

He was always there for us kids, and he was always there for my mom. It was hard to see him in such a fragile state, but I was very thankful he was still with us. And he has certainly always been there for the girls. They love their grandparents and have always spent a lot of time with them. Even as they both have gotten older, they're still not embarrassed to run up and give my dad a big hug and kiss in public. He certainly loves them with all his heart as well.

I sat at the bench for a while and thought about the past. I thought of when my dad used to drive me to hockey and golf practices and games. He was and always has been a great father. Right before I got up to leave, I looked up to my dad's window. He had a room facing the front yard. My mom was standing in the window looking down at me. I smiled and waved to her, and she waved back. Then I got up and went out through the gate and walked back home.

As I walked up the back steps of the house, I glanced in through the window to the kitchen. Allison was making some more coffee, and I just stood and watched her for a while. She didn't notice that I was standing at the window on the back steps. I always felt so lucky to have her in my life. She's such a beautiful and caring woman and a great mother. I watched her for a moment and thought of all the little features that attracted me to her when we were young. Even at forty-eight years old, she was a very attractive woman. I smiled and went in through the back door and was met by my number-one fan.

"Hello, Rosie," I said as I bent over and gave her a rub on her ears with both my hands. Her smile was ear to ear, and her tail was wagging a mile a minute. I then looked up at Al and walked over and embraced her as she rested her coffee cup on the counter.

"Hi, honey," I said softly and then gave her a kiss. I rubbed her back as we looked at each other, and we both exchanged warm smiles. I then noticed the full coffee pot to my delight and proceeded to pour myself a cup.

"How's your dad?" asked Allison with a look of concern in her eyes.

"He's doing good, Al. It was a good morning. Mom and I sat with him for a long time and watched golf and ate cookies. He was in good spirits and asked about the girls, too," I replied and then took a sip of coffee.

"I'm glad. I know it's hard on you guys to have him there, but it's definitely the safest and most caring place he can be. And he's right around the block from us, too," said Allison.

"Yes, I'm happy he's safe. It's tough on Mom to not have him home, but it's for the best. It's different not visiting him at his own house, and I think we're still just getting used to it. I guess it's just going to take some more time for me. It was fun watching the Open with him, though. He also asked about you, of course," I added as I leaned against the kitchen counter and looked back at Allison, feeling a bit melancholy.

"Are the girls up?" I asked as I strolled toward the dining room and looked around the corner. I didn't see anyone at the table, but I heard them coming down the stairs together. Most everything was in its original state in our home, so there were a lot of creaks in our old stairs. You couldn't go up or come down without everyone hearing you. Al and I just stood together in the kitchen doorway as Liz and Gracie staggered down the stairs and took seats at the dining-room table. Al and I looked at each other with a smile and then back over at the girls. It was almost noon, but you would have thought it was three in the morning by their body language. They had stayed up in the yard last night and had a small bonfire and just talked till the wee hours of the morning. Even though they were very competitive, they were each other's best friends. We always felt they were at their best when they had time to sit and talk with each other. There were plenty of times when we would stay up and just listen to the girls talk and share stories about sports or school or boys.

"You girls stay up late last night? It's a little late for breakfast, you know," I said teasingly as I looked at them resting their heads on the table and then over to Al.

I knew how to perk them up, though. "Since it's too late for breakfast, how's about we go get some Pinesburgers?" I asked.

Both Liz and Gracie raised their heads quickly and produced huge smiles and became energetic almost immediately.

"Oh, yeah, Dad!" they shouted in conjunction. Then they came over and gave me a hug and ran upstairs to change for lunch.

Allison looked over at me with a smirk. "Sure, I get to tell them to clean their rooms, and you get to announce lunch at Glenwood Pines. I guess you'll win the best parent award this year," Allison said sarcastically.

"Just motivating the little darlings, Al. Don't worry; we'll squeeze them for some chores later on today," I said in a confident tone.

It was a great Sunday afternoon in Ithaca. We drove up the west side of the lake and had lunch, and then we came back down and stopped at Purity for ice cream. "Best ice cream on the planet" has always been Allison's motto. Then we headed to Buttermilk State Park to swim and lie in the sun. It was a great family day. By the time we arrived back home, it was six o'clock and still pretty warm outside. We decided to grill up some hamburgers and hotdogs and eat outside at our picnic table. While I grilled and Allison prepped the table, Liz and Gracie played with Rosie in the side yard. By the time dinner was ready, everyone had worked up another appetite and Rosie was totally content just to rest on the cool slate patio in the backyard. As everyone ate, I stared over at Allison, and she smiled back at me. Again, I always thought she had the most beautiful smile.

3

BACK TO WORK

"It's impossible. How do Monday mornings come so fast?" Allison asked as the alarm in our bedroom went off. She was still lying in bed with her face wedged between two pillows. I was up and standing in front of my dresser mirror, fixing my tie.

"I'll bring you up some coffee, Al," I said as I watched her stir in the mirror. Then I made my way downstairs and fixed each of us a cup of dark roast and brought it back to her. She still had her face between the pillows and was sprawled under the covers across the entire bed. I put her cup down on the nightstand and then grabbed the remote and turned on the television, which was positioned up in the far corner of the bedroom. We usually watched a little news as we sipped coffee and got ready for work each morning.

"It's already seven thirty, Al," I said softly as I rubbed her back.

She then turned over, and I handed the cup to her. She yawned and then produced a big and easy smile. "I don't know why I'm still so tired," she said as she took a sip and turned her head to the television.

"I have a busy day, Al. I have a lot of back-to-back meetings this morning and then a conference call in the afternoon. I'd better get going. I'm sure Maggie wants to review all the paper work before the clients come in this morning," I said as I stood up.

"She sure keeps you organized, doesn't she?" said Al, referring to my trusty assistant.

"Yes, she sure does. If it weren't for her, I'd be very disorganized at work. And if it weren't for you, I'd be very disorganized at home. I'm grateful for both of you."

Allison smiled at me, and I leaned over and kissed her good-bye.

"Have a great day yourself. I'll catch you at dinner. If you want, I'll cook some spaghetti tonight too," I said as I made my way down the stairs.

"Sounds good. See you later," she yelled back.

My office was less than a mile from the house, and it only took a few minutes each morning to get there. I could actually walk to work, but since I wear a suit, I was more comfortable driving to the office. Stanford James had a real nice business model. There were usually just two or three financial advisors, an administrative assistant, and a receptionist at each office. They were a community-oriented firm, so they usually were found in small towns across the country. The home offices were located in Connecticut and Long Island. We had a terrific location in Community Corners, which was a small section at the northern end of Cayuga Heights. It had a few restaurants, shops, and businesses, and it had a lovely, quaint feel about it.

The other two advisors in my office were Teddy Rodgers and Rocky Flynn. Rocky's real name was Ralph, and he told us that his mom nicknamed him Rocky in junior high school. Apparently he was getting beaten up a lot in school, so his mother wanted to give him a tough name to help out his image to try to protect him. She named him after Rocky Balboa, the character that Sylvester Stallone played in the Rocky movies. I guess it just stuck. He always kids us that it never really helped him, but since his mother picked it for him, he never had the heart to change it. Since Rocky is only around five foot three, we had a lot of fun with the name and teased him a little. He had a great sense of humor and could give it back just as well. Teddy, on the other hand, was six foot four and a little straighter laced than the rest of us. I believe he was valedictorian of his class in high school and did just as well at Syracuse University. He was a marketing major, and it came in handy in promoting his business over the years. We were all relatively the same age and had great chemistry. Stacey was the receptionist and was just out of community college and perfect for the front line. She had a tremendous personality, and the clients loved her. She was quick with a cup of coffee or water and greeted them with a huge smile. Maggie was the main cog of the engine in our office. Without her, we would be running into one another all day long. She kept us totally on schedule and organized and did it with great temperament. It's not easy to keep three guys in line, but she had it down to a science. We paid her very well, and she was worth every nickel, if not more. Every morning there was a *Wall Street Journal* on each of our desks, and then she brought us each a cup of coffee and sat down with us separately to review our schedules. She had been there since the office started almost twenty years ago, and she was the first one aboard, working with a couple of older guys who had since retired. Then Teddy and Rocky came onboard, and I joined up a few years after them when we moved to town. It's easy to say that we all felt very lucky to have her on our team.

"Good morning, Stacey," I said as I walked through the door.

"Good morning, Jack," she replied with a big smile as she looked up and adjusted her headset. "How was your weekend?"

"Great weekend, Stacey. Weather was perfect, and I got to spend a lot of time outdoors and do some swimming, too. Did you have nice weekend?" I asked as I checked messages on her desk.

"Yes. My boyfriend and I went up to the state fair and saw a few horse shows and then pigged out on all the goodies up there. Oh, Maggie is ready to go through your schedule with you. Rocky and Ted are out meeting with clients in Trumansburg this morning," she said.

"T-burg. The Rongo. Great place," I said as thoughts came to me about the times we had spent in one of my favorite haunts when I was a younger man. I then strolled up to my office and saw Maggie going through my files and checking my schedule as she sat at the chair in front of my desk.

"Good morning, Maggie," I said as I walked in and took my seat.

"Good morning, Jack. Good weekend, I hope. Cup of coffee?" she offered with a smile.

"Of course. Thank you, Maggie. How we looking today?" I asked as she prepped the coffee just outside the office.

"We are booked. We got Helen coming in for a review at nine a.m. Then you have Peter and Edith coming in at ten a.m. And it keeps going from there," she replied with a whimsical smile.

"Happy Monday," she then said with a smirk and a wink of the eye.

Allison woke slowly that morning, but after a cup of coffee, it didn't take her long to take a shower, grab something to eat, pet Rosie, and get out the door for her walk to work. It was just a short stroll down Thurston Avenue and then over the bridge to Bergman Hall. She was only about a half mile to work, or a fifteen-minute walk, and she really enjoyed a little exercise and time to think and prepare mentally for the day ahead. She ran the Biophysical Department, which was a pretty large and high-profile engineering school at Cornell. She really enjoyed her job and had a great staff, but satisfying the professors' needs was a pretty challenging task. They were always under strict and strenuous guidelines, and she did everything she could to keep the ship sailing on a smooth course every day. Amanda was her right-hand lady. She was the one who made appointments and set up all Al's conference calls with the other administrative managers. Amanda was a great worker with tons of initiative, and she was also a wonderful person. Not only was she Al's assistant and main point of contact at work, but she was also one of Allison's best friends. Amanda was a single mom with a fourteen-year-old daughter, Kylie, and they both were on the run at all times. Kylie was into soccer and softball, and it was standard practice for Amanda to finish all her tasks, set up for the next day, and then run off to one of Kylie's games.

"Good morning, Miss Amanda," Al said as she breezed up to Amanda's desk.

"Good morning, Allison. I hope you had a nice weekend. And I hope it was relaxing, dear, because we are back to back all day long. No worries, though, because I got you nice and organized and gave you a little breathing room here and there for coffee and lunch," replied Amanda as she got up and grabbed Allison by the arm and led her into the adjoining office.

"Great weekend, Amanda. Did you have fun with Kylie? Any soccer games?" Al asked as she took a seat at her desk and turned on her computer.

Amanda then sat at one of the chairs in front of her. "Oh, yeah. Four soccer games in two days. This tournament team that Kylie is on is very demanding—for me and for her. But she loves it, so I go along with the program. The sacrifices we make for our kids, right?" she said with a look of chagrin on her face.

"Don't I know that drill all too well. Between hockey and golf with Liz and Gracie, we've been all over the country, it seems. It's going to actually be a nice little break to have them both in college and let the school worry about a lot of the transportation. So, with that said, what do we have on the agenda today?" asked Al as she took off her sneakers and slipped on her work shoes.

"Well, to start with, you have a conference call with the Architectural Engineering Department at eight forty-five.

After that, you need to meet with the other administrative managers at Bard Hall. That meeting should take about two hours. The afternoon is full of meetings with our professors, and I have all their needs written out for you in these folders right here," she said as she placed the folders in front of Al.

"I appreciate all you do, Amanda. You know that, right?" Al said with a warm smile.

"You know I do, girl. There is one other thing, though," said Amanda as she raised her eyebrows and pressed her lips together.

"What's up?" Al asked.

"Well, it's Robert. His divorce has been taking a toll on him, and he looks terrible and has been just sitting in his office by himself a lot of the time. A lot of us have been worried about him, and we were hoping you could have a chat with him," Amanda said.

Robert was one of the professors in the department, and he had been going through a tough divorce for the past few months. He had two younger boys, and it had been tough on the whole family. He carried his feelings into the workplace, which made for an awkward environment at times. Actually, Robert had gone to Cornell and graduated with Allison and me, and I think they knew each other pretty well during the college days because they had some classes and labs together. They were pretty friendly during school, and Robert was in the department the year before Allison came onboard. He was a handsome and pleasant man and could easily turn a girl's head and get her attention. His wife was a professor as well, and she traveled quite extensively, and I guess the stress and strain of life just caught up with them. She now lives and works in New York City at Columbia University, and Robert is here with the two boys.

"I'll check in with him this afternoon. I've noticed how glum he's been, too. I guess it's understandable. Especially when there are kids involved," Al said in a slightly sad and consoling fashion.

Liz and Gracie had gotten up early and had been playing golf down at Newman till about one in the afternoon. Most of the players were older men and women, but the girls loved being down there and competing with the more seasoned players. The older gals and guys loved to have them down there just the same and appreciated their energy as much as their skill at such a young age. The girls had been going down there since they were ten and eleven years old, so they knew everyone at the club. We were members of the county club as well, but they enjoyed hanging around the Newman course. Since they had been going there from an early age, it held a special place in their hearts. They would always talk about their matches at the dinner table, and both of them always had quite entertaining stories. They would also brag that Newman had the best greens in town, and they liked putting on really true rolling greens.

"Why did you have to give him that putt?" Liz asked in a miffed tone of voice. Liz and Gracie had left Newman and were driving up to see my dad at the assisted living facility. They were both competitive young ladies, but Liz never missed an opportunity to drive her opponent into the ground. Gracie, on the other hand, had a touch more etiquette and was a hair more compassionate.

"It was only a foot and a half, Lizzie," said Gracie, shaking her head and looking out her window on the passenger side. They loved each other, but when it came to sports, they could bicker with the best of them.

"I would have definitely made him putt that. He was missing the short ones all day. That guy's always bragging, too. We had him," said Liz with a grimace on her face.

"Can we just drive to Grandpa's, please?" asked Gracie, rolling her eyes.

That was the last of the conversation until they made it to Bridges. The two girls parked the car, walked up the slate path to the front door, and, after greeting the receptionist, made their way to their Grandpa's room, which was the first room on the left at the top of the stairs. Grandpa's door was open, and they stopped and stood in the doorway and spotted Grandpa sitting at his small dining table, having lunch and watching television.

"Hi, Grandpa," said Gracie as both girls looked into the room and smiled at their grandfather.

He looked right back at them and paused for a moment, a tad perplexed. And then he smiled ear to ear. "Hi, girls. Come on in," he said jovially. Ben loved his granddaughters and had become very close to them through the years. He loved watching them play their sports and went to their functions at school. But most of all, he just loved sitting and talking with the youngsters about life.

"How are you doing, Grandpa?" asked Liz as they strolled up to the table and leaned over and gave him a big hug and kiss on each cheek.

"I'm doing great. Come and sit down, girls. I'm just finishing up lunch. Grandma made some cookies. I know you girls love those. Have some," he offered as he extended the basket of treats to the girls.

"What have you two been up to? Looks like you might have been playing a little bit," said Grandpa as he took the remote and lowered the volume on the television so he could hear the girls.

"We just finished a match down at Newman, Grandpa," said Gracie with a smile.

"Yeah, and we would've won if Gracie hadn't given that old guy the last putt. I would have made him sweat it out a little," Liz said.

Gracie looked over at her sister with a mean look that possessed tight lips and squinty eyes. "I was just showing good etiquette, Liz. Maybe you'll have some one day," she said.

The two girls then got into a little staring match at the table, which made their granddad chuckle to himself.

"Now, ladies, take it easy. Both are important. You have to know when to apply the pressure, but you also have to know when to show good sportsmanship."

The girls turned their faces to their grandpa. He then continued his explanation. "Now, you're both great athletes and excel in different areas. Liz, you always want to run your opponent into the ground. You've always been that way, and that's good. That's why you've won so many golf tournaments. Your aggressiveness and tenacity is your biggest trait. But it's also important to know how to lose gracefully and be a good sport. Gracie, you're a great athlete as well. You're a little more compassionate than your sister in golf, but you make up for it on the ice. I guess that's why a lot of the players on other teams wind up sitting on the ice when they come face to face with you. I want you to remember something, ladies. You're both terrific kids. Both of you will do well with anything you pursue in life because you are very driven kids. I'm biased, I know. But I've seen you kids at a very early age and have watched you develop into great young ladies. I'm very proud of both of you," he told them as they both looked at him, and appreciation filled their eyes.

"Sounds like you're ready for your second year at Siena, Liz. Where's the first event this year?" he asked his eldest grandchild.

"The first one is the Cornell tournament, Grandpa. We're gonna crush the field and win the whole damn thing this year," replied Liz as Ben smiled and Gracie shook her head.

"If I remember right, you were top ten last year. Maybe it'll be your time this year," continued Grandpa, and he was a little sad thinking about possibly missing the event.

"I hope you'll be there, Grandpa. I love having you at my matches," replied Liz as she rubbed his hand on the table.

Grandpa then turned his attention to his other granddaughter. "How do you think things will shape up for you this year at…uhh…Clarkson, Gracie?" he asked, struggling a bit to piece together his question.

"I like my chances to make the lineup, Grandpa. I had a good camp earlier this summer, and the coach likes the way I move the puck out of the zone in the breakouts too," answered Gracie with enthusiasm.

"I think you'll make the lineup, Gracie. Both of you girls always showed your best stuff when you were competing with older kids. It'll be fun to see you come down here and play Cornell at Lynah. We'll have to sit in the visitors section, I guess," he said. He laughed, and then they all laughed together.

"Oh, and I forgot to mention it to you, Grandpa. The coach is trying to put together some preseason games, and we might be coming to Ithaca and playing Cornell. I'll let you know as soon as I find out. I would love for you to be there," said Gracie.

"Girls, I'll tell you right now. Come hell or high water, I'll be at both of your events. You can count on it," said Grandpa sternly as he smiled at both his granddaughters.

"So, what has your dad been up to? I haven't seen him in a while. Tell him to stop by, would you please," said Grandpa.

"I thought he was here yesterday with Grandma," said Gracie as she looked across the table.

Grandpa had a confused look on his face, and he looked deep in thought. Liz, being the older, recognized the look on his face and was a little sympathetic.

Gracie, on the other hand, did not recognize the forgetfulness of her grandfather. "He came, and he watched golf with you, Grandpa," she continued.

Liz then gave Gracie a little kick underneath the table.

"It's okay, Grandpa. We'll tell him to come by tomorrow," she added with a smile.

The three of them ate cookies at the table and talked for another couple of hours. The girls really enjoyed Grandpa's stories of where he and Grandma had played golf in different parts of the world. Grandma and Grandpa were well traveled, and the girls always imagined that they would follow in their footsteps one day. After a while, they both gave him a hug and kiss and rubbed his back and said they would visit again in the next day or so. Dad looked at both of them with warm but sad eyes and told them that he loved them.

The girls then walked down to the parking lot and got in Liz's old Jeep. Liz looked over to her sister, who had started to cry and would not look back at Liz. She just stared out of the window. Gracie was a big and tough young lady, but she also had a tender side to her, and she wore her heart on her sleeve, especially when it came to her grandfather.

"Why can't Grandpa live in our house?" she asked Liz as she wept.

Liz was not one to cry. She was very emotional but tried her best to keep her feelings in check. She was truly the big sister. "It's just not safe, Gracie. He needs extra care and attention. Don't worry; he'll be fine. Let's go home. I'll bring you back tomorrow, okay?" She started the car and put her hand on her sister's shoulder.

"I'd like that," replied Gracie as she gave her sister a loving look and wiped the tears from her eyes.

Back at the Cornell campus, it was a long workday for Allison. She had been in back-to-back meetings with staff and professors all day long and wanted to save her meeting with Robert for the end of the day. She knew he was going through a tough divorce and that he was having a hard time dealing with it. His office was just down the hall from hers, and he had been doing most of his work from there and staying till late at night. She knew he would be easy to track down and wanted to meet with him after five o'clock, when most of the staff would be gone and they could have more privacy. After Amanda left for the day, she took a walk down the hallway and peeked in his doorway. He was sitting and staring at his computer.

"Staying late again, Robert?" she asked as she stood in the doorway.

Robert looked up and gently smiled at Allison. "Hi, Allison. I didn't notice you there. Come on in and sit down," he said in a soft and somber tone of voice.

As Allison walked over to one of the chairs positioned in front of his desk, she noticed how messy his office was and knew that this was the opposite of his true character. There were open textbooks in front of him and along the ledge of his window. Behind him were the remainders of a sandwich and some empty soda cans with potato chip bags. A couple of jackets and a sweatshirt were strewn across the back of the chair in the far corner of the room. Yes, indeed, Robert was in disarray, as was his present life.

"How are you, Robert? I wanted to check in with you again. How are you and your family making out?" she asked as she leaned forward and showed compassion to the situation.

Robert was a very good-looking man with masculine features. He stood about six feet tall with wavy brown hair that was gently combed back and had blue eyes and a perfect smile. He always wore his tortoise-colored, horn-rimmed glasses, which gave him an even more debonair look, especially when he was wearing his tweed coat in the fall and winter months. There wasn't a woman on campus who didn't notice his features, and it was easy for him to turn heads. But everyone also knew he was a married man with kids. Now he just looked like a broken man who needed a friend.

"Remember our heat transfer lab when we were sophomores, Al?" he asked as he thought of a fun memory they shared from the past.

"Actually, I do remember that class. You were a little unfocused, and I had to do most of the work. Most of your concentration was on the frat house and the girls at the parties, if I recall correctly," she replied with a slight grin.

He proceeded to lighten up and gave her a smile in return that was both boyish and genuine. "Yes, you certainly horsed me through that class. But I picked you up in some others. Remember differential equations?" he said as he raised his eyebrows and kept twiddling his pen between his fingers.

"Those were the days, Allison. No worries. Life was easy. You studied and you partied. It was as simple as that. Then it gets hard and becomes complicated," he continued as the look on his face changed from happiness to sadness in one fell swoop, and his eyes wandered around the room.

"Now, Robert, I know you're going through a rough patch right now, but things will get better, you know," said Al as she leaned forward to show compassion and concern.

He then focused on Al and looked right back at her. "I know it will, Allison. It's just tough for me now. I'm confused. The kids are confused. I'm just feeling the weight on my shoulders," he replied with sad eyes and a turned-down smile. Then he rested his hands on his desk with his head held low.

"Listen to me, Robert. You must move on in this situation so you can be at your best for your family. You probably feel as if a part of you is missing, and that's understandable. When the time is right, you'll meet someone else and things will come together again. You're a smart, considerate, and good-looking man. I just want you to know that I'm here for you if you need a friend. I'm just right down the hall if you need someone to talk to or you're just feeling down, okay?" Al said as she put her hand on his on the desk and gave him a sweet and understanding smile.

"Thanks, Allison," he replied. I think he really appreciated that she had taken the time to have a heart-to-heart talk with him during a tumultuous time in his life.

Back at my office, I was well organized for my hectic day, thanks, of course, to Maggie. Our client, Helen White, had arrived right on schedule, and Maggie escorted her back to my office. "I'll bring your coffee back in a sec, Helen," said Maggie as she left for the break room.

Helen was a great client. She had inherited a large trust from her parents, and we managed it, along with a few other gifting accounts, to blend into her lifestyle. She was really just a socialite and didn't work at all. She didn't have to. We were able to generate a lot of tax-free income for her on a monthly basis, and she had excess income because she really didn't have any expenses. She lived in a huge house in Cayuga Heights and spent most of her time at the country club playing tennis or golf or bridge, and then she just attended charity and fund-raising events. She was in her early fifties and had short and sassy dark-brown hair. Helen was an extremely attractive woman and had never been married. She was a bit flirtatious, and her big brown eyes could draw any man's attention in a heartbeat.

"Good morning, Helen. How was your weekend?" I asked as I rose from my chair and gave her a nice handshake and smile.

"Busy. Busy. Busy, as always. But a lot of fun, too," she replied as she put her light white sweater across the back of the extra chair and took a seat.

"Here you are, Helen. Black, just the way you like it," said Maggie as she put the coffee on a napkin in front of her on the desk.

"I'll leave you two to your business," Maggie said as she smiled at me and then closed the door behind her.

"She's great," said Helen, and then she took a sip of coffee.

"Yes, she is. I'm very lucky to have her. She's great with the clients and always has my back," I replied as I watched Maggie go down the hallway, and then I returned my attention to Helen. "So tell me about your weekend, Helen," I said as I leaned forward in an eager and attentive manner.

"Well, I went out to dinner with a group of gals at the club on Friday night. That was fun—a real fun group of ladies. We had a few drinks and shared some stories and had a few laughs. Then I played some tennis Saturday morning and bridge in the afternoon. Then I had the hospital fundraiser to go to on Saturday night. Yesterday I played golf with a group over at the Cornell course. I didn't play very well, but we had a good time. That course is always in marvelous shape. And then I just put my feet up at home the rest of the day. It all goes so quick," she finished and then took another sip of coffee. Helen was very energetic and talked in a very upbeat and quick manner.

"How was your weekend?" she asked as she rested the cup back on the desk.

"It was a lot of fun. The girls got to spend some time with each other, and we also had some nice family time. Went out to eat and had ice cream and even did some swimming. Took Rosie for a few walks too. And went to see my dad too," I replied.

"How is your dad doing these days?" she asked as her eyes got a little more focused.

"He's doing okay, Helen. He seems to be hanging in there. His memory comes and goes, and he's on a little more medication now, but he'll surprise you every once in a while and be pretty sharp. It's up and down, I guess...and a little confusing to me at times. My mom misses him at home, but we all know it's for the best. I guess he has good days and bad days," I answered in a mellow tone of voice.

"Dreadful disease, that Alzheimer's. I wish we could come up with a cure. I know so many people suffering from it. It's a shame. But hang in there, Jack. Spend as much time as you can with your dad. That's the most you can do. Enjoy every minute. And if it ever gets you down and you need anyone to talk to, don't hesitate to call, okay?" she said as she patted my hand.

"Thanks, Helen. I really appreciate that. Your friendship has meant a lot to me through the years," I said as I looked back at her. It was quite amazing how good she looked at nine o'clock in the morning. Not a hair out of place, and her makeup was perfect. She was wearing dark-blue pleated dress pants and a white blouse, and she had on pearls that sat in a perfect arrangement around her neck in a distinguished fashion. Actually, there was never anything out of place whenever I had seen her, which was usually at my office or the club.

"Now, with that said, let's talk about your income stream. All the tax-free money seems to be going to your bank on the first of every month, as planned. The market has been doing well, so your equity side is performing nicely, too. There is also plenty of cash for liquidity and emergency purposes. We have one bond coming due this month, and I'll check our inventory and see if there are any high-quality bonds out there with good rates that we can add to the portfolio. I think we're doing great, and your income is way more than your expenses. Do you have any concerns, or is there anything else I can do for you?" I asked in a businesslike tone.

"Well, actually, there is one thing you can do for me. My alumni fundraiser at Cornell is in a few weeks, and I could use a handsome man as my escort. Do you know anyone who'd be interested?" she asked. She gave me a big grin and took another sip of coffee.

I smiled back at her. I must admit, I enjoyed her company, and I always thought her flirtatious nature was harmless.

"I'm sure I could easily find someone to go with you, Helen. I'll check around," I replied with a boyish grin.

It was a long Monday, but we all made it back to the house and ordered pizza for dinner. This was the time to get together with the family and review the events of the day. I told Al that I would order the food from my office before I left for the day and see her at home just after five o'clock.

"Hi, Al," I said through the screen window on the back porch. She was having a glass of red wine and looked exhausted.

I went into the house through the back door and met her in the kitchen. I gave her a kiss and rubbed her shoulder.

"You look whipped, honey. Tough day?" I asked as I walked over to the refrigerator and pulled out a beer.

"Yeah, you can say that. It's tough to deal with these professors all the time, and some of them aren't getting along with their students. A couple of them haven't gotten their grant money, so they feel stymied with their research. And I have a professor who has personal issues, too. I guess it's all just hitting the fan at one time," she said and then she took another sip of wine.

"How was your day?" she asked.

Just then the doorbell rang. It was the pizza delivery guy, and we could hear the girls and Rosie come bustling down the hallway stairs. All three of them moved pretty fast when there was the involvement of food, especially pizza and wings. Gracie and Liz grabbed the pizza after smiling at the cute delivery guy and placed the boxes and soda in the middle of the dining-room table.

"Hello, girls. Hello, Rosie," I said as the girls and Rosie scrambled into the dining room. I then bent down to greet Rosie as the girls grabbed chairs and pizza at the same time.

"How's my special little lady? Did you have a good day, girl?" I asked Rosie as I gave her a big kiss and good long pat on her head. She loved the attention and gave her love right back to me in the form of licks and waggles.

"I don't know if you can be jealous of a dog, but she always gets better kisses than I get," said Al as she moved from the doorway and took a seat at the table.

"I love all my girls, Al. Don't I, Rosie? Don't I? I love all my girls. But you're my special little lady, aren't you?" I said as I ruffled and petted the sides of her face and then took a seat at the table.

"How was your day today, girls? What did you do?" I asked Gracie and Liz as I grabbed some wings for my plate.

"We had a great day today, Daddy," said Gracie between bites of pizza. "We played some golf down at Newman and then went up and spent time with Grandpa."

"Yeah, we had a lot of fun today, Dad. We both played pretty good, too, and we both made some nice putts," added Liz as her younger sister glared back at her.

"Great. How was my dad?" I asked.

Gracie looked down at her plate, and her sister continued the conversation. I sensed there was something wrong by their body language.

"He's doing great, Dad. We talked about school and about golf and hockey. And we had some of Grandma's cookies, too. We watched television with him for a while. He always has the best stories," said Liz as she nudged her little sister under the table.

Gracie picked up her head and looked at her sister, and then she looked over at me. "Dad, can Grandpa come and stay with us? I think he'll be happier here…especially if he can't be with Grandma," she asked in a pleading manner.

It's times like these that you realize life can have some tough spots and be full of hard decisions. The girls were very attached to their grandfather, and I realized that they might have noticed him have some forgetful moments and were concerned for him. My girls would easily give up college to take care of their grandpa. That wasn't realistic, though, and I had to reiterate my stance and make it sound as rational as humanly possible.

"Gracie, I wish it were that easy. There is nothing I would want more than to see my dad living back with my mom...or have him living here with us. He needs special attention now and has special medications, and it just wouldn't be safe for him. I'm sorry, but it's not possible," I looked over at her, and then her sister, and back at Allison.

Gracie's eyes began to well up, and she shrank in her chair.

Liz tried to console her by rubbing her leg, and Al showed support as well. "With this disease, Gracie, this Alzheimer's... it's just not that easy," Al said as she looked compassionately at Gracie across the table.

Gracie just began to shake her head back and forth and didn't want to hear any reasons. "It's just not fair. It's just not fair!" she yelled. She got up and ran up the stairs into her bedroom and shut the door behind her.

I held my hands against my face, rested my elbows on the table, and closed my eyes. Allison and Liz were quiet for a moment as a sad reality had taken over suppertime.

"I'll go up and sit with her, Dad," said Liz. She got up and tapped me on the shoulder and went upstairs.

Al and I stayed at the dining room table and talked for a while.

"I'm going to take Rosie for a walk, Al. Do you want to come?" I asked, looking over at Allison. She looked whipped, and I already knew the answer.

"I think I'm going to sit this one out and go up and take a nice, hot bath, Jack," she said. She walked over, kissed the top of my head, and then headed up the stairs.

I looked down to my left, and Rosie was sitting there as if she was trying to cheer me up and tell me she was there for me. I just looked at her and smiled.

"What an amazing dog," I whispered as I reached down to acknowledge her presence. I then got up and grabbed her leash and attached it to her collar, and we headed through the kitchen and out the back door.

It was a quiet night, and the sun was just about to set. The students wouldn't be back for another couple of weeks, so the neighborhood was just full of the local residents. Summertime was pretty wonderful in Ithaca, and I could hear the crickets chirping as we walked along the uneven sidewalks in Cayuga Heights. Some of the trees in this neighborhood had been in existence for over a hundred years, and their roots were pushing up the slabs of concrete, which made for a very cautious stroll.

I made my way to Bridges underneath all the large oak trees that overhung the sidewalks and came to the front gate. I opened up the iron latch and walked up the stone path and went inside. It was pretty late for this facility, as most of its residents went to bed pretty early, and I inquired about my dad as I met the receptionist in the lobby. Anytime I stopped by with Rosie, someone always offered to watch her for a bit as I visited my dad. They always went above and beyond the call of duty in this establishment, and that was why it was held in such high regard in the community.

The receptionist sent someone to check to see if he was awake, and shortly after that, a young man came down the stairs and reported that he was already asleep in his room. He also told me that he had had a good day and that he even played a game of chess with my dad. I thanked him and made my way out of the lobby with Rosie at my side.

We walked down the steps and out through the gate and took a seat on the bench, which looked toward the front of the building. It was a beautiful sight; I could see in through the main dining room, and all the chandeliers were lit up and blended so elegantly with the outside lighting, which emphasized the walkways and yard. What a beautiful place and such wonderful people, I thought. I looked up to my dad's room and could see his lights were off. I envisioned him sleeping soundly. Rosie lay down at my feet and remained patient as I sat and thought about all the wonderful times I had spent with my father. The way my girls felt about him made me miss him more.

After a short while, I got up, and we walked through the neighborhood back to Thurston Avenue, up to the entrance of Beebe Lake, and then down the dirt path that led to a granite bench that was tucked away about hundred yards beneath two young maples, positioned just off the path and a few feet from the water's edge. This is the bench I sit at when I'm having sad thoughts or a tough day. It's a peaceful spot, and it somehow provides me comfort in times of need. I don't consider myself to be very spiritual, but I always feel at ease after I sit down and stare out over the lake here. I think Rosie feels the same way about this little area. She never lies down here. She always sits to my right side and stares across the water with me.

I looked down at her and petted her head, and we watched the slight ripples and listened to the summer noises together.

4

A SUMMER'S END

Work for Allison and me went along in an uneventful manner the following week. Both of us stayed as busy as possible as we tried to keep our minds off what was about to occur the coming weekend. It was the kind of weekend that put most parents in a frenzied and emotional state of mind. Both of our girls were leaving for college. Throughout the week, we spent as much time with Liz and Gracie as possible. We had a few lunches together and went to a movie as well. I was also able to go hit some balls on the Cornell range with them and then get down to Newman, where Al and I got to sneak in nine holes one evening. Not to brag, but every once in a while, I tend to surprise the youngsters and beat them on a hole or two. They actually love it when their old man wins every once in a while.

The girls really loved when Al came along, too. Al didn't play athletics growing up, as she was concentrating most of her efforts on the music club in high school. She was a fantastic clarinet player and still connects with some of her friends to reminisce about the old days and how much fun they had competing against other schools and traveling in a beat-up old school bus around the country.

She was quite a natural athlete, though. It was really amazing that she never practiced but could step up on the first tee with her driver and stripe one down the middle. The girls and I would look at one another with our mouths hanging open, and then the two youngsters would go over and pat their mom on the back. Al got a real kick out of it and loved that her girls appreciated her knack for doing so well without spending hours on the driving range.

The girls also spent a lot of time with their grandparents that week. They played nine holes with my mom, and then she treated them to lunch afterward. My mom has always liked to treat the girls to ice cream or a Pinesburger, and the girls loved hanging around with her and spending time with someone who was very pleasant and also a good listener. They stopped in to see their grandpa every day, too. We even set up a time on Thursday night for the entire family to have dinner with my dad. My mom had prepared a huge home-cooked meal, and all of us met up there at six o'clock on Thursday night.

"Well, hello everybody. Come on in," said my mom cheerfully as the four of us peered in through Dad's doorway. Mom was putting the finishing touches on the table, and she had a huge meal with all the trimmings laid out for everyone to enjoy. It was just like Thanksgiving in August. Since we were kids, my mom had always enjoyed having everyone over to her house for Thanksgiving and Christmas and cooking a big meal. She loved to play music and cook all throughout the day, and there were always tons of treats in the form of cakes, pies, and cookies to finish off the festive gathering. Most of the time, we ate all the dessert items before dinner even started, and she really didn't mind at all.

She was dressed in a pretty pink-and-white summer dress, and Dad was wearing a nice white polo and dark-blue cardigan sweater. They were both all smiles as the girls ran over and hugged both of them. Needless to say, the girls spent a little more time hugging my dad. They each gave him a big kiss, and Gracie stood by his side and grabbed him by his hand. The table was set up beautifully, with a big turkey, mashed potatoes, gravy, and all the different vegetables surrounding the big golden bird.

"This is absolutely wonderful, Kate. You did a great job. I can't believe it," said Allison as we all stood around the table. It was a small room, but that didn't matter. We were all one big happy family, and we were all together.

"Well, I say, let's eat this fat ole bird while it's hot," blurted out my dad.

We all laughed and took our seats. Liz and Gracie sat on either side of Grandpa, and Gracie held his hand until she looked at him and decided he needed it to hold his utensils. He took a few moments and looked around at everyone at the table. He wasn't an overly sensitive man, but he was touched that everyone had come to his room and wanted to share time with him. He was a very strong man but a very appreciative soul just the same.

"Before we start, I just want to say how happy I am that everyone has taken the time to come over and have dinner here. I want to thank you, Kate, for preparing this meal and bringing us all together. I want to thank my son and his beautiful bride for checking in on me from time to time too. Most of all, I want to thank God for giving me the two best grandchildren an old-timer like me could ask for." He then grabbed them each by the hand and looked at Gracie, and then back at Liz.

"I love you girls, and you're both going to have a great school year. I'll miss both of you, but always remember I'll be with you in spirit and see you when you come home for Thanksgiving," he said to them.

"We love you too, Grandpa," said Liz as she rubbed his back.

Gracie didn't say anything. She just rested her head on his shoulder for a moment as Dad brushed her hair and kissed her head.

"Well, with that said, we're here to spend time with each other and enjoy Kate's cooking and have some laughs. So, Jack, why don't you carve this sucker so we can enjoy it while it's hot," said Grandpa in an amusing tone of voice.

Everyone laughed again and started to get in a much more uplifted spirit. We had a great meal and finished it off with Mom's most famous recipe, the immortal chocolate pudding pie with whipped cream. Throughout the meal I noticed my dad's right hand shaking a bit, but I didn't mention it at all. I'm sure Allison noticed it too. He was trying to hide it and hold it underneath the table in his lap as much as possible. My heart sank a little, and I was definitely concerned, as this was the first time I had noticed tremors in his hand.

We decided to give the girls a break Friday night, thinking it would be a good idea to let them spend some time with their friends. It was the last weekend the local kids would see each other for a while, as most of them were off to college again or making the first trip for their freshman years. We had made plans with our two closest friends, Peter and Edith Glickstein. Peter and I had hailed from the same hometown, Pleasant Beach, on Long Island, and we had crossed paths about twelve years ago. Peter was a local attorney, specializing in estate planning, and has helped many of my clients with the intricate formalities that people endure after the passing of loved ones. Edith and her family had been heavily involved in local commercial real estate since their dad had started the business over fifty years ago. Throughout the years, we'd spent a lot of time together, either going out to dinner or attending local plays or concerts at the State Theater. Tonight we had set up a plan to meet for a drink down at Simeon's on the Commons at seven o'clock and then head over to see a production of *The Producers* at the Hangar Theater. The Hangar Theater was just past the entrance of Cass Park as you go up the west side of the lake and was a local staple, providing Ithacans with some of the greatest plays in the area. It was a smaller venue, and you could really enjoy the actors' performances by being a little closer to the stage than at some of the larger places. Allison and I just loved going there, and we had had many date nights and celebrated many birthdays there over the years.

"What's on the agenda tonight, ladies?" I asked as I walked into the living room and spotted Liz and Gracie lounging together on the couch and watching television. They had spent most of the day just hanging around the house and taking it easy. Basically, they were a couple of couch potatoes after they had woken up at the early hour of one in the afternoon. As I said before, young and growing kids can really sleep and eat like nobody's business.

"Meeting our friends at the Nines tonight for pizza, Pop," said Liz, as Gracie was glued to the television and not very coherent or paying attention to her surroundings.

"Okay, you guys have fun tonight. Mom and I are going to see a play at the Hangar Theater, and then we'll be back around ten. Now, remember what I said about drinking, right?" I said firmly to the little darlings. I was pretty fortunate in this regard, as they were too busy with practice and sports schedules most of the time to be involved to any great extent with underage drinking. When I was in college, the drinking age was eighteen, and as a freshman, everyone was allowed to participate in the consumption of wine, beer, and liquor. But times had since changed, and with the drinking age being twenty-one, one had to be a lot more creative to indulge with the upperclassmen. Still, we were a very lucky family, as the girls would rather be on the golf course or hockey rink than drink in the evenings. Allison and I always thought that it was best just to enjoy it while it lasted and let them make their own decisions and just try to keep them safe while we had that opportunity. After all, we didn't want to be hypocrites, knowing full well that we had attended many parties till the wee hours of the morning while we were at school.

I can't tell you how many times I've waited an extra twenty or thirty minutes for Allison to come down the stairs, I thought as I patiently waited for her in the living room, checking my watch and feeling a little anxious that we would arrive late for our scheduled date with friends. But each time she did come down the stairs, I also felt very lucky and it was definitely worth it. She was a beautiful woman, and when she casually strolled into the living room wearing a light-green-and-white summer dress, I felt the same way. She had on one of her favorite necklaces, which I had picked up at a local artisan shop downtown for her birthday, and she looked adorable as she held her little white purse and made a full turn in front of me. Two of my favorite local shops, American Crafts by Robbie Dein and Hand Work, have bailed me out of a lot of tough spots through out the years, as I usually wait too long to pick up birthday or Christmas gifts. In my opinion, nothing compares to local artwork. It's always so unique and original, and, simply stated, it's just better. I would always prefer that Al and the girls wear something made by a local artist rather than a mass-produced item. It always made it special.

"Well, what do think? Not bad for an old gal, huh?" she said, finishing up her turn and looking for my approval.

"You look wonderful, Al. You always do," I replied as I stood up and got close to her and gave her a kiss. As I looked down to my side, I noticed my faithful companion, Rosie, at our side looking up to us, and wanting to be part of this group hug.

"He's mine tonight, young lady," said Al playfully as she looked down at Rosie.

And so we set out for our date and made our way to the Commons to meet our friends for a preplay drink. As we walked into the bar, we knew exactly where Peter and Edith would be seated. The bar had two nice window tables on either side of the entrance, and we had been having drinks and dinner in the same two locations for years. All of us enjoyed looking out onto the Commons and people watching as we enjoyed our drinks and dinner.

"Up here, guys!" yelled Edith so that we could hear her over the music. As we looked up, Peter and Edith were waving to us with big smiles as their glasses of white wine sat in front of them. Allison and I took our seats, and then Peter poured us each a glass of chardonnay from the bottle that sat in a shiny bucket of ice on the table.

"So, how are the parents of two college kids holding up?" said Edith with a compassionate smile. She knew we were having a little bit of separation anxiety, and, since their kids were a few years older, they could understand what we were going through.

"Hi, Edith. Hi, Peter. Well, I think we're both just hanging in there," said Al.

"Don't worry, you two," Peter said. "You'll pull through. You'll get used to it; you'll see. I remember when our youngest began her freshman year, and Julie was already out of the house, it was definitely hard to swallow. And then I remember coming downstairs one morning and the living room was clean. And then I went into the kitchen, and there were no dirty dishes strewn about the counter. And then I popped into her room, and it was totally clean, and clothes weren't thrown all over the room. And the house was quiet. I fixed Edith a cup of coffee, and we sat out on the back porch, and I thought, this isn't so bad."

Everyone had a good laugh.

"Now, don't get me wrong. I still miss them. And I guess we still miss some of the chaos of raising children. But you get used to it. Trust me; you'll be fine," he said, and Edith nodded in agreement.

"See, honey? They've been through it too. It'll be okay," I added as I rubbed Allison's back.

It was always great to get together with Peter and Edith. We could always count on them for support. They were such positive people to be around, and they made us feel good when we spent time with them. It was true friendship at its best, and it was totally reciprocal, as we had helped them through some tough times, such as when Peter lost one of his good friends in an auto accident. We shared a glass of wine with our meal, along with some laughs, and then it was off to see the play.

"Every time I pass this place, I just laugh," I said to Allison as we were driving past Cass Park, on the way to the Hangar Theater. Cass Park was the oldest ice rink in town, and if you had young hockey players in the house, you spent a lot of chilly weekend mornings at this facility. The rink was exposed to all the elements of winter, as it had no walls and really and truly was just an outdoor hockey rink with a ceiling. On the plus side, the wind would whip through, and, combined with the cold air, would produce some of the smoothest and most perfect ice surfaces I've ever come across in all my travel hockey days with the girls. Actually, some of the best times with our daughters was waking up on the weekends in the middle of February, on cold and blustery winter days, and bringing them to play hockey at seven in the morning. All the parents would huddle in the stands, with their cups of coffee and hot chocolate, and have a great time watching the kids skate in a practice or game. It was a pretty big social event for the grownups. Only a hockey parent can understand the mentality that went along with youth hockey, and we all loved it.

"I remember, Jack. The girls pretty much learned to skate here. Those were good times. It was so much fun. I miss those times," she replied as she rested her head on my shoulder and I pulled into the parking lot.

"Me too, Al. Me too."

We had a great Friday night, and the play was tremendous and full of laughs. Saturday we got up around six, and I proceeded downstairs to make a pot of coffee. As I was making the coffee, I looked through the kitchen window above the sink and noticed Liz's Jeep wasn't in the driveway. I smiled to myself and shook my head and walked back upstairs to our bedroom and rubbed Allison, who was still sleeping under the covers, with a pillow over her head.

"Al, you're not going to believe this, but I think the little darlings went to adult pickup hockey this morning. You know, the six o'clock skate they have up at the rink," I told her.

She barely acknowledged my statement.

"I bet my dad is up by now. I'm going to shoot over there and pick him up," I added.

Al just waved one of her hands without uttering a word in reply. So I went back downstairs and fixed a couple of travel mugs of coffee and headed over to pick up my dad. He was awake in his room watching the news.

"You interested in watching a little early-morning hockey, Pops?" I asked as I showed him his travel mug.

He smiled at me with an appreciative and genuine grin. "I would love to do that," he replied, and he got up from his chair and found his baseball cap and coat.

We headed out of the parking lot and cruised through Cayuga Heights and up the east side of the lake and pulled into the rink's parking lot. There were about twenty cars in the parking lot that belonged to a faithful group of players who had awoken in the wee hours of the morning to get some exercise and enjoy the coveted ice slot time of six in the morning. We headed in through the doors and parked ourselves up in the stands. Needless to say, we were the only ones up there.

Right away, I was able to point out Liz and Gracie skating at the same time. Liz was in her usual position on the right wing, and Gracie was playing the off-side defense, which gave her great positioning for her one-time slap shot. We noticed something else that brought a smile to our faces. Liz was tracking down Joe Nieuwendyk, an ex-Cornell hockey player and NHL Hall of Famer who took residence here in the summer months. And in goal was his friend, Mike Richter, a retired New York Ranger and another Hall of Fame hockey player who came up to visit Joe during the summer. Joe had given much of his time, energy, and resources back to the community that had cheered him on during his college days at Cornell. Besides being a world-class hockey player, he's just an outstanding guy, and I don't think I've ever seen him turn down an autograph or invitation to skate in a fund-raising event. He's just a classy individual, and the locals have really appreciated all his support through the years, to say the least.

After the girls finished their shifts and made it over to the bench and took seats to catch their breath, my dad and I started waving to try to catch their attention. They spotted us standing up high in the stands and waved back to us in a very excited manner. I know it made their morning to see their grandpa up in the stands again. And I know it made my dad's morning, too.

"Thanks for thinking of me, Jack. I miss watching them," he said without turning his head.

"You're welcome, Dad. They miss you too," I said as I looked at him and grabbed him around the shoulder.

After an hour of watching the kids skate, I dropped Dad back off at Bridges and headed back home. I knew I had made his morning, but I could also tell that the shaking of his right hand was a lot more noticeable. I didn't mention anything to him, though, as I thought it would be better to talk to my mom and the doctors a little bit later that day.

As I rolled back into the driveway and came up to the back door, I noticed Rosie standing at the storm-door window. I thought, I know that look. She had a look on her face as if she had been left out of a road trip or an adventure. Rosie was twelve years old, a little bit long in the tooth, but she was always full of energy and eager to do anything. I gave her a good pet, walked into the kitchen, and noticed Al sitting at the dining room table in her pajamas reading a magazine and enjoying a cup of coffee.

Liz and Gracie certainly made the most of their time together that day. They came in from playing hockey later that morning, got something to eat, changed into golf attire, and headed down to Newman to play nine holes. They didn't have a match or competition set up, as they just wanted to play with each other.

Allison and I thought it would be a good idea to take Rosie for a walk down at Stewart Park and enjoy the beautiful day too. You can see a couple of the holes on the golf course from across the inlet, and we thought we might be able to catch a glimpse of the girls. I called to invite my mom for a walk, but she was already set on going to spend the morning with my dad. I didn't bring up anything about his hand, thinking she'd be well aware of everything he was going through, as she kept in close contact with his physicians. I felt it better to just let it be for today.

"Ready, Al?" I asked as she finished up putting together a basket of sandwiches and drinks for us to enjoy down at the park. I always admired that about Allison. She worked her butt off at Cornell but always found time to do all the little things too. She really enjoyed the role of being a mother to the girls and enjoyed doing things for me, too.

"Yep, I'm ready, captain," she replied with a salute and smile.

We then loaded up the Volvo with Rosie and the food and started down to Stewart Park. We wiggled through the neighborhood and then down the road that brought us past the Fall Creek House and behind the High School, and we then proceeded into the parking lot of the park. We set up at a picnic table just off the lake and made a nice little spot to have lunch. Then we decided we'd take Rosie for a walk around the park and work up an appetite.

This park was always pretty special to us. We had taken the girls there many a time in the summer months to enjoy the views of the lake and everything else the park had to offer. It was a beautiful sunny morning, and a warm and humid one as well. As we walked, Rosie took her usual spot out in front to lead the way. There were already plenty of people up and enjoying their day. The lake was full of sailboats, paddle boarders, and kayakers, and the park was full of kids in full swing on the playground. The backdrop of the lake made for a nice walk, and there were plenty of things to point out as we strolled on the path that surrounded the park. The shoreline was full of huge willow trees that had beautifully cropped branches full of dangling green leaves, and they looked as if they had all gotten their hair cut at the same barber. They provided such a wonderful outline to the lake as we walked along the path. We could see everyone sitting on benches or blankets, and there was always a little live music somewhere along the walk. Whether it was bongos or guitars or harmonicas, the local music lovers loved to congregate there, and we were so fortunate to have so many wonderful musicians in Ithaca. I guess we were spoiled in that regard.

"Remember how the girls liked to play over there in the water park, Jack?" Al asked. We both looked over at some kids who were laughing and running through the dozen water spouts that made up a little water park for the younger kids as their parents watched and talked on the outskirts. It brought back fond memories of Liz and Gracie chasing each other through the spouts, which projected water up around six feet off the ground. All the younger kids just loved this spot.

"I certainly do, Al. How can I forget?" I replied as we continued our stroll. We walked past the pavilion and tennis courts and up past the old boathouse. On the other side of the park, there was an inlet that separated Stewart Park and the Newman Golf course. There were a lot of spots to sit and relax, but our favorite was a bench that sat underneath a youthful Yellow Buckeye tree. It overlooked the seventh hole, which was a par-three along the inlet. Al and I had been coming to this spot for the last ten years, to watch the kids from a distance and give them a wave as they played the hole. As a fan and spectator, it had always been my favorite angle to watch golf. You could see them hit off the tee and watch the trajectory of the ball as it hopefully landed on the green. That is, if they didn't push their drive and land in the water to the right. Unfortunately, I've seen that too. Only a junior golf parent knows the feeling of his or her son or daughter hitting a shot into a hazard, but that's golf.

"I remember when this tree was first planted," said Allison.

"Me too," I replied as I reached to hold her hand.

We sat quietly for a few minutes and enjoyed the serene and picturesque view of the course and the ducks and Canadian geese that made their home on the inlet. Allison also pointed out a blue heron that was hard to notice, as it was standing still in the marsh behind the number-eight tee box. Just then we noticed our girls on the sixth green, and, after they finished their putts, they walked up to the seventh tee. Liz had honors and was placing her ball on the tee as Gracie took a seat on the bench.

"Jack, there's something I wanted to talk to you about. I have a doctor's appointment coming up, and—" began Al.

But I unknowingly cut her off midsentence. "One sec, Al," I replied. Liz had hit her ball, and it landed right in the middle of the green, just five feet from the pin. I could then see Gracie give her a high five as she took her turn on the tee.

"What's that, Al?" I asked as I watched Gracie get ready for her shot.

"Oh, it's nothing," she replied as she joined me in watching our daughters.

As I think back, I wish I had been more attentive to Allison and her needs, and I think this was one of those times. I wish I had been a better listener. She gave so much to the three of us, and when it was my turn to give back, I guess sometimes I just came up short. I always felt bad about not paying closer attention to what she was trying to tell me that day.

Needless to say, we sat and watched the girls walk down the fairway, and we both began to wave to them. They were very excited to see us and waved back with equal enthusiasm. It was a great mutual feeling of love and appreciation. When they got up to the green, we waved good-bye and headed back to have our lunch. We gave Rosie a nice big bowl of water and ate some sandwiches as we sat at the table and watched the sailboats go by and listen to the waves ripple on the shore. It was a perfect afternoon, but it was also a melancholy one. We knew the girls were taking off for college the next day.

Mom came over for dinner on Saturday night, and we had a nice supper and followed it up with a bonfire in the backyard. Allison and I cleaned up inside, and Mom spent time talking and laughing with her granddaughters by the fire. She had certainly taught them a lot throughout the years and was a perfect complement to my dad's athletic and competitive spirit. She was a great listener, just like Al, and gave them their caring and sensitive side. We were lucky to have my parents so involved with our kids, and it always made me feel good inside. My mom stayed till about nine o'clock and then gave the girls each a big hug and some spending cash for school, and then she drove her Subaru back to her house down the road.

Allison and I let the kids stay outside, and we went up to bed. The girls were all packed and their stuff was in the hallway, and I would get to loading up the cars early the next morning. Liz and Gracie wound up staying up well past midnight, but we knew they could catch up on their sleep tomorrow as they rode in the car.

The next morning came pretty early for all of us. Al and I tossed and turned most of the night, and we had the coffee pot going full bore by six in the morning. Al sat at the dining room table, with Rosie underneath, and watched me as I loaded up the two cars. I would drive Gracie in our car, and Al would go along with Liz and follow us to Siena. Gracie didn't own a car yet, and freshman weren't allowed to have a car on either the Siena or Clarkson campus anyway. I always thought that was a good rule, as they wanted to give the incoming kids a chance to acclimate to their new surroundings and get used to being on their own and making good decisions. Liz, as a sophomore, on the other hand, was allowed to have a car on campus, and she mostly used it to come back and forth for breaks and holidays. Siena was about four hours from our house, so it wasn't too long a drive home.

"Well, we're all packed up," I said. I refreshed my coffee in the kitchen and then sat down next to Al at the table.

"Should I wake them up?" I asked as I looked at Rosie under the table and then over to Al. I noticed she was having a tough time letting both her chickens fly the coop today. It was always a nice cushion to have at least one girl home as we waited for the other one to come home on break or when we all could get together at one of Liz's golf tournaments. Now, Al realized that after today, it was just going to be us at home. Neither of us had slept great last night, but she was having a real tough time with the transition and was acknowledging the separation anxiety that had filled our home for the last few weeks of the summer.

"Give them a few minutes more to sleep in," she said with a glum look on her face. Then she used her foot to pet Rosie's stomach as she lay on her side underneath the dining room table.

"I don't want them to go, Jack," she continued as her eyes watered and she rested her head on my shoulder.

"I don't either, honey," I replied as I rubbed her back.

I then decided it was best to have another cup of coffee each and give the girls another ten minutes in their own beds. That little bit of time made a big difference as Allison came to grips with going upstairs and getting them up and ready for the departure. I watched from the bottom of the stairs as Al poked into each room and gingerly woke up Liz and Gracie. They had stayed up pretty late talking last night, so they didn't exactly spring out of bed. But we got them in the shower and then downstairs to have a little breakfast at the table.

"Well, here's the plan, ladies," I said energetically as I rubbed my hands together and looked around the table at three people who were a lot less eager to get a start on the new day.

"I'll drive Gracie in my car, and Mom will drive Liz in hers. That'll give you girls a little extra time to catch up on some sleep. And then we'll stop for coffee about halfway up the throughway. I just walked and fed Rosie, so she's all set. Grandma said she would come and take her for a walk later this morning and keep an eye on her today, too. And with that said, what do you say we get on the road?" I looked around the table again. It was pretty much the same results: looks with a lot less enthusiasm than I had mustered up.

But Allison chimed in and provided some much-needed support, and they finished their breakfast, grabbed their phones and coats, and loaded up any remaining items of in-terest into the cars. It was now time for them to say their first set of good-byes. It was time to acknowledge the four-legged queen of the house, Rosie, who had been running around the cars with us in excitement as we were loading up. The girls knelt down next to Rosie and gave her tons of pets and kisses and put a big smile on her face. After a few minutes, I put

Rosie inside, and we headed out of the driveway and down Thurston Avenue.

Both of the girls slept till we arrived at a rest stop about halfway to our destination. At the rest stop, Al and I woke up the girls, and we all piled out for bathroom breaks and drinks and then reloaded to complete the first leg of the trip. The extra sleep made all the difference in the world for the two tired girls, and they were up and ready to converse with their parents.

"Well, are you excited to get back to school and see your friends and teammates, Liz?" asked Allison as she drove and Liz was fiddling with the radio station.

"Totally, Mom. Everyone is meeting at the golf training facility on campus, so you can drop me off there. Coach said he will have some food and drinks for everyone, and then we're going over to Shaker to play today. We want to show the new girls the home course and get them used to playing with the team," replied Liz in an excited manner. She always made an easy transition to anything new and was a very social young lady. She had been the same way when we dropped her off her freshman year. She made friends with all the kids in her dorm and got along with all the kids on the golf team, too. We were always very comfortable with Liz leaving the house because she was so confident and could blend quite easily into her new surroundings.

"Are you happy to finally be starting your first year, Gracie?" I asked, looking over to my youngest as she was staring out her window. Gracie was always a little quieter than her sister, and she was always a lot more pensive about getting involved in new things. She needed a little more transition time.

"You know, Dad, I am ready. I think I'm going to really like some of the other girls on the team. Since I got to skate with them a little in the summer, I think I'm really going to get along with them. There's another player from Syracuse, too, and we've already talked about carpooling together next year.

"I think living in the dorm is going to be a lot of fun, too," she continued, but she still had a slight worried look in her eyes.

"Looks like you have a good perspective, Gracie. You're going to do real well. You'll have to juggle the hockey and the schoolwork, but you should be used to that by now. I think you're going to meet a lot of new friends and have a great time up there," I said as I glanced at her and then back at the road. I still sensed some trepidation and wanted to give her a moment before I continued the conversation.

"You look a little concerned, Gracie. Is anything bothering you?" I asked after a short while.

She grimaced a bit and looked over to me and then turned to face her window again. "Dad, I'm worried about Grandpa. Is he going to be okay?" she asked as she turned and looked at me.

Knowing that she was a very sensitive girl, I knew exactly how she felt and what she was going through now. I took a minute to think, and then I answered her as best I could as I rubbed her hand.

"Gracie, I know you and Liz have a special bond with my dad. He loves you girls, too. It's not easy to have him in an assisted living home, but it's necessary and the best for everyone. He needs special medicine and full-time attention, and they do a great job at this place. Grandma sees him multiple times during the day, and your mom and I will be there as much as possible, too. He'll be fine. He's just getting older and needs more supervision, as he's dealing with the Alzheimer's. And on top of that, he has a heart condition. He's got the best doctors and is in the best care," I said warmly as I checked to see if she was all right.

She just kept looking out of the window and stayed quiet for a while.

"I promise you he'll be fine. When you come down for the home game against Cornell, I'll make sure he's in the stands. How does that sound?" I said in a more cheerful tone as I patted her leg to give her some reassurance.

She nodded but remained quiet as we continued down the road. Then she turned to me with teary eyes. "I just don't want him to forget me, Dad. I always want to him to be able to remember me," she said as she leaned over and put her head on my shoulder.

I held her by the hand tightly as she moved closer to my side.

"He'll never forget you, Gracie. I promise you that," I said as I looked ahead of me. I must admit, I was misty eyed as well as we continued down the road in a peaceful silence.

Al and Liz had passed us on the throughway, and we followed them in through the main gates at Siena, which was in the small hamlet of Loudonville, just twenty minutes north of Albany. Siena had a great historic look to it as you pulled onto campus, and the gold dome that housed the great clock on the main administrative building gave a real majestic quality to the school. We drove in through the gates and then back to the Raymond Golf Training Center, which was located on the east side of the campus. There was a big buzz, and all the kids were making their way back and forth from their dorms to their cars as they moved their belongings to their dorm rooms. We pulled next to each other in the parking lot, and Liz had a huge smile on her face when she got out of the Jeep. I could tell she was really excited to be back to college, and she had already noticed some of her friends by the entrance of the facility. They exchanged waves and smiles of excitement. Gracie made her way around her side of the car, and we all stood together.

"I want to bring Gracie over to say hi to the girls, Dad. Give us a few, okay?" said Liz. She grabbed her sister, and they walked fast over to the kids in the doorway. A lot of hugs and high fives were exchanged, and then they disappeared into the facility. Al and I looked at each other and just smiled.

"I think she's excited to be back, Jack," said Al with a grin.

"Looks like it, Al. She really has made some nice friends here," I replied as I put my arms around her shoulder.

We made our way alongside the adjoining baseball diamond and up to the golf facility doorway and went inside to say hello to the other parents and kids. The golf facility was totally amazing. It had multiple hitting areas, a swing-analysis room, a putting area, and lockers. The kids were all enjoying the golf wonderland, and we got to meet some of the other parents and say hi to the coach. After about a half hour, we all walked outside and gave one another hugs as we said our good-byes. We gave Liz and Gracie a little extra time together and sat in the car and watched as they talked and then embraced.

And then Gracie made her way back to the car. It was time to head up the Northway and make our way through the Adirondacks to Potsdam, New York.

"Next stop, Clarkson," I said cheerfully, to set an easygoing and upbeat tone for the second leg of our journey.

The ride through the Adirondacks was wonderful, and we really enjoyed the backdrop of lakes and humongous pine trees. We passed through a lot of small towns, and some of the roads were extremely winding, with treacherous turns. But we made it safely up to Potsdam and made our way to Gracie's dormitory, Reynolds, which was situated on top of a hill on the west side off campus. Her room was on the second floor. Her roommate was not there just yet, so we lugged all her stuff up the stairs and got her situated in her room. The hallways were packed, and all the parents were helping their kids get set up for their maiden voyage.

After we got the room situated, we headed over to Cheel Arena to check out the rink and locker room and to say hi to the coaches and a few players who were getting in a skate. I could tell Gracie was a little nervous, but she started to feel at ease after talking with the coaches and some of the other players who skated over to the boards. They invited her to come out and skate and shoot around for a little while, and Gracie said she would grab her gear and be right back to join them on the ice. We were going to take her out for lunch and meet her roommate. But Al and I thought this would be a good time to say good-bye, since she was feeling a lot more comfortable, with her teammates starting to show up in the locker room. She also noticed her name on one of the lockers and a big number four right next to it. I guess it made her feel at home, knowing that she had a spot all to herself. Yes, I think it's safe to say that she had made the mental transition to the next phase of her life.

We decided to walk out to the car and say our good-byes so we could have a private moment for some last-minute conversation. Al held Gracie's hand all the way to the car and then gave her a big hug.

"You're ready, girl. It looks like you have some nice kids on the team, and the coaches are great gals, too. You're going to have a great year," said Allison. She gave her another hug and then rubbed her arm with affection.

"I'm excited, Mom. I feel good about everything. I've got to admit, I was really nervous all the way up, but now that I'm here, I feel a whole lot better. Thanks for everything. I love you," she told her mom as she hugged her again, and then she came over and gave me one.

"You're going to do great, kid. Enjoy yourself and work hard. We'll miss you, but we'll see you soon, and we're just a phone call away. And let us know if you guys ink the preseason game at Cornell, too," I said.

"I'll miss you, Dad," she said as she hugged us one more time. I did everything I could to stay composed, but Allison welled up a bit as she watched her youngest say good bye to her father. After we made sure she had some money and all her things, we said good-bye, and she left us and walked in through the hockey-rink doors. We stood for a moment and then looked at each other and smiled. Then we got in our car and made our way off campus. It was now time for the final leg of the journey, back home to Ithaca.

We were both pretty content, as both of the girls were happy to be at school, and Gracie had looked and felt happy to be with her new teammates. That made us both feel at ease, and we looked and smiled at each other as we headed down the road. I was looking forward to talking to Allison and having some conversation, but after about twenty minutes of driving, she fell asleep and didn't wake up till I pulled into our driveway in Ithaca. I knew she needed to catch up on her rest, and it was very relaxing for me to look at her sleeping quite soundly as we made our way home. As I pulled into the driveway and turned off the car, I gently rubbed Allison to wake her up from her four-hour nap.

"Where are we?" she asked softly as she looked at me with a slight smile and sleepy eyes.

"We're back in Ithaca, Al. We're home," I replied as I rubbed her hair, and then I kissed her head.

5

BACK TO WORK

Monday mornings come too quickly, we thought as the alarm clock went off. I leaned over and turned off the clock and then looked down at Al, who was still underneath the covers with her head resting on her pillow and eyes still closed.

"I vote for the four-day workweek," she said as struggled to come to grips with yet another robust workweek on the Cornell campus.

"Rise and shine, honey," I replied as I looked down at her, and she seemed to wedge her head deeper between two pillows.

"I'll get the coffee. You just hop in a nice hot shower, and you'll feel a lot better," I said as I rose from bed. I then grabbed my glasses from the nightstand and stared over at Rosie, who was still half asleep on her bed, which was positioned just to the left side of my dresser. I gave her a rub of the belly with my foot and made my way downstairs to start the coffee pot. Allison and I didn't know how anyone could start Monday mornings without coffee. It seemed impossible to us.

"Good morning, Maggie. Where's Stacey?" I said merrily as I strode into the reception area and greeted my trusty assistant, who was sitting at the receptionist's desk.

"Happy Monday, Mr. Jack. Stacey needed two hours off this morning, so I'm filling in for her till ten," she replied with a smile. That was one of the best things I'd noticed about Maggie through the years. She always had a big smile and great attitude, whether it was first thing Monday morning or late in the afternoon on a Friday. She had a perfect disposition, and that really helped her deal with three demanding guys around her all the time. She was the main piston that was driving all our business, and she was crackerjack. All of us required attention for our clients and certain reports all day long, and she knocked it down without any complaints, always with a big smile. Maggie had gotten divorced about ten years ago from a high school sweetheart and remarried a great guy and lived in the town of Lansing, which was about five miles outside of Ithaca. Her husband, Jim, was the editor of the local paper, the *Ithaca Journal*. It was a rocky and turbulent time for Maggie ten years back when she was going through the divorce. Her previous husband was a real nice man as well, but Jim certainly filled a void in her life, and they were a great couple. They didn't have any kids, but she said that they were discussing that part of their life right now, and the two dachshunds, Frank and Beans, were a full-time and enjoyable job for now, constantly keeping both of them on their toes.

"Did you have a nice weekend, Maggie?" I returned as I rested my hands on the front of her desk.

"Great weekend, Jack. Jim had the weekend off from the paper, and we spent most of the time up at Long Point. We brought the dogs with us. Jim kept them entertained by throwing sticks for them in the lake, and I just read my book and sipped some wine. We had a little lunch at one of those picnic tables that sits along the shore, and it was under a tree that gave us tons of shade. It was perfect," she said.

"Long Point State Park. Another hidden gem," I replied with a nod.

"Well, how did the big drop-off go?" she asked.

"Smooth as silk. Some tears here and there, but for the most part, everyone got off to a good start and got acclimated pretty easily once they saw their friends. I think Allison had the toughest time dealing with it. She's starting to realize that there will only be her in the house and that she'll have no buffer from me. She's lost all her girl power," I said in jest.

"At least she has Rosie to soften the blow," Maggie said with a smirk. Maggie always had a great sense of humor.

"The boys are in the conference room," she then said.

And so I made my way back to our conference room to catch up with Ted and Rocky. As I pushed open the glass door, I found my two office mates seated together with cups of coffee in hand.

"There's the big guy," rang out Rocky as they both smiled up at me. I was also so blessed to not only work with the world's greatest assistant, but to have a couple of great guys as office mates and business partners.

"What do you say, Jackson? Come on in and have a seat. It's your turn to listen to Rocky talk about how great the single life is and all his doings this weekend. I'll get you a cup of coffee," said Ted in a jovial manner as he walked behind me and patted me on the back.

Then he went into the break room to get me a cup. It was usual protocol to have a cup of coffee together in the conference room first thing Monday morning if our schedules were all open for at least a half an hour. That was the time we took to ourselves and caught up with one another. Rocky was still single, but he did have a steady girlfriend, and they spent most of their time together on his boat on the weekends. Ted was married and had two boys. The youngest had just finished college, so he and his wife usually were off visiting them or spending time at their cabin in the Adirondacks. He usually was the one who gave me pointers about how to get used to home life again without any kids in the house. We were all a little different, and it worked out to be a perfect little smooth-sailing office. We all cared for one another, and we were interested in each other's lives, and it certainly showed to anyone who entered through our front doors.

Back on the Cornell campus, Amanda and Allison were reviewing their work schedule in Allison's office.

"Well, Allison, it looks like you're booked from nine to one o'clock and then from two thirty to six today. I know it's a little bit later than you'd like to stay on a Monday, but I couldn't reschedule some of these people," said Amanda. She looked at Allison sympathetically with raised eyebrows.

"I just appreciate your keeping me organized, Amanda. Thank you, and happy Monday," said Allison. She smiled back at Amanda and raised her coffee cup for a toast to her trusty assistant.

After another few minutes of going through the work detail that was involved in the day's meetings, an unexpected visitor poked his head in the doorway.

"Good morning, ladies," said Robert, standing in the doorway with a hazy grin on his face and looking a little tired.

"Good morning, Robert," Allison said, a little surprised by his unannounced entrance.

"Al, do you have a minute to chat?" he asked. He looked at Allison in a hopeful manner and then over to Amanda.

Amanda looked over to Allison to see how she felt about this interruption.

"Sure. Of course," Allison said. "I'm set for the first few meetings, Amanda. We can catch up again just after lunch."

Amanda put together the folders that were spread out on Allison's desk and excused herself from the room. She smiled at Robert as she walked by and closed the door behind her to give them some privacy.

Robert took a seat in the chair in front of Allison's desk. "Al, I'm sorry for barging in on you like this," he began in an apologetic tone.

"No problem at all, Robert. You know that. What's up?"

"Well, I just need some advice, Al. I had a tough weekend with the boys. They're arguing a lot, and then I butt in to break it up, and they yell at me. The whole house seems to be off balance. I just don't know what to do here. Then I come in to work, and I can't get focused on my research or my class. I just can't get a handle on things," he said, looking overwhelmed.

Allison nodded and gave him a look that said she was really concerned and sympathetic to his situation.

"I can totally understand what you're going through, Robert. And I want to help you. What exactly are the boys saying when they're arguing with each other or yelling at you?"

"It's tough to explain. It's just a lot of things," Robert replied, shaking his head and focusing his eyes on the floor. "I have a class in a few minutes, Allison. And I'm sure you're busy too. And I know it's Monday morning and you're just getting started on your day. Can we talk at lunchtime?" he asked.

"Sure. I'm free at one o'clock. Where do you want to meet?"

"How about lunch off campus? We can go over to Agava on the East Hill. That way it can be a little more private," he said.

She took a moment to digest the offer and then made a decision. "Sounds good. I'll meet you there at one," she said in an uplifting tone, and then she noticed right away that the acceptance had put him at ease.

He got up, thanked her, opened her door, and rushed down the hallway to make his way to his next class.

Back at my office, I was going pretty hard all day long with back-to-back appointments with my clientele. I loved my work and it was really gratifying to help people reach all their financial goals, but sometimes it could be stressful. People relied on me for growing and protecting their net worth, generating income streams to handle expenses, and making sure their financial future was on solid ground. It could be daunting at times, but I had great clients who were also great friends, and it was also very rewarding for me on a personal level. Needless to say, the office had been growing so dramatically and so quickly that we were going all day long with portfolio reviews and consultations for new clients.

Since we were all booked through the morning, Maggie ordered pizza for us and delivered it to our conference room. We were having a little lunch in the conference room when Maggie poked her head in and relayed a message to me.

"Hey, Jack. Helen is holding for you on line four," she said with a smile. Maggie thought that Helen had a thing for me and would tease me a little here and there when she called or came into the office. It was our own little inside joke.

"Thanks, Maggie. Well, I'll see you boys in the trenches," I said to Ted and Rocky in an amused tone.

I walked back to my office and picked up the phone. "Well, how we doing today, Helen?" I said as I pulled her accounts up on my computer screen.

"Hello, Jack. I'm doing great; thank you. I have some great news. I golfed with some new members at the club today, and they're in the market for a new financial advisor. They just came to town from San Francisco and would like to relocate their accounts to Ithaca and work with a local financial advisor. Well, I, of course, suggested you, and, long story short, arranged to meet them tonight at the club for a drink and possibly dinner. I know I'm catching you off guard, but these people can be tremendous clients. They just sold a startup Internet company and have oodles of money," Helen said enthusiastically.

"That's wonderful, Helen. I really appreciate your thinking of me like that. Sounds like a great opportunity. Let me check with Al, and I'll give you a call right back to confirm the meeting. I just want to make sure we don't have anything on our agenda tonight," I said, feeling grateful that she kept me in mind for referrals.

"Sure, of course, but I hope it's okay with Allison. These could be great clients for you, and they have a lot of money and connections too. It would be great for your career."

I paused for a moment and then told Helen to hold for a minute. I gave Al a quick call on the other line. I knew she had mentioned she had a doctor's appointment this week, but I didn't remember the day or time. I tried to call her, but it seemed her phone was turned off, and I couldn't get through to her. I sent her a text, just as a backup, and let her know that I had client meetings tonight and to call if she needed me. I didn't know it at the time, of course, but she was having lunch with Robert at Agava.

After leaving Allison a message, I switched over. "Helen?"

"I'm here, Jack."

"I couldn't get Al, but I'm sure it's okay. What time would you like to meet at the club?"

"Why don't we meet for a drink at five thirty?" she suggested.

"Perfect. And I really appreciate you thinking of me, Helen. I'll see you later today," I said.

"Great. I'll see you at the club later, Jack. I think it'll be a successful meeting, and we'll have some fun, too," she said.

And so my schedule was now booked through the evening, too.

Agava always had a nice lunch crowd, so the place was bustling as Robert and Allison sat down at a small table for two.

The place was immaculate and the service was impeccable at this place, and it had a loyal following.

"Jack and I love this place," Allison started as she put her napkin on her lap and then looked up at Robert.

"Me too. Carol and I used to come here all the time for dinner. Seems so long ago," Robert added with a slight sigh.

"I really appreciate you meeting me, Al," he added.

"I'm happy to try to help, Robert. Now, what's going on with the boys? What's going on with you? Obviously, I can see you're having a hard time with this breakup, and that's understandable," replied Allison as she rested her arms on the table and held her hands together and focused on her colleague.

After a big sigh, Robert filled her in on his weekend. "Well, where do I start? Let's see...the boys were fighting all weekend with each other...about who knows what. And then I'd step in and try to see what the argument was about, and then they would both start yelling at me to stay out of it and that it was none of my business. It really hurts, because they look at me with disgust in their eyes. Then each of them went back into their own rooms and shut the door behind them. Then Carol's attorney called, and apparently she wants more assets, and she feels she's not getting a fair shake in the settlement. My attorney isn't worth crap, and he should be handling this stuff. And I'm falling behind on all my research, and some major deadlines are coming up for my grants to get funded again. Just seems like everything is happening all at once," he said in an exasperated tone as he slowly moved his head from side to side. His eyes became slightly watered, and he looked like a broken man. It was a little hard for Allison to believe that such a strong and confident guy could be so broken a soul.

"Robert, listen to me," she began. "Take a breath and have a sip of water."

She waited for him to finish his sip and then continued. "It seems that this is obviously hard on you and your boys. This is what I would do. I would go back to your office and start there. I would clean up the office and throw out all the old sandwiches and coffee containers and make your work surroundings nice and neat again. Then I would lay out a nice plan to schedule how you can finish your research projects on time. Put together a calendar and set your times and block your time, and that way you will hit your goals.

"Then take off for home and go see your boys. Judging by what you're telling me, they'll probably be in their rooms when you get home. Knock on their doors, but don't intrude. Use a gentle voice and tell each one of them that you want to have a family meeting in the living room. When you're all together down there, tell them that you sympathize with how they feel and realize that they can be carrying around a lot of mixed emotions and that it is not their fault. Tell them that this is just a situation in which their parents couldn't work out their issues and feel it's the best for the family that they have separate lives. Tell the boys you love them and their mother loves them too. Whatever you do, please don't say anything negative about Carol, as that will just make this a much more difficult situation. After that, tell them things will work out and they will feel better in time and that you love them and always will.

"Then give each of them a hug and order some pizza and watch some television with them. I think you'll feel better if you let them blow off steam, and just be a little gentle and understanding with them. How does that sound?"

"Now I know what Jack sees in you. Thank you, Allison. I wish I would have asked you out a long time ago. Things might have been different for me."

"Don't lose hope, Robert. Stay positive. You'll meet someone as special as you."

Just then a couple of visitors stopped by the table. It was Peter and Edith on their way out of the restaurant.

"Well, hello, Al. How are you?" asked Peter as they came up to the table.

"Hi, Al," said Edith as she bent over and gave Allison a hug.

Robert then got up to introduce himself and shake hands with Peter and Edith.

"Edith, Peter, this is Robert Parker. He's a professor and colleague of mine at Cornell," Allison said.

"Nice to meet you," said Peter. Edith smiled but remained quiet.

"Glad to meet you as well," replied Robert, feeling slightly awkward.

"We had a great time with you guys the other night, Allison. We have to get together again," Edith said.

"Well, enjoy your lunch. I'd like to stay and chat, but I have to drop Edith back off to work and I'm due in court in a half hour," said Peter as he and Edith started to move away.

"See you, Al. I'll call you," said Edith.

"Bye. Talk to you guys soon," replied Allison.

Robert sat down and looked across to Allison. The situation was slightly uncomfortable for her.

"They look like great people," said Robert as the waiter came to the table.

"Yes, they are great people. Great friends, too," said Allison as she looked at Robert and then turned her focus to her menu.

I parked my car over by the practice green, which was at the rear of the parking lot of the country club. The parking lot was full, and I remembered that there was a big get-together for the Ithaca Garden Club at the club's catering hall adjoining the bar. This club was very popular and had a few hundred members, and besides the entire gardening itinerary that they discussed at these meetings, it was a huge social event for all of its attendees. A few of my clients were members of this esteemed association, and I had actually had the pleasure of seeing their work as I visited their homes throughout the year. I must say that the gardening skills they possessed were utterly amazing, and I had been quite astonished a few times as I walked into their yards to witness the impeccable displays of plants, flowers, and shrubbery that encompassed their homes. To say the arrangements were breathtaking would almost be an understatement.

I made my way through the front doors and into the bar area, and Helen immediately came into view at the far end of the bar. She saw me as I turned the corner and waved for me to come down. I noticed that she was sitting alone at the bar and having a lively conversation with the bartender, Matt.

"Hello, Jack. Glad to see you," said Helen as she got up and gave me a cordial embrace.

"Been a long day. Glad to be here. Nice to see you, Matt," I said as Helen and I sat down together. Matt and I had always had a lot of fun together picking on each other and teasing some of the other members here and there. In my book, you can't beat a friendly bartender who pours a great drink. And that was exactly what you got with Matt.

"Tanqueray and tonic, Jack?" he asked with a big grin as he wiped the area in front of me.

"Absolutely. Thank you, sir," I replied. He then went to make the drink, and I turned to Helen. "How are you, Helen? Oh, and where are the new members?" I asked as I grabbed a couple of peanuts from the bar.

"They'll be along in a few minutes. Carol called me and said they were running a little behind schedule. Jeffrey is the husband. You'll like these people, Jack. They're really nice and a lot of fun. They're not too good at golf, but a lot of fun. And, like I said, they have large accounts that they want to bring to town. Jeffrey is a Cornell alumnus, and he's being considered for the board of trustees as well," she said with raised eyebrows.

"Besides, I never get to spend any down time with you. It's nice to have a few minutes and just sit and talk as we wait for them," she continued as she patted my hand.

Just then Matt brought over my gin and tonic. I looked at him with welcoming eyes and tried his concoction. "Perfect, as usual," I said as I looked at him.

He gave me a wink and then headed off to take care of other members coming into the bar.

"Well, how about a toast, Jack?" said Helen with a gleam in her eyes.

"A toast? And what are we toasting to, Helen?" I asked, a little perplexed.

"Well, Jack, let's have a toast to possibly a huge account for your office. A toast to bigger and better business, of course," she replied as she raised her glass in the air.

I smiled and picked up my glass to meet hers, and we tapped them lightly together and then followed it with customary sips of our cocktails.

"I appreciate your thinking of me, Helen. I really do. Thank you," I said with sincerity.

"You're quite welcome, Jack. You do such a nice job with my accounts and my trust, and I know these people will love you just the same," she replied.

I then remembered that I should try to call Allison again and excused myself for the restroom. I stepped away and headed around the corner and placed the call to Al. There was no answer, so I shot her out a text that I would be having dinner with clients at the club and would see her around eight o'clock tonight. After checking my other work e-mails on my phone, I made my way back to Helen. She was sitting but turned around in her chair and talking to a sharply dressed couple who were standing just behind her.

"Well, there he is. Jack, I want you to meet Jeff and Carol Wagner. These are the new members," said Helen in an upbeat spirit.

"Glad to meet you, Jeff, Carol. It's always a pleasure to meet another Cornell alumnus and any of Helen's friends," I said as I extended my hand to shake Jeff's hand first and then Carol's directly after.

"My pleasure, Jack. Helen says you're a whiz with money, and that's what Carol and I are looking for, you know," said Jeff in a friendly but stern fashion.

"Well, you're certainly right, Helen. He is very handsome," said Carol.

Jeff chuckled, and Helen produced a big smile. I, of course, was utterly embarrassed but handled it fine. "Well, thank you, Carol. You're too kind. And I'm only too happy to help you with your finances. Can I get you guys a drink?" I offered, looking at Carol and then to Jeff.

"Yes, I'll have a martini. Gin, of course. Three olives. Carol will have a Chardonnay," Jeff said, looking at Matt, who was standing right behind me and ready to serve the new members.

Matt nodded and began making the drinks.

"I'm hungry, though. I really haven't eaten much today. Would it be okay if we grabbed a table?" asked Carol.

We all agreed, and off to the dining room we went with our drinks in hand. I extended my hand to show them the dining room and let Helen lead the way. I picked up the rear, and, as I walked behind everyone, I pulled my phone out and checked for messages. There were none, so I shut my phone off, which was my usual protocol whenever I sat to down to eat.

Allison walked in through the back door and put two bags of groceries down on the counter. There were other bags in the car, but before she went back to get the remaining groceries, she picked up her phone and tried to call me again. Rosie had greeted her with a big smile, but Allison was in a rush, so all she could offer was a big bowl of food and a fresh bowl of water. She had missed my call while she was shopping in Wegmans and had tried to call me a couple of times but couldn't reach me. Still there was no reply. She was forwarded to my voice mail and realized I probably had turned off my phone.

She put the phone back into her purse and went outside to finish unloading the groceries. She put most everything away but was running behind schedule due to her hectic day. She headed back out the door to try to make her doctor's appointment. She had been running all day between meetings at Cornell, and it didn't help her schedule at all having to dedicate a lot of her work time to Robert's personal plight. But that was how Al was built. She was always available to help anyone at home or at work. When you add all the homemaking stuff and raising a family on top of her career, it was an unbelievable workload. She never once complained, either. She just did it all.

After pulling into the parking lot of the Ithaca Medical Center, she walked briskly to the receptionist's window to announce herself. She had made it on time, and she finally got a chance to catch her breath in the waiting room as she sat down and picked up a magazine to wait for Dr. Liebenthal to see her. After a few minutes, a nurse came out and announced her name, and Allison followed her back to a private room and waited for the doctor. She made herself comfortable in a chair that was tucked in the corner and sat with her dress coat folded in her lap. This was a follow-up visit from her last appointment, which she had had just before the girls left for school.

"Good evening, Allison," said Dr. Liebenthal as he knocked on the door and then entered the room to see Al sitting and smiling nervously in the chair.

She greeted the doctor with a smile but remained in the chair. "Hi, Doctor. How are you? I'm sorry for being a hair late," said Allison in a meek tone of voice.

"You're not late at all, Allison. Actually, you're never late, and I appreciate that, too. Not everyone is on time like you. You're a model patient," he replied, looking at the chart and flipping through some pages. He then paused and sat on the dressing table to the side of Allison.

She looked to the doctor and felt a little awkward that he had sat down to give her the report.

"Allison, your health is basically good. Blood pressure is good. Weight has always been good. Cholesterol is very good. As we did a complete physical last time, there was one item I wanted to discuss with you," said the doctor, and then he paused for a few seconds.

"Allison, during our last visit, I suggested you make an appointment for a mammogram. Did you do that?" he asked with a straight and slightly serious face.

Allison began to get really nervous. She rubbed her hands together and thought for a minute as her face showed signs of worry. "Sorry, Doctor. I guess I've just been so busy with the kids and Jack and everything...I guess I just didn't get to it."

The doctor removed his glasses. "Allison, you are extremely healthy. The only thing that concerned me when I checked you out last time was the slight redness underneath your left breast. Now, it could be nothing at all. There was no hardness or substance to the skin area, as we discussed. But overall, I think it should be checked out. I wanted to see your blood tests before I addressed this with you. I don't want to worry you here. I just want to be proactive and have you go in for a mammogram to check this out and make sure of it," he said as he held his charts and posted a concerned look toward his patient.

Allison closed her eyes for a few seconds to digest the doctor's thoughts and then reopened them. "Doctor, you're saying that I'm healthy though, right? I mean, I feel good. I don't feel any different. And you mentioned that the redness could be from stress or maybe a tiny rash. And my mammogram a couple of years ago went perfect," she said, looking for his confirmation that this was just a formality.

"Allison, you are healthy, from everything I can see and from all your other tests. But the only way to make sure that this is nothing at all is for you to have more x-rays, and I want you to do that as soon as possible, okay?" he replied in stern fashion.

"Now, I will let my assistant know that you need to make an appointment with Dr. Connors, so when you leave here, just stop by on your way out, and she will set everything up for you," continued the doctor.

Allison had been exhausted before showing up for the appointment, and now she was worried, frazzled, and even more worn down from the news.

"Listen, Allison. You're going to be fine. I just want this checked out so we're sure of everything," he said gently as he put his hand on her shoulder.

She nodded back to the doctor. He spent a few more minutes talking to her, and then they left the room together. She made another appointment with his assistant and then headed out of the building.

On the way back home, she just shook her head back and forth in disbelief and felt drained on every level. She pulled into the driveway, got out of the car, and walked into the house. Rosie was there waiting for her with a smile and wag of the tail, and that made her feel a little better as she petted her head and scratched underneath her chin.

"Nice to see you, girl," she said softly to Rosie as she walked into the dining room and hung her coat over a chair. Then she found a bottle of wine and poured a nice big glass and sat at the dining room table to collect her thoughts.

Back at the Ithaca Country Club, we had just finished our dessert, and the party was starting to disband for the night.

"I had a great time, Jack. I think I can speak for both myself and Carol that it was certainly our pleasure to meet you and get to know you," said Jeff as he held out his hand for a goodnight shake.

Carol was giving Helen a hug and saying good-bye, and then she came over and shook my hand. "Yes, I really enjoyed meeting and talking with you, Jack. Let's get together for lunch or dinner again real soon. Please let Jeff know when we can stop by your office to move our accounts there, too. I know my mind is made up, and I'm sure that's what Jeff wants to do. Right, Jeff?" she said as she held my hand and looked to her husband for approval.

"Yes, absolutely. I'm a pretty good judge of character, and I think we would mesh perfectly. Give me a call tomorrow, Jack, and we'll set a date to come to your office to work out the details. Does that sound good to you?"

"That's wonderful, Jeff, Carol. I really appreciate the opportunity to manage your assets. Thank you," I said, holding my hand out to shake Jeff's hand once more.

Then I went over and hugged Helen and thanked her as well. They had decided to have an after-dinner drink at the bar, but I mentioned that it was a work day for me tomorrow and I needed to get home to get some rest so I would be bright eyed and bushy tailed for tomorrow's appointments. We all had a little chuckle, and then I made my way through the bar and out through the front doors.

As I walked briskly to my car, I reached into my coat pocket and pulled out my phone and turned it back on to see if I'd missed any calls or messages. When I got to my car, the one and only message came up on my phone.

"Jack, sorry I missed your call. I was unloading the groceries. Tonight is my doctor's appointment. Will you go with me, please? Love, Al."

I closed my eyes and couldn't believe I had forgotten the date and time of her appointment and felt terrible. A selfish feeling rumbled through my body as I shook my head and looked up to the sky.

"Damn," I muttered. I jumped into my car and sped to the house. I pulled into the driveway and hustled out of the car and up the steps to the back door. Rosie had heard my car rumbling down the gravel driveway and met me at the door.

"Hello, Rosie. You're up late. Where's Mom?" I asked her as I petted the top of her head and walked into the kitchen. Al was sitting at the dining room table and got up quickly to meet me in the kitchen.

"I'm sorry, Al. I had my phone off for the dinner meeting, and I didn't see your message, and I—"

But Al cut me off. "It's okay, Jack. Never mind. Listen to me. Your mother just called and was very upset. She's over at Bridges, and your dad is having a bad day, and your mom was crying. She wanted you to meet her over there. I just hung up with her a second ago, so could you go over now and see if everything is okay?"

"Jesus. What did she say?" I said as I put my briefcase on the floor.

"She was crying, Jack. She said your dad was having a tantrum and wouldn't cooperate with the nurses. Could you just go over, please, and check on them," she continued as she came closer to me and grasped my arms.

I told Al I was sorry again and put my car keys on the counter and moved quickly out through the back door and down the street and made my way to the nursing home. As I walked down Wycoff, I could see my mom sitting on the stone bench on the corner of the property. I walked quickly toward her and called gently. "Mom?" I said softly.

She turned and stood up. She'd been crying, and she moved to me and squeezed me tight and rested her head on my chest.

"Jack, I'm so glad you're here," she whispered as she held on.

I looked down and could see huge concern in her watery eyes. "It's okay, Mom. It's okay. Shhhh…shhhh. It'll be fine. Just relax and tell me what's going on with Dad," I said easily as I rubbed her back, and then we both sat down together.

I kept rubbing her back, and she started to calm down and then took a deep breath and told me about Dad.

"Well, I just came over to bring him some cookies for after his dinner, and when I got there, he was arguing with the staff. He was very upset and telling the nurse to leave his room in a real angry tone. And they were just trying to calm him down. And then I was in the doorway and went inside, and…"

she said quickly in an excited state, and then she had to pause to catch her breath.

"Slow down, Mom…it'll be fine," I said lightly as I consoled her and rubbed her back some more.

"Then I went right behind the nurses to get closer to him, and he was just yelling, and he looked like he didn't want me there and was just telling everyone to get out of the room and he didn't want strangers in his room," she continued as she started to weep again.

"It's okay, Mom. I'll go and check on him, okay?" I said as I pulled her close to me. We sat there quietly for a few minutes. I held my mother and rocked her a little bit, and it seemed to calm her down. She continued to lean her head against my chest, and I gave her a kiss on top of her head, and then I got her to look up at me.

"It's just that this was the worst I've seen him, Jack. He's always been very easy to deal with, and this time he was just so flustered and angry and…" she said with sad eyes.

"It's just that he looked at me as if I'd let him down, and he was so angry. He kept saying he wanted to go home. It was horrible," she finished and then put her head against my chest again as she squeezed me hard.

"Mom, listen. I'll go in and talk to the staff, and I'll make sure he's doing okay. And then I'll come back out and sit with you and then take you home," I said to her in a consoling way as she started to calm back down.

"No, Jack, you can't go in now. The doctor said they were giving him some medication and that he was in good hands and to let him rest for the night," she said as she lifted her head from my chest.

We sat at the bench for a while, just talking and looking up to his room. I held my mother's hand, and we sat and comforted each other as we remembered a man so strong and confident with a huge heart for everyone around him. It was a strange feeling to look up at night toward this building and see all the beautiful antique lamps and chandeliers that were shining so eloquently on such a dark and quiet night. I was extremely sad but couldn't show my true feelings, as I knew this would upset my mother even more. She was in a very fragile state. I wanted my mother to come and spend the night at our house, but she wanted to go back to her own home.

We got up from the bench and began to walk to her house. It was a quiet walk underneath the maple trees that hung over the sidewalks. I thought we would talk till we reached her doorway, but we didn't. I just held her hand all the way there, and then we hugged and I told her I would call her in the morning. She smiled and closed the door behind her, and then I walked home by myself. It was a lonely walk, and it felt strange that it was so quiet. I've always felt that quietness seems to appear more during sad times.

I reached my back door and went into the kitchen. The light was on, but the house was also very still, and it felt awkwardly silent. I stood for a moment and looked out the kitchen window into the backyard. I poured myself a glass of water from the sink and then walked upstairs, taking my tie off as I made my way up the creaky steps and into the dark bedroom. I could see Rosie asleep on her bed on the floor by my dresser, and Al was sleeping peacefully on her side. I sat down on the bed right next to her and put my hand on her back. She woke easily and looked up at me.

"How's your dad?" she asked with eyes half open.

"He had a bad day, Al. Mom said he was just very confused and angry, and it really got to her. She was really upset and broken," I replied.

"Sorry to hear that, Jack. But listen to me. He's in good hands over there. He's got a lot of trained professionals, and they're the best at what they do. I'm sure the doctor and the staff have everything under control right now and he's sleeping peacefully. Come to bed, and we'll call and check on everyone in the morning," she said as she rubbed my arm, looking up at me with sleepy eyes.

I sat for a moment and realized Allison was right, and then I wanted to let her know what I was thinking. "I'm sorry I missed your doctor's appointment, honey," I said softly and wanted to continue.

But she just looked too tired to talk more. "It's okay, Jack. I'm fine. Let's get some rest and talk in the morning."

"Okay, Al," I replied. Even though it wasn't okay.

6

A MATTER OF TRUST

The next morning was a little uncomfortable, to say the least. I couldn't sleep with so much on my mind and had gotten up early and made a pot of coffee. Allison was still sleeping soundly when I went downstairs, so I just had a cup of coffee in the living room and watched the morning news. Rosie came down after a while and lay down beside my chair, and I petted her as I caught up on the day's happenings on CNN. As I started my second cup of coffee, I heard Allison stirring about upstairs, and then I heard the shower and the bathroom door close. I thought I'd make her some breakfast while she got ready, so I put an English muffin in the toaster and poured some juice and made a setting at the table for her, and then I waited till she came down. Only about ten minutes went by, and then I heard Al's footsteps making their way down the staircase. This was a record for her, as she usually took at least a half hour every morning to slowly get ready and make her way out the door. I had set out her muffin with some marmalade and a glass of juice and cup of coffee at the dining room table. I sat at the table and waited for her to turn the corner into the dining room. As she came around the corner, I was reminded once again of how beautiful she was and gave her a sincere smile.

"Good morning, Al," I said as she came into the room. Rosie had gotten up and came upstairs and into the room to greet her with a wagging tail and happy face.

"Good morning," she replied easily as she petted Rosie and then looked at the table at the small breakfast that I put out for her.

"That's nice, Jack. Thank you," she said as she came over and placed her briefcase on the table, and then she sat down beside me. She still looked a little tired as she took a sip of coffee.

"How did you sleep, honey?" I asked as we nursed the coffee together.

"All right, I guess. Not totally sound, but good enough to face the day. And my schedule is packed and starts early today, too," she replied as she started to stand back up. She seemed to be in a rush to start her workday and get to her office.

"Tell me more about your mom and dad, Jack. Was your mom a little better when you left her?" she asked as she put her suit coat on and then put her briefcase strap over her shoulder.

"A little bit. She was very upset last night and worried about my dad because he had a bad night. But she calmed down, and I sat with her for a while and then walked her home. I told her I would check with the doctor this morning and would call her as soon as I finished speaking with him," I said.

"Well, I'm glad you were there for her, Jack. I talked to her for a while last night, and she was pretty upset. I would give the doctor a call early and get back to her as soon as you can," she said as she sipped some juice and put the glass back on the table.

"I'll be in meetings most of the day, so I'll catch up with you when I get home tonight, okay?" she continued as she grabbed her keys on the kitchen counter and made her way to the back door.

"Al?" I said.

She stopped briefly and looked over at me.

"I'm sorry about yesterday. Is everything okay? Did everything go well at your doctor's appointment?" I asked sincerely.

"Yes, it went fine, Jack. Everything is okay," she replied as she smiled back at me.

"I'll see you tonight. I got to go." She gave me a slight smile, shut the door behind her, and then walked hurriedly to her car and quickly made her way out of our driveway.

I sat for a while at the table, thinking. My mind-set switched back to my dad, and I thought it best to place the call to the doctor as early as possible. It made me sad to think that my dad was in this state, but it was worse knowing that my mom was completely and utterly worried about her husband of over fifty years. I sat for a few moments at the table and started to reflect about my dad. Worry started to creep in, but I immediately felt better as I looked down and noticed Rosie was sitting at my feet and looking up at me with a big smile. I gave her a rub of the head and knew that she had to go outside. It was also time to give her a fresh bowl of water and some breakfast. Rosie always had a way of making me feel better during the toughest times. She was always right at my side, and I know it sounds so simple or foolish, but I loved having her with me, especially when I was alone in the house.

"Come on, girl. Let's go outside," I said to her as we made our way to the back door and then went outside together.

As I walked into my office, Maggie was standing with Stacey at the front desk, and they informed me that my mom had already called for me. I filled them in on yesterday's events and then made my way back to my desk to check my calendar and e-mails and get ready to place a call to the doctor. Maggie came into my office with a cup of coffee and placed it on my desk and smiled at me and then rubbed my shoulders. She then left and closed the door behind her so I could have some privacy.

"Good morning, Doctor. This is Jack McNamara. How are you?" I asked.

"I'm doing well, Jack. Thank you. I'm sure you're calling this morning about your dad. So, just to set you at ease right away, I'll let you know he's doing a lot better this morning," replied the doctor.

"Yes, I am. Thank you, doctor. That's great news. I was worried, and I know my mom was extremely concerned and upset last night," I said as I closed my eyes and felt grateful.

"Now, let me fill you in, Jack. As you know, your dad is going through the different stages of this disease. He will be more prone to these episodes as it progresses, so we need to be mentally prepared for some off times as he moves along. There will be changes and sometimes there will be outbursts when he becomes unable to control his emotions, and this is triggered by the forgetfulness and memory loss. Last night was one of those times. With that said, we had to change the dosage on some of his medications. I will review this with your mom, and then we can get together for a consultation later this week. Again, rest assured that he is in good hands, and he is in good spirits this morning," the doctor continued.

"That makes me feel a lot better. Thank you again, Doctor. And I just want to say I really appreciate everything that you and your staff have done for my dad. It's really comforting to know he's in good hands during these difficult times, and I know my mom really feels good that he's in a great facility. And with that said, I think I'll let you go and give her a call right now to set her at ease," I said, feeling a lot better.

"No need to, Jack. Your mom is here already and sitting in the room with your dad. She's been here since four in the morning. The staff called me, and I came down and checked on the situation. She actually slept in your dad's room for a while, and they had breakfast together after he woke up. I spent some time talking with them and then left them alone most of the morning. I walked by the room about ten minutes ago, and they were both sitting and watching the news together," he said.

I paused for a moment and smiled to myself. "I should have known she'd be there," I said, shaking my head in disbelief.

"I'll be right down, too. Thanks, again, Doctor. Good-bye," I said and then put the phone down.

I sat in my chair for a while, smiling to myself. I grabbed a baseball off the corner of my desk and stared at it and rubbed it. It was my lucky baseball that was signed by Tommy Agee of the New York Mets. He was a center fielder, and my favorite player of the team that won the 1969 World Series. My dad had given it to me for my fourteenth birthday. I felt both blessed and lucky this morning. My heart was at ease, and I knew my parents were both okay and together again. I stood up and put my suit coat on and grabbed my briefcase and got ready to make my way out of my office. Maggie was standing at my doorway with the door slightly ajar.

"Peter is on line four, Jack. Is everything okay with your dad?" she asked.

"Yes. Thank you, Maggie," I replied as I sat back down in my chair.

"I'm glad. I'll be up front with Stacey if you need me." She closed the door and walked down the hallway to talk to Stacey.

"Hi, Peter. How are you?" I said in good spirits.

"Great, Jack. It's a beautiful sunny morning, and it looks like it's going to be a better afternoon. I'm all caught up here, and I wanted to know how your schedule looked and if you wanted to play eighteen at Cornell today," he said.

"Wow, that would be great, Peter. Except I'm kind of dealing with something today. My dad had a bad night last night, and I'm on my way over to see him right now and talk to the doctor," I replied.

"Sorry to hear that, Jack. Is everything okay? Can I help in any way?" he asked.

"Everything is fine, but thank you, Peter. Dad had an episode at Bridges last night, but everything is better this morning. I'll find out more later this morning. So I can't do golf today, but maybe we can get together for dinner later this week," I replied.

"Sounds good, Jack. I know Edith wanted to have you guys over. We saw Allison the other day down at Agava, but she was with someone—a colleague, I believe. And Edith didn't want to intrude on the conversation," he said.

"Really? I didn't know she was at Agava. When was that?" I asked.

"I think it was Friday afternoon. She was having lunch. She introduced the gentleman she was with. I think it was Robert Parker? Yes, that was his name," he said.

I paused for a moment and then wondered why Al hadn't mentioned she had had lunch with Robert. I had an uneasy feeling all of a sudden.

"Oh, yes, that's the fellow she works with in her building. We all graduated together. She's known him for quite some time. Anyway, I'll chat with her today and give you a buzz tomorrow at your office, Peter," I said. I then hung up the phone and scratched my head. I had really never had a reason to ever be jealous, as Al and I always had had a great relationship; but this was one of those uncomfortable times. I just shook my head and put down the baseball, grabbed my briefcase again, and started down the hallway to make my way to see my parents.

I felt a little uncomfortable on the car ride over to Bridges. Allison and I had both had lunches and dinners with clients and coworkers throughout our careers. It was part of our jobs. I didn't know why, but this time it just felt awkward to hear about Al having lunch with Robert. As I thought about it for a moment, a memory came to mind of a time when we were students at Cornell. When Al and I were dating, she introduced me to Robert, and afterward, she mentioned she had had a crush on him when she first met him. Then she said it was nothing and always told me I was the better catch. We were kids back then, and I knew it was immature to even think about that now, but I guess my emotions were getting the best of me. As I pulled into the parking lot, I shook my head and laughed at myself, that I was even slightly jealous that Allison would have another relationship. Robert and Al worked together, and it was just plain silly to think anything odd about them having lunch together. I put myself at ease, made my way in, and, after greeting the staff, went upstairs to my dad's room.

I reached my dad's doorway, peeked inside, and stood quietly for a moment. My dad and mom were sitting together and watching television, and I noticed they were holding hands. Ever since I was a kid, it always made me feel good inside when I saw my parents showing affection to each other. It always put a smile on my face. They didn't see me standing there, so I just stood quietly, smiled, and reminisced for a little while. Mom and dad were always together and loved spending time with each other. I smiled, but it was bittersweet because times were totally different now, and I guess no one knew that more than my mom.

"Hello, lovebirds," I said lightheartedly, and their eyes shifted from the television. Big smiles broke out on their faces as they looked over to me.

"Hi, Jack," said my mom, happy to see me there.

My dad just turned and smiled as I walked over to greet them. My mom stood up, and I gave her a big hug and rubbed her back. Our eyes met, and I could tell she was so happy I was there. My dad stood up gingerly, and I gave him a hug and wanted him to know and feel that I really cared about him. I didn't hug my dad as much as my mom through the years, but this time I felt it best to show my love to a man who was always there for his family.

"How are you doing, Pop?" I asked softly.

"I'm good, Jack," he replied. He paused for a few seconds and looked at Mom, and then back toward me.

"I'm just a little embarrassed, I guess. And maybe a little afraid that it's going to happen again," he continued.

Then Mom came over and grabbed him by the hand and put her arm around him. "It's okay, honey," she said.

I sighed slightly and felt for my dad, and I could see the anguish in his face, as he knew he was fighting a battle he would never win.

"Dad, let me tell you a story," I said as he put his arm around my mom.

"I remember a ten-year-old boy who was in a little-league baseball game. He was on a team called the Pleasant Beach Chemists, sponsored by one of the local pharmacies in town. It was the league championship, and this boy was up to bat. The bases were loaded, it was bottom of the ninth, and there were two outs. There were a lot of parents and kids watching this game on the sidelines, and it was very loud. The team was losing two to one, and if this boy got a hit, he would surely tie or win the game. The pitcher was just too good for this young kid. He was too fast for him, and the boy wound up striking out," I said.

Then I paused and looked for an expression on my dad's face. "Does that sound familiar, Dad?"

He nodded.

I continued the story. "That little boy was me. It was a really tough day. I remember how the coach looked at me. I remember the sighs and groans from the parents on our side. I remember the loud cheers from the other side and seeing the other team celebrating. It felt terrible, and I stood and cried at the plate. None of the coaches or players came over to me. Only one person came and put his arm around my shoulder. My dad. I remember you putting your arm on my shoulder and telling me it was okay and saying there was always another game and not to take it so hard," I said, starting to get a little choked up myself.

I paused for a moment and then started again. "Afterward, you took me to Gianelli's for a pizza and soda, and it made me feel a whole lot better. That was an embarrassing time for me as a little kid, but my dad was there to pick me up. Just like he was always there for me.

"Now, I want you to know something. This disease you're fighting is terrible. I know you recognize that, and it's frightening to everyone. But you have nothing to ever be embarrassed about, and there's still going to be a lot of good times. And most importantly, I want you to know I'll always be here for you—every step of the way. And I know Mom will be right by your side too," I said and then reached over and gave him another hug.

"I love you, Jack," he said with teary eyes.

"I love you too, Pop," I replied. My mom stood to the side with her hands clasped and held to her lips.

"Now, how about watching a little golf with your kid?" I asked Dad.

"Sounds good, Jack," he replied, and we all walked over to take a seat at the table. Mom had brought over some cookies and snacks, and for the next couple of hours we watched the European Tour on television and talked sports. It was a great feeling to sit with my parents and have a cup of coffee and not think of anything else. My mom and dad held hands under the table the whole time. Unfortunately, I also noticed that my mom was doing her best as she tried to soothe Dad's shaking hand.

As we were talking, a call came in on my cell phone. It was Gracie.

"Hello, Gracie," I said.

"Hi, Dad. Liz is also on the line with me," she said.

"Hi, Dad, how are you?" Liz asked.

"I'm good, girls. I'm over at Bridges with Grandpa and Grandma."

"Yes, we know. I called your office, and Maggie told me where you were and filled us in on everything. I called Liz, and we thought it would be a good idea to say hello to Grandpa. Is he okay? Can we talk to him?" asked Gracie.

"Yes, he's fine. I'll put him on. Dad, it's Gracie and Liz for you," I said as I handed the phone over.

My dad's eyes lit up in excitement to hear from his granddaughters. "How are the best granddaughters in the world doing?" he asked.

At this stage I thought it would be a good idea to give my dad some time alone as he talked to Liz and Gracie. Mom and I got up, and we motioned to Dad that we would be down the hall. We walked down the hall and took a seat on one of the couches in the main sitting room by a huge window that overlooked the front yard. Mom had filled me in on her visit with the doctor. The doctor had changed his medication to try to keep pace with combatting the progression of Alzheimer's, and he had also made some slight modifications to his heart medicine. He was doing all he could to put together a plan that would try to keep my dad in good spirits and make his time as comfortable as possible. The doctor also said to expect more episodes, but the staff would be very attentive and everyone would be close by in case something should happen again. Mom said she would spend even more time with my dad, if that was possible. She was already down there most of the day, but she said she would come earlier and leave a little later and make her trips more frequent. She also said that a specialist would be brought in to check in on dad and do some more testing and then would meet with us to give us his findings and more advice.

Both of us knew that the waters would be rockier going forward, but we agreed we would enjoy every possible minute of the good times. Mom and I talked a bit about the past and about how Dad used to be and what a great father he was all through my childhood. Then we sat quietly for a while and looked out the window. I held my mom's hand as I stared at the bench that we usually sat on just off the front corner of the property. We sat and watched the rain drip from the large maple trees that surrounded the front yard. The different colors made for beautiful fall foliage, and it always made me smile when I looked at all the brightly colored leaves. I had mixed emotions today, though. I was happy to spend some quality time with my parents, but I was also worried about them going through this uncertain time.

After about twenty minutes, I motioned to my mom that we should get back to the room. We walked down the hall and came to the door and looked inside the room. Dad was still on the phone with the girls. He was laughing as he was hearing about their college experiences and also giving them some pointers for golf and hockey. As I looked at him, he seemed exactly as he always had to me. Having fun and giving advice to his family was what he did best of all. We all loved him for it. So I let him talk to the girls and just sat with Mom on the bed. Dad wound up talking for another fifteen minutes, and then I thought it would be time to give them some privacy. I gave them each a hug and told them I would call later to check in on them.

I made my way down the hall, then downstairs past the reception desk, and proceeded outside to my car. I got into the car and started it, and, as I was pulling out of the driveway, I noticed it was just a few minutes before noon on the car clock. I thought it would be a good idea to drive over to Allison's office and surprise her and take her out to lunch. So I headed over to the Cornell campus.

I pulled into an empty parking space in front of Bergman Hall and turned off the car. Just as I was about to get out, I saw Allison and Robert walk out of the building and stop just outside the entrance. They stood face to face and were talking, and Allison had her arms crossed to her chest. It looked like a deep conversation, so I just sat in my car and watched them from a distance. After a few minutes, Robert leaned toward Allison and gave her a big embrace and held her for a while. He then kissed her on the cheek. Then Robert walked away from her, got in his car, drove past me, and exited the parking lot. Allison just stood there for a while and watched him drive away. She didn't notice me in the car, and she turned and went inside the building.

I sat quietly for a while in my car and stared at the entrance of the building. I felt very confused at this point and very nervous. Allison was my soul mate, and it had been that way since we were barely sophomores in college. Our family was everything to me, but I felt very vulnerable at this moment. All I could think of was Peter telling me how he had seen Allison having lunch with Robert the other day. Again, I knew Al had had a crush on Robert in college for a while, but that was old news. They had worked together for many years. I knew Robert was married with kids and just never thought any more about the past crush between the two. He certainly was a good-looking man, and I could see how he could turn a lady's head, but I never thought it could be Allison's.

As I sat in my car, I thought about all the office romances that had hit the rumor mills through the years, but I had never thought I could possibly have to deal with one myself. There were a lot of mixed emotions inside me, and I thought it would be best just to drive away. So I started the car and headed back home. As I drove through campus, I had a lot of bad thoughts in my mind, and my stomach got queasy. I reached Fall Creek Road and pulled into my driveway and parked the car in the back, just in front of the garage doors. I really needed some fresh air, and it felt good when I stepped out of the car. I rested on the hood of my car for a few minutes and tried to clear my head. Then I walked over to a big wooden swing that sits in our backyard and leaned on the frame. I looked at our house and started to remember when we moved here long ago. I remembered how happy Al was and how funny the kids were as they raced around the yard on our first day. It brought a smile to my face, but I also felt worried. Had I let Al slip away from me? Could this possibly be happening to us? I had so many thoughts rushing through my mind that I just shook my head and walked up to the back door. As I opened the back door,

Rosie was right there with a big smile, wagging her tail. I knelt down in the doorway and rubbed her neck and back.

"You're always here for me, Rosie. I can always count on you to cheer me up. You're the best. You're my special little lady," I said to her as she licked my face while her tail was moving a mile a minute.

"How about we go for a walk, girl?" I asked as I rubbed her head and stood up. Of course, I knew Rosie lived for walks. She especially loved to walk around her home field, Beebe Lake. She was twelve, but she always mustered up enough energy to walk around the lake or play with Liz and Gracie in the yard. I knew it would do me well, too.

I put my jacket over a chair in the dining room and called my office. I told Maggie I would be taking the rest of the day off, and she could tell right away that I needed a mental break. Maggie has always been very supportive through the years, and I don't need to say or do much to let her know how I'm feeling. She can recognize it in my mannerisms or tone of voice immediately. I hung up with Maggie and then went upstairs to change for the walk. I put on a pair of jeans and grabbed my sneakers and sweater. Rosie had followed me upstairs, as per usual, to make sure I would honor my commitment, and kept a watchful eye on me. If I was blue, she could always sense it, and she always made me feel better. We headed downstairs. I grabbed her leash and strapped it on her, and we headed down Thurston to the entrance of Beebe Lake.

As I reached the canoe house, I stopped to take off Rosie's leash. During weekdays there weren't that many walkers, so I usually let Rosie walk by my side without the leash. She was very well behaved, and for the most part, she would just walk alongside or slightly ahead of me. The slight rain had subsided, the sun started to peek out, and it felt good to be out for a walk. My thoughts seemed to go back and forth from my Dad to Allison, but it felt less stressful as I moved along down the path. I usually noticed all the beauty as I walked along Beebe Lake, but this walk was filled with sadness and uncertainty.

I stopped at the granite bench that was tucked away off to the right and sat just off the edge of the water. Cornell alumni had donated it, and there never seemed to be anyone there to use it. There was a sign that designated it a beach, but I had never seen anyone swim there since I had been in town.

Rosie positioned herself right beside me, and we both sat and stared at the lake and the surroundings. The water was very still, and there was a small gaggle of Canadian geese about twenty yards off shore. I started to think that maybe I should have gotten out of the car at Bergman Hall and gone into Allison's office to talk with her. That would have probably been the mature way to handle the situation, but it was too late now. Then my thoughts switched to my mom and dad. I started to think about how my mom must feel as she watched her husband lose his memory right before her eyes. I started to think about how afraid my dad must be, knowing that this was happening to him and there wasn't a damn thing he could do about it. I started to think about how I wished there were cures for these awful diseases such as cancer and Alzheimer's. My emotions seemed to fluctuate between heartache and pain and anger and hopelessness. I started to think of Liz and Gracie and how I missed them already and how they felt about their grandfather. It just got to be too much, and I put my head in my hands and slumped over.

Rosie, of course, sensed my anguish and came closer and rested her head in my lap. I lifted my head after a moment and tried to gather my senses and compose myself. Then I turned to the side and saw an older woman standing next to me with a dog on a leash.

"Is everything okay, sir?" she asked as her golden retriever kept busy sniffing Rosie. It was younger female golden, and she had plenty of energy and was very excited to meet another dog. Rosie, being a lot older and more mature, was totally fine with the other dog's explorations and enjoyed the visitor.

"Yes, thank you," I replied, and I gave the younger dog a pat on the head. "Just having a bad day, I guess. But it's always nice to see another golden," I continued as I tried to crack a slight smile to my visitor.

"She's five years old and still full of energy. Her name is Libby, and she's got to meet everyone. And she loves to say hi to any dog that comes along," she replied, looking at her pet with much adoration.

"My name is Marion Bennett, and I live just past the Plantations. That's where I usually take Libby for a walk. But we needed a change, and we've been coming here for the last week to get a longer walk," she said.

"Nice to meet you, Marion. I'm Jack MacNamara, and this is Rosie," I said, starting to feel better just talking to someone.

"Well, Jack, it seems you have a lot on your mind, so I'll leave you to your thoughts. Now, I'm a little older than you, and one thing I always realized is that tomorrow is a new day," she said as she slightly tugged at Libby to start away.

"Thanks, Marion, and nice to meet you," I replied with an easy smile.

"You're welcome, Jack. Libby and I will see you around the lake again," she said as she made her way down the path toward the canoe house.

It's funny how a complete stranger with some kind words can give you a different perspective on life. What a kind and thoughtful person to take the time to see if I was okay and to stop and talk to me. I started to feel a little more positive, and, after a few minutes, I got up, and we continued our walk on the gravel path between the trees and wild flowers. Rosie was moving slowly in front of me and paused here and there to sniff the ground or a tree, and I let her be. And then she just ran past me to take the lead again.

About a hundred yards or so up the path, there was a small wooden bridge that crossed a small inlet of the lake. This was another one of Rosie's spots. Since I could remember, she had been coming to this bridge and then perching herself down in the middle of it, taking a seat facing the lake. She would sit there for a few minutes each time we came. I didn't know why she did it, but it had been her routine for years. It was as if she were staring out over her kingdom or something, and she was the guardian of the lake and it was her duty to keep a watchful eye over her territory. I usually walked by her as she sat on the bridge, and I would get to the other side and give her some time. After a minute or so, she would break away, as if released from her trance, and joyously trot up the path again. It just cracked me up, and it gave me something to smile about—which really helped more than ever this time. It was hard to take my mind off my parents and Al, but I tried to just soak up my surroundings for a little while, and it settled me down. We had the path all to ourselves, which was the best thing about weekdays, as all the students were in class, supposedly, and most people were working. You might run into a retiree here or there, or a visitor, but for the most part, it was a very inactive time. It was my second-favorite time to walk the lake. My first, of course, was early mornings or lunchtime on the weekends with Allison.

As we started to approach the granite bridge, Rosie took off into an all-out sprint. Then I heard a high-pitched yell for help. It sounded as though it was from a young girl.

"Rosie!" I yelled as I started to run in the same direction. The bridge was about thirty or so yards away, and as I got closer, I could see a young girl and older woman at the top of it. They were both looking down at the water, and the older woman then frantically scampered down the other side of the bridge. Rosie reached the start of the bridge and made her way down to the edge toward the water in a hurried state.

"Oscar! Grandma, get him!" yelled the young girl to the older woman.

As I came to the start of the bridge, I could see a small dog flailing around in the water beneath the bridge. Most dogs are decent swimmers, but this little guy was having a tough time. As I reached the young girl, I saw Rosie leap from the edge into the water and paddle to the dog in distress. Rosie's splash startled the little dog but also propelled him in the right direction, and the little guy began to make his way to safety on the other side of the shoreline. The little dog was doing the best he could with his tiny legs to move to safety as Rosie nudged him along. It was as if the little dog had picked up the skill of swimming in a matter of seconds as a mother-like figure forced her to learn quickly to save her life. The older woman was screaming in Chinese and stroking the water toward her as she stood knee deep in the reeds. The young girl was also yelling in Chinese and then switched to English.

"My grandma can't swim. Please help her get my dog!" she yelled to me, and I made my way down to the old woman as fast as I could, keeping my eyes on the little dog at the same time. As I raced down the embankment and prepared to jump in to retrieve the dog, Rosie snatched up the little one by its neck and made her way to the old woman. The woman started to calm down, and the little girl ran down the embankment to stand with us. I just stopped and stood in amazement as Rosie dragged the dog to shore, released the little Pug puppy, and gave it one last nudge in the behind toward its owners. It was as if Rosie had been taken over by maternal instinct and knew a little one was in dire need of her services.

The girl swiftly picked up the dog, and the grandmother grabbed them both and moved them to dry ground. Rosie made her way through the reeds and then stood at my side. She was panting and sopping wet and shook off a few times. Water and saliva were being flung all over me, but I didn't care. I just rubbed her head and ears with both my hands.

"Great job, girl," I said.

The little girl and her grandmother were very much relieved, and I don't think the little girl wanted to let her dog on the ground anytime soon. She gave the pug to her grandmother and knelt down in front of Rosie and gave her a big hug and kiss on the head.

"Thank you for saving Oscar. Thank you. Thank you," she said over and over again as she gave her continuous hugs and pets.

Rosie loved the attention and was just plain tuckered out and panting as the little girl kept rubbing her. Then Rosie gave another huge shake to dry herself off, and the little girl got wet and laughed hysterically at the event and went over to check on Oscar again. I don't know what it is about pugs. I love the breed, but they always look as if they're crying or upset about something. They always have this tearful expression, even if they're elated or having the best day of their lives. But they're cute and adorable dogs just the same. All in all, the little guy definitely had a right to display his concerned and worried facial expressions this time, and I'm sure he felt a lot better on land and with his owners at his side.

"What's her name?" she asked me as she came back over with Oscar in her arms.

"This is Rosie," I said with a warm smile and wet jeans and sneakers. The little girl held Oscar's face to Rosie's, and then she put the smaller dog on the ground at Rosie's feet.

"Oscar says thank you, Rosie," she said and then picked the puppy back up quickly.

"She says you're quite welcome," I said as I gestured to the little girl, and then I looked over to the older woman and nodded my head.

It turns out that the little girl was a daughter of a graduate professor at Cornell, and she was taking a walk with her new puppy and her grandmother who was visiting from China. They had stopped during their walk at the top of the bridge, and the girl had put the dog on the wall and wanted to take a picture. As the grandmother grabbed her camera, the dog slipped down into the water, and that was when we heard her scream.

That seemed to be quite enough excitement for all of them, and after the little girl hugged Rosie again, they made their way back to their apartment just a few blocks from the lake.

Rosie and I made our way back to the other side of the bridge, and I let her lie down in her spot underneath the big maple tree as I sat down on the granite bench that surrounded the tree. I looked out over the lake and thought about the day I had just had. It wasn't even dinnertime yet, and I couldn't remember a more eventful day. Rosie just rested on her side looking as if she could've taken a big nap right there, so I gave her a lot of time to catch her breath before we started home. I stared at her and shook my head again as I thought about the natural tendencies that must have caused her to react so swiftly and strongly to help a little one who was in dire straits.

As I looked down at Rosie and then across the lake, my thoughts quickly turned to Allison. I wanted to talk to her and find out what was going on between her and Robert. Also, I still owed her an apology for missing her doctor's appointment. The joy of watching Rosie save little Oscar slowly slipped away, as now I was thinking about my relationship with my wife. I wanted to get home and pull myself together to have a conversation with her tonight.

I let Rosie rest a little longer, and then I got her up and told her we were going to start home. This time I put her leash on.

7

A QUIET EVENING

When Rosie and I got back to the house, I let her in the back door and she ran right for her water bowl. She lapped the whole bowl up in seconds, so I refilled it and gave her some food. Then she walked into the living room and lay right down on her bed that sits to the left of the fireplace. I followed her into the living room and watched her get settled in, and then I walked back into the kitchen. As I looked down at the floor, I noticed all the muddy tracks that both of us were leaving all over the house. At least Rosie had an excuse. She had rescued a young dog.

I didn't have a good excuse and felt that it would be a much better night if I got the mop out and cleaned up after both of us. So I took off my dirty sneakers and put them on the rack just outside the kitchen door and grabbed a mop and bucket and went to work on the house. It cleaned up nice, and I felt a lot better. I checked on Rosie and she was sleeping away on her bed, so I took a break and went back into the kitchen and made some coffee.

As the coffee brewed, I stood in the kitchen and leaned on the counter and stared out the window above the sink. It was quiet in the house, and that gave me a chance to think about things for a while. I felt a little numb. I just focused on the double swing in the backyard. I thought about Allison and the kids. I thought about my parents again and was trying to figure out what my next course of action would be in helping my mom and dad. Mostly, I thought about my wife and my marriage. A lot of questions rattled through my brain again. How could I make it better? Did I give Al enough attention? I started to get overwhelmed again, and then the coffee timer went off in the background. I poured myself a cup and went into the living room and sat in the recliner and just sipped my coffee and watched Rosie sleep.

I started to put together a game plan for the evening. The first thing I would do is give Rosie a bath and get cleaned up myself. The next thing was to go down to Wegmans and get some food to make a nice dinner for Allison. Then I'd stop at Triphammer Wines and Spirits and pick up a nice bottle of wine. As I nodded to myself that it sounded like a pretty solid plan, I finished my coffee and started to put it in motion. I put my cup in the kitchen sink and went back and got Rosie going, and we headed upstairs to the shower. Needless to say, she didn't like to get cleaned up, so it took a little coaxing and pleading every time we went through this procedure. She was twelve years old and had rescued a dog, so I was extremely patient with her this time around. I kept her cleaning quick and washed her fast in the shower stall and then dried her off and let her mosey downstairs. I hopped in myself and took care of business and was in and out quickly and then tidied up the bathroom. Then I went downstairs and peeked into the living room and noticed Rosie back in her spot by the fireplace. So I grabbed a jacket and headed out on my mission.

Liz and Gracie had definitely made my dad's day by giving him a call and talking to him for a long time. When you have a special bond with your grandparents, sometimes it's harder to be apart from them than from your own parents. I knew it was hard for them to accept my dad's condition, but they were trying their best to handle it on their own terms. Apparently, after they hung up with Grandpa, Gracie had called Liz to talk about the conversation. It had lifted her spirits, but she had still noticed how Grandpa was getting more and more forgetful about things. Liz, being the big sister, always played the role of trying to calm Gracie down and give her a little more perspective on the situation. They had talked with my dad for half an hour, and the conversation that took place afterward between the girls was about the same amount of time. Liz handled Gracie's feelings quite well and told her she needed to concentrate on her schoolwork and hockey and that she would check in with me and talk with her again in the morning. I got Liz's call around five o'clock that evening as I was preparing dinner for Al and me.

"Hi, Dad, how are you?" she said in a high spirits.

"I'm doing good, Liz. I'm in the kitchen making some dinner for us and trying not to burn anything along the way," I replied as I checked on the main course in the stove.

"What's on the menu tonight, chef?" she said in a whimsical tone.

"Well, we have salmon with roasted potatoes and asparagus. We also have a nice bottle of chardonnay. I think your mom will like it...that is, if it comes out the same way she usually cooks it. But I know that's highly unlikely," I replied.

"I'm sure it will, Dad. You've always done a pretty good job in the kitchen," she said.

"Thank you, Liz. Well, how is everything else? Oh, and by the way, thank you for calling Grandpa. I'm sure he was delighted to hear from you girls. How was your conversation?" I asked.

After a brief pause, Liz said, "Well, Dad, that's why I'm calling. Overall, we had a great talk. Grandpa was in very good spirits, and I know he loved hearing from us as much as we loved talking to him. It's just that he doesn't remember a lot of little things...and sometimes he called me Gracie. I noticed his mood change a little bit as he became agitated about not remembering things. Now, I know he's older, and I guess we just wanted to see what you thought...and, well, you know Gracie; she always gets overemotional, and I'm trying to calm her down, too," Liz said with a slight sigh of exasperation.

I closed the oven door and put the oven mitt on top of the stove. After a deep sigh, I said, "Well, Liz, I'm just really proud of the fact that you guys love your grandpa so much and care about him. It makes me feel really good inside to know that you girls have such a special relationship with my parents. With that said, I want you to know that this Alzheimer's is a real bitch. It affects the person and everyone around them. I've talked extensively with the doctor, and so has your grandmother. It's hard to grasp everything that's going on and understand the best way to deal with this whole thing. There are different stages of this disease, and it doesn't get any easier.

Forgetting conversations and memory loss are just a small part of it. There are going to be these changes in mood and defensiveness, and, unfortunately, it's going to get worse. Depression and disorientation will also become part of the equation."

"Now, I know this is hard to swallow, but all we can do is support my dad and show our love and be there as much as possible and enjoy his good days, but recognize that he will also have bad ones. And believe me, you girls have always been there for my dad, and he loves you for everything you do for him. Believe me when I say that, Liz."

"Grandma, Mom, and I will take care of Grandpa. I want you girls to enjoy your college days and concentrate on school and your sports. That's what Grandpa would want you to do. And I know you're the older and a little more mature then Gracie, so I need you to tell her that as well. Grandpa is in good hands with us and the staff at Bridges, and you and Gracie can check in with him as much as possible. But just try to keep things in perspective and be patient with him, as you always have been. How does that sound?" I asked.

"Thanks, Dad. Now I have a better understanding, and I'm going to read up on this a little more. And I'll talk to Gracie in the morning," she said. I could sense her calmness over the phone.

"Is everything else good, Liz? How's golf going?"

"It's going real good. I practiced with the team at Shaker yesterday, and I was driving the ball great. My chipping is spot on, and I'm putting lights out. Totally looking forward to first tournament of the season, which of course is the Cornell Invitational. Remember, we're coming to town in a week and a half. I hope you and mom are going to follow me around. You will, won't you, Dad?" she asked.

"I always do, don't I, Liz? I love following you. And you always play well at Cornell. Remember, your mom wants your team to come over for dinner one night during the tournament. So tell your coach, okay?"

"Yep, I already did, Dad. Everyone, including Coach, is looking forward to coming over the house. Oh, yeah, and I forgot to tell you: Gracie just found out that the Clarkson team is definitely having a preseason game against Cornell. It's going to be the same week as my golf tournament. She said she'd call you guys in the morning. You'll be getting a double dose of us," she said comically.

"And, Dad...could you bring Grandma and Grandpa to the course to watch me? And could you bring them to Gracie's hockey game, too? I know it will be a lot for them, but I really think that Grandpa would like it."

"Liz, I promise you, they'll both be there," I replied.

She paused for a few seconds. I knew that was what she had wanted to hear me say. "Thank you, Dad. I can't wait to see you and Mom at the tournament," she said.

"Looking forward to it, Liz. I miss you. I miss you and your sister a lot. Now, how about letting your old man get back to cooking for your mom so I don't burn the dinner," I said.

"Will do. I love you, Dad."

"I love you too, Liz. And tell your sister the same. Please tell her she can call me at work tomorrow, okay?"

"I certainly will. Good-bye, Dad."

"Good-bye, Liz." After hanging up, I felt much better. I guess it's always better to talk about the uncomfortable things, and I knew Liz would make Gracie feel at ease, as she always did.

I checked the stove, and the meal was looking close to being ready. Then I checked my watch. Al was usually walking in the door around now, so I set the table and poured us each a glass of wine. I lit a candle that sat in the glass casing in the middle of the table, and then I took a seat. I started to feel uncomfortable again about seeing Allison embrace Robert and get a kiss from him, and uneasy thoughts rattled through my brain. I knew it was just on the cheek, but it still made me jealous and uncomfortable. Also, I felt childish that I hadn't approached her at that moment, but I guess I had too much going through my head to deal with it. Just as my mood began to grow somber, Rosie walked up to me and sat to the side of my chair.

I smiled at her and petted her on the head and under her chin. "You always know when I need someone. Don't you, girl?" I said to her.

She seemed to acknowledge the feeling, and then she licked my hand and rubbed her head on my thigh. Then she lay down on the floor by my chair. What a genuine and sweet animal, I thought. I still was utterly amazed as I thought of her rescue at the lake and just shook my head back and forth as I petted her.

As I took a sip of wine, I heard Al's car come down the driveway. I got up from the table and went into the kitchen, and Rosie followed alongside me. I looked out through the window and watched as Al stepped out of her car and made her way to the back porch. She noticed me through the window and gave me a gentle smile, but she looked exhausted as she made her way into the kitchen.

"Hi, Al," I said as she came in through the back door.

"Hi, Jack," she replied in a tired voice.

Rosie was right at the door and gave her a warm and friendly greeting which help set the mood for my special dinner.

"Hello, Rosie. It's nice to see you, too," she said as she gave her a pat on the head and came over to me and gave me a small kiss that made me feel better right away.

"I hope you're hungry, Al. I've got your favorite dinner lined up—salmon with roasted potatoes and asparagus. How does that sound?" I asked as I opened the stove door to show her my masterpiece.

"Oh, and I poured a glass of wine for you on the table," I continued.

"This is wonderful, Jack. Thank you. It's been a long day, and I could use a glass of wine. And I can't believe you've made dinner. It's very sweet. Thank you very much," she said as she made her way into the dining room, draped her coat over a chair, and put her briefcase down by the hutch. Then she grabbed her glass of wine, took a sip, and sat at the table.

"It's pretty much ready, Al. I'll make our plates and bring them in." I said as I opened the oven door and checked one last time. Then I grabbed the oven mitts and put the glass pan on the stovetop. I prepared our plates, brought them into the dining room, and set them on the placemats on the table.

Allison gave me a warm smile and acknowledged my effort in making dinner. I must admit I didn't cook very often, but everything came out pretty good, and the salmon went very well with the wine. Al usually did all the work in the kitchen, as she was the better chef, and my duties were at the grill for steaks, hot dogs, and hamburgers. I guess that has always been the way, but she definitely enjoyed my stepping up to the plate and cooking dinner every once in a while and giving her a break.

Dinner, for the most part, was a soft and quiet time. Allison appeared very tired and pensive, and she seemed pretty hungry, too. I thought I'd keep the conversation to a minimum and let her eat and ease into the evening. She seemed to enjoy the dinner, and I poured us each a second glass of wine.

"Thank you, Jack. That was very good. I had a long day today with lots of meetings, and it's nice to come home and have dinner already prepared. Thank you," she said again with a smile.

"How was your day? Did you check in with your dad?" she asked as she took a sip of wine and looked at me.

"Yes, I did. I called there this morning and had a good conversation with the doctor. He filled me in on everything and talked a lot more extensively about what Dad's going through and the different stages. He said that there are a few different stages with Alzheimer's and that Dad will have times of confusion and big mood swings, too. He says he will become defensive and confused from time to time and that it's just part of the disease. Unfortunately, the memory lapse is part of it as well. All in all, we just have to support him as much as possible and be gentle and patient with him through this thing. The doctor said it's going to be tough, but he will watch him closely and so will the staff. Mom was already there when I called, too. Apparently she had been there since four or five in the morning and sitting in the room with my dad," I said.

I sighed and looked at Al and then down at my plate. "Actually, Liz and Gracie called me together while I was with Dad, and they talked to him for a long time. I could tell he really enjoyed that," I continued.

"Jack, your dad has a lot of support around him. He'll be fine, and we're right here to help with anything he needs. And the staff over there is phenomenal," she said as she reached over and put her hand on mine.

"How are the girls? What are they up to?" she added.

"They're great, Al. Liz is excited to bring the golf team over for dinner one night, just like last year. Oh, boy, and I got some big news. Liz told me that Gracie's team is definitely coming to town to play Cornell in a preseason game. She said it'll be the same weekend that Liz's golf team is coming here, too. I don't know what Gracie's plans are for dinner with the hockey team. I thought you could talk to her about that tomorrow," I said sheepishly. And as soon as I mentioned Gracie's team coming on the same weekend and possibly having them to the house, I immediately knew I had put too much on her plate. I guess I should have thought it through a little more.

"I don't know, Jack. Having the coaches and six players on the golf team is a little easier than cooking for thirty players and coaches on the hockey team. I'll talk to Gracie and see if the coaches have any dinner plans yet and come up with something. I can't wait to see them, though. I miss having the girls around here," she said in a sad tone.

I could tell I had overwhelmed her a little bit. She loved having the kids over, but cooking for entire teams was a lot of work. Especially for someone who already had a big workload with her job.

"I miss them too, honey. And don't worry; I'll help out with the team dinners. I'll be your number-one assistant in the kitchen," I replied, trying to bring some humor into the air as I held up my hand to declare the scout's honor.

"Both of the girls really want my mom and dad to come watch them play. I know Dad can't walk much, but if he's doing okay, maybe he can come out and watch Liz tee off and watch a little with Mom from the clubhouse. And I'll ask Peter for his hockey tickets, since they're right next to my parents' seats, and we can all watch Gracie together—of course, if he's still up for it," I said, trying to piece together a game plan.

"Sounds good, honey. Actually, I saw Peter and Edith at lunch the other day. I was having lunch with a colleague, and they stopped at our table to say hello," she said.

I was torn about approaching her on this topic and wanted to see if she would offer any more about her lunch with Robert. But she didn't, and I felt it best to leave the subject alone for now. Also, I guess I didn't want to let her know I had stopped by her office and didn't go inside to see her. And then I realized I couldn't bring up the fact that Rosie had rescued a puppy today. Things seemed to get more complicated, so I just let it go.

We talked a little more about having Peter and Edith over for dinner after Thanksgiving, and then I got up to start cleaning off the table and told Allison to just sit and relax. The conversation then switched to her parents.

"About Thanksgiving, Jack. What do you think about going down to North Carolina and spending it with my parents? We haven't seen them in a while, and I know they would love it if we could go down there and spend some time with them," she asked.

I put a dish in the sink and came back into the dining room. "I would love to go down and see your mom and dad. It's just that it's not the best time right now, Al. I just think I need to be around home for right now, just in case I need to go over and help out with my dad. And we got the girls coming to town over the next couple of weeks. And I seem to be getting a little backed up at work with all this going on," I replied in a slightly overwhelmed tone. And as I looked at her, I could see the disappointment in her face.

"I understand we have a lot going on here, Jack. We always have a lot going on. I mean, we both work and then follow the girls around all the time, and your parents," she said. I could see a little bit of frustration start to build in her eyebrows.

"What I'm trying to say is, there is never a perfect time to go away and see my parents. But we have to make time to visit them, or we'll always be putting it off. I know your dad needs help right now, but I miss my mom and dad, and I need to see them more often," she said as she got up from the table.

I stood in the archway between the dining room and kitchen, thinking for a moment. Then I walked over and put my arms around Allison and looked into her eyes. "I miss them too, Al. Could you let me think about it for a while?" I asked her.

She nodded and put her head on my chest. I rubbed her back and kissed the top of her head as I embraced her.

"I'm exhausted, Jack. I think I'm just going to go upstairs and take a shower and go to bed. Maybe read just a little bit."

"Okay. I'll finish cleaning up. You go on up," I said as she pulled away and made her way upstairs. As I picked up her plate and walked it to the sink, I realized I hadn't followed up and asked her about her doctor's appointment and felt very foolish. I guess I had just gotten distracted watching the girls that day down at Stewart Park, and she was half asleep the other night, and that didn't seem like a good time for a conversation either. I walked quickly to the stairs and looked up. She had just reached the top.

"Al, I forgot. How did everything go with your doctor's appointment? Is everything okay?"

She looked back down at me and paused for a moment. "Yes, Jack. It was just a routine checkup. I'm fine." She gave me a weary smile and walked down the hall toward the upstairs bathroom.

I stood there for a minute and then walked back into the kitchen and finished cleaning up. I sat for a while in the living room and thought about how it had been an awkward day all around, from beginning to end. The dinner had been good, and the conversation had been soothing for a while. But the uneasy feeling had returned, and it seemed entirely my fault. I started to regret not asking Allison about Robert. I regretted shooting down her thoughts about going to North Carolina for Thanksgiving. I began to feel more and more selfish and confused about my decision. My plan had been to come to terms with my wife tonight, and I was disappointed at myself for not making that happen.

At this point, I thought I would give Al some space and let her get some sleep. I started a fire and sat back in my easy chair and tried to think about how I could make things better. Rosie wandered in from the dining room and lay down next to my chair. I petted her back as I continued to think about how I would approach tomorrow. I sat by the fire for a long time that night, and by the time I made my way upstairs to bed, I still didn't have an answer.

8

OUR GIRLS COME HOME

Time seemed to go by really slow the following week. I was still torn in a few different ways. Allison and I fell into our routines at work and home and focused on the girls coming back to Ithaca. *Tranquility* was the perfect word to describe the essence of the house. We both seemed to work longer hours and then come home and have dinner and go to bed. The intimacy was certainly not there, but it was indeed peaceful. Al had an alumni fundraiser for her department and worked the following weekend, which she would do on occasion. I wound up opening accounts for Jeff and Carol, and I called Helen to thank her for the referral. Actually, I offered to take her to lunch at the Heights Café to thank her, and she gladly accepted the invitation. Since Al and I were not really having a lot of deep discussions lately, it felt good to talk to another woman. It was a very pleasant lunch and a good way to break up the workweek.

I kept busy at work but couldn't help but think Allison might have started a relationship with Robert. Still, I didn't bring it up at home. I guess I was just hoping she'd be the one to open up about it if indeed it was true. This was probably the worst thing I could have done. Looking back, it definitely would have helped us if I had approached her right away about Robert. But communication wasn't and isn't one of my strong suits, and it's quite ironic, since I spend all my time talking to people in person and over the phone. My conversations at home with Allison seemed to revolve around Liz and Gracie coming home. And when that weekend finally came, we were in much better spirits. Allison always needed a little bit of a buffer from me, and the girls provided that in the house and in our lives.

Liz and the Siena golf team were the first ones to make their way to Ithaca. It was customary to play a practice round on Friday and have all the participating teams play the course before the actual tournament started Saturday morning. Saturday consisted of thirty-six holes, with lunch in between, and then the event finished Sunday morning with eighteen holes. There were fifteen teams in the tourney, and five players got to play for each team. The lowest scores for teams and individuals were then calculated to figure out the winners and placements of the players and their teams. Liz was just a sophomore, but Al and I had been going to junior golf tournaments for a long time, as we loved watching the kids play. We usually let them have the practice round to themselves and then caught them on the tee box for the opening round. So we each got a call from Liz on Friday morning, announcing that the team had arrived from Latham and was in the Cornell golf course parking lot.

"Good morning, Liz," I said cheerfully.

"Good morning, Dad. I just wanted to let you know we're here and unloading our clubs now," Liz said in a sleepy voice.

She and Gracie have both attested to the fact that whenever either of their teams go on the road and depart in the early morning hours, everyone usually sleeps all the way to the destination. My two girls were notorious sleepers, so this was right in their wheelhouse.

"Great. How was the ride from Siena?" I asked.

"Easy. Everyone slept. Coach sang a little with the radio to his old music, but he wasn't that loud," she replied. Apparently, the coach liked to put on his seventies and eighties music and sing along to old songs on their drives to tournaments. At least it was what the girls considered to be old music. This usually prompted the girls to put on their earphones and listen to their own music or watch movies along the way.

"Well, Dad, I got to get going. We start teeing off in an hour, and everyone wants to hit the range and the putting green. I already called Mom, but remember, we'll be over to the house around five tonight," she continued in a rushed tone.

"I remember, honey. And Mom is excited to see you and the team, too. She cooked up a big pot of pasta and meatballs for the team. And we'll have some red wine for the coach," I said, remembering that the coach enjoyed a glass of red wine—especially after spending an entire day with five girls. So I said good-bye, hung up the phone, and put it on my desk. I was at work and had a busy day in front of me, but I felt good inside. It felt great to hear from Liz, and I was excited to see her and spend some time talking to her.

I looked out through my office window. It also felt good that it was a beautiful, crisp, sunny fall day and was shaping up to be nice weather for the golf tournament, which was a blessing because this tournament had a history of some pretty severe weather consisting of high winds and rain. But it looked perfect this year.

I started to get anxious, as I knew I'd hear from Gracie when she arrived with her team in a couple of hours. I started to daydream a little at my desk. I started to think about when the girls were young, and I thought about all the good times Allison and I had with them in their youth. It felt like a good time to reach out to Allison and talk to her. Just as I picked up my phone and was about to dial Al's number, Maggie showed up in my doorway. She was holding a stack of manila folders and had a big smile.

"Well, are you ready to get started and review your files for today, Jack?" she asked, knowing that my mind wasn't on work today.

"Yes. Yes, I am, Maggie. Come on in," I replied as I put the phone back on my desk.

It was a real busy Friday, but I was in a great mood. I heard from Gracie just after lunch, and she was excited to get back to town. She had already talked to Allison, and they had arranged to have the hockey team over to the house for lunch Saturday afternoon following their morning warm-up skate at Lynah Rink. The coach thought it was a great idea, and the team could actually walk to our house after the skate, as it took only about fifteen minutes and would give them a good stretch after their practice. This was a preseason hockey game, and the first game for either team.

I also talked to Allison in the afternoon, and we had a great conversation. I think the girls coming back to town really put her at ease. She seemed as if she was getting back to her old self and was thrilled to have the whole family back together. I knew it was going to be a lot of work to have both teams over back to back, but she was excited to have kids in the house again. The house had been very quiet over the last couple of weeks, and a little bit of activity with players and coaches seemed like a wonderful remedy. Either way, with about forty players and coaches passing through our doors, it was going to be eventful. Of course, Allison had absorbed most of the workload and had done quite a lot of food shopping to prepare for this weekend. When we had company in the summertime, I did a lot of the grilling outdoors, but in the fall and winter, we relied on pasta. When kids would come over, Al would cook up big trays of pasta with meatballs and have plenty of salad and bread. This weekend was going to be more of the same, only the quantities would be quintupled.

"Liz and the team will be here at five o'clock for dinner, Jack. I'm taking off early from work today and will start preparing the dinner. I have everything under control, but I could certainly use some help in setting the table and getting the extra chairs out of the garage. Could you come home by four o'clock and help with that part?" Allison had asked earlier that afternoon.

"Of course, Al. I'll be home by four and do my bit. Don't worry; I'm your wing man."

It felt good inside to have a nice exchange and connect again. I was looking forward to getting home all throughout the day and knew Al needed help setting up for dinner. I had called my mom between appointments, to check on Dad's situation and see how they were making out. Dad had had a tough week, but he was doing okay today. I knew Mom would love for them to come over and be with the teams, but I also realized it would be too much to ask at this stage. She said that Dad had had an episode last night, not as bad as the one before, but he was extremely flustered and irritable and she just wanted to stay and sit with him. I had dropped in most every day to see him myself, mostly at lunchtime or just after work, before I went home. We had some good conversations, but he was definitely more forgetful and more defensive and agitated at times. He was also a bit more sullen and depressed, which made me sad. It was hard for me to see the toughest man in the world brought to his knees by an opponent he couldn't beat.

The day was hectic, but thanks to Maggie's organizational skills, it went along smooth as silk. She had set up my final client meeting at three o'clock and promised she would have me out the door forty-five minutes later. Again, she was spot on. I walked my clients to the door at a quarter to four and said good-bye, and then I walked back to my office to grab my coat. Just as I put on my coat, Maggie came to my door, and she had a perplexed look on her face.

"What's up, Maggie?"

"Well, Jack, we have some unannounced visitors. Jeff and Carol are up front and want to see you," she said with a concerned look on her face.

Right away my shoulders slumped, as the unexpected client visit was throwing a wrench into my game plan. I shook my head and took a deep breath and tried to think about the best course of action. These people were new clients, but they were now the biggest clients on my books. I wasn't a fan of people just showing up out of the blue, but I certainly couldn't turn them away.

JESS WILLIAM ESPOSITO

Maggie knew I was torn, so she offered her advice. "Why don't you meet with them for a few minutes, Jack. I'll call Allison and let her know you might be a little late. Sound good?"

I thought for a moment and then nodded. I put my coat down and went out to greet Jeff and Carol in the waiting room. "Hello, Jeff. Hi, Carol. Nice of you to drop in," I said cheerfully as I shook Jeff's hand and gave Carol a hug.

"I hope it's okay to drop in like this, Jack. Our last advisor always made time for us. Jeff and I are going to an event tonight, and we had some questions about gifting," said Carol.

"Of course it's okay, Carol. Anytime. Come on back to my office," I replied. I felt uncomfortable as I led them back to my office, but at least Maggie had my back and was going to call Al for me.

The questions that Jeff and Carol had were pretty involved and took up a lot of time, and I wound up sitting with them for over an hour. By the time I showed up at the house, it was a quarter after five, and as I walked up the back steps and looked in the window, I saw that everyone was sitting at the table and eating dinner. I always felt terrible when I let Allison down, and tonight the feeling I had was no different from any other time I had come up short. I walked in through the back door, and, of course, Rosie was right there to greet me. I gave her a good pat and looked toward the dining room table. The first set of eyes that I caught were Al's, and they didn't lie. I saw right away that I had let her down again. We had an old set of sleigh bells hanging from the top of the door, so you could hear when someone came in and out. We had put them up to keep track of the girls coming and going at night. They were both great kids but could be little devils every once in a while. There was music playing in the dining room, and it looked quite festive. All the players, as well as Coach Miller, were sitting around the table, and everyone turned when they heard the bells ring. Liz came running into the kitchen and gave me a great big hug. It felt wonderful to hold her again.

"Hi, Dad. I missed you," she said as she held me tight.

"I missed you too, Liz. I'm glad you're home," I replied as I rubbed her back and looked over to the table.

Everyone was smiling at us, and the coach stood up to greet me. I looked at Liz and kissed her forehead. Then I put my arm around her shoulder and she put hers around my waist, and we walked in to say hello. It looked as if Al had done a marvelous job with dinner. I looked across the table and saw a ton of ziti and meatballs and Italian bread and salad. The kids all had soda, and there was a big bottle of Chianti on the table for Coach Miller, who Liz had told me loved his wine. I shook the coach's hand and told him how nice it was to see everyone again. Some of the players I had met last year, and there were some new ones on the team that we met for the first time. All the girls were in good spirits and were excited for the tournament. They seemed to think the course was in great shape, and all the players had had a nice practice round. There was an open setting for me at the table, right next to Al. I sat down and kissed her on the cheek.

"Sorry I'm late, hon. Some clients came in at the end of the day, and—"

"It's okay, Jack. Don't worry about it. Just dig in while it's hot, and I'll pour you a glass of wine," she said.

When you've been together with someone for so long, you know when he or she is being truly genuine or just polite. Al knew it wasn't the right time to talk about my lateness, and deep down I knew she was angry with me. But she also knew that Liz was home and there was an entire team and the coach at the table with us.

And so the party continued, and all the girls and Coach Miller had a great time. It felt good to have a lot of chatter at the table again. After the girls finished their food, they drifted into the living room and watched television while Al and I remained with the coach and talked awhile and had a couple of laughs. After an hour, the coach announced that they should be getting back to the hotel, as they had an early start and long day tomorrow. He thanked Al for the dinner and walked into the living room and got the players together to board the van. The players thanked us for everything, and I hugged Liz one more time, as did Allison. All the girls gave some love to Rosie on the way out, and then they were off to the hotel. Al and I stood in the kitchen and looked out the window together as they made their way out of the driveway.

"I'm sorry, again, Al. Some people showed up at the end of the day, and I couldn't get out of it," I said sheepishly as I turned to face her. I could tell she was disappointed with the reply; she had heard it a few times already under different circumstances.

"Couldn't or wouldn't? I just needed you to help set up a little, Jack. That's not much to ask. It's okay to tell the clients you have other commitments, isn't it?" she replied softly. Allison never raised her voice or got too upset, and that always made me feel worse.

I apologized again for being late and reiterated that I had been in a tough spot. It was a little quiet and uncomfortable for a few minutes, but then we looked at each other and came to terms and made peace. We started to clean up together and talk about Liz and the coach and players and what a wonderful bunch they were. Liz was certainly in good hands, and she was growing up right before our eyes.

We finished the cleanup and had a half of glass of wine at the table together. Liz teed off at eight o'clock the next morning, and we were going to follow her on the course. And then we had the Clarkson hockey team coming over for lunch. So we thought it would be a good idea to get to bed early ourselves. Allison headed upstairs, and I let Rosie out one last time before bed. As I stood on the back porch and waited for Rosie to finish her business, I kept thinking about Allison. I thought about the look on her face when I showed up late and let her down. I thought about her having lunch with Robert. I knew one thing for sure. I loved her, and I wasn't going to be late for anything tomorrow.

When Al and I pulled into the Cornell golf course parking lot the next morning, I saw my parents right away. They were standing just in front of the putting green and appeared to be looking for Liz. I parked the car, and then we walked over to meet them. It was a brisk morning, but the sun was shining and there was no wind in the air. It was a perfect fall golf day. There wasn't too much talk between Al and me this morning, but we were excited to follow Liz today. Both Al and I enjoyed walking the tournaments together, and it was even more pleasurable if we had a beautiful sunny day. Also, since I loved the game, it was awesome to see the shot-making skills of all the talented players. It boggled my mind sometimes to see them pulling off great bunker shots or showing no fear and attacking pins that were tucked in the most ruthless spots on the green. I loved to watch them think their way around the course, and to see your kid have a great outing is truly a special feeling.

My parents loved to watch the girls play too. Liz had picked up a lot of my dad's gamesmanship and mental toughness, and it was naturally displayed when she was on the course. I had always noticed a gleam in his eye when he watched her at an event. My mom was truly not as competitive as my dad, but she thoroughly enjoyed having the family together. And since we were a sports-minded family, it was a way for us to spend a lot of time together and be outside, not parked in front of a television. We've had a lot of great conversations and laughs walking around the golf course together, too. It's a little nerve racking to watch your kid have a tough hole or round, but when they were firing on all cylinders and in the zone, it's a great experience. Plus, most golf courses have phenomenal scenery with breathtaking views that contain wonderful flower arrangements and bushes and magnificent trees and holes surrounded by the golfer's main enemy, water. That's the cool thing about golf—the courses are all different, and you get to appreciate all the unique qualities they possess as you stroll the fairways as a player or fan.

We walked across the parking lot, and as we came close to the putting green, I called over to my parents. "Good morning, you two. Great day for golf," I said with a big smile.

"Good morning, Mom. Good morning, Dad," Allison said as she leaned in and put her arm around my dad.

I hugged my mom and looked into her eyes and then gave my dad an arm hug around the shoulders that made him smile.

"Hello, Jack. Hi, Allison. We're so excited, right, Ben?" said my mom, looking at my dad.

He looked happy but confused to me. There was a distant look in his eyes. "Yes, I love coming to the golf course," said Dad as we all looked toward the putting green at all the stand bags that surrounded the area while twenty or so players rolled balls in preparation for their rounds. They would look up from time to time to the first tee, which was adjacent to the putting green and just on the other side of a long arrangement of sea grass and red and white pansies. All the players were well aware of their tee times and the two-stroke penalty that was issued for being late, and not one of them wanted to start the round on a sour note.

"I don't see Liz on the green. Have you seen her yet?" Al asked as she looked over the players and then tried to spot a green-and-gold golf bag with her name on it.

"No, we didn't. We only got here just before you guys," replied my mom as she glanced toward the green again and then over to the clubhouse. There were a lot of parents and players there as well. They always had a nice setup for breakfast for the players, and this was where the parents loaded up on coffee and reacquainted themselves with parents of teammates.

"How are you, Dad? Did you get a good night's rest? Are you ready to walk a little bit today?" I asked as I rubbed his back. He was wearing a Siena windbreaker that we had gotten him for Christmas and a plaid hat he had picked up at the Royal Troon Golf Club In Scotland when he played there years ago with my mom.

He looked at me with slightly glazed eyes and a tender smile and appeared a little cold, too. "I slept okay. I'm kind of tired, but I can't wait to see my granddaughter. I really miss her," he replied as he searched the grounds.

"Where do you think…um…" he started to say and couldn't remember her name.

"Liz, Ben," interjected my mom as she took hold of my dad's hand.

He looked at her with an embarrassed but appreciative glance as his slight smile faded. But the smile was soon resurrected.

"Grandpa. Grandma," a voice called out, and we all turned around to see Liz walking toward us. She was coming down the path from the driving range. She looked fantastic in her green-and-gold Siena golf attire and had a big smile that went from ear to ear. She moved quickly toward us, and she had her golf bag slung across the back of her shoulders. My dad was filled with happiness immediately and started to walk to her. As she got to him, she put her bag down quickly and gave him an enormous hug. Liz was a strong and athletic young lady, but it still looked like a big bear coddling one of his offspring. My dad looked as though he didn't want to let go of her.

"I missed you, Liz," he said.

"I missed you too, Grandpa. I'm glad you and Grandma came," she replied as she took her head off his chest and looked slightly up to him.

Then they walked arm and arm over to my mom, and she gave her a warm embrace.

"Thanks for coming, Grandma."

"We wouldn't miss this for anything, Liz. And you have such a great day for the event," she replied as she looked up at the sun, which sat alone across a clear, pastel-blue sky. Just a few soft white clouds rested off in the distance.

Liz talked to us for a couple of minutes and Dad gave her some advice, as he always provided to both Liz and Gracie, and then she had to move along.

"I'm going to hit a few putts. My tee time is in ten minutes, so I gotta go," she said as she gave us all an appreciative look.

"Go get 'em, Liz. There's no wind today, so attack those pins and don't give those other players an inch of breathing room. Remember, a little gamesmanship goes a long way," said Dad in General Patton–like fashion as my mom slightly shook her head.

"Will do, Grandpa," she said as she turned and headed over to the putting green.

Al and I left my parents by the putting green, and they watched Liz putt a few balls while we walked to get a cup of coffee and something to snack on before setting out to follow Liz. Al and I both acknowledged the fact that Dad seemed a more forgetful and irritable and looked confused at times, but there were also glimmers of his old self here and there, and that was the most confusing part of the equation. It was depressing to see it all unfold right in front of our eyes, but it felt good to see him outside the assisted living home. And even though Al and I had had an uncomfortable moment last night, we were both putting those feelings aside and were ready to have a great day together.

When we got back to Mom and Dad, we saw that Liz had made her way over to the first tee. She had her driver out and was taking some practice swings. She had always been long off the tee, and she was unbelievably straight as well. There were three players in her grouping, and she was the third to tee off.

"Next on the tee, from Siena College. Please welcome Liz MacNamara," bellowed the starter. All the parents who were standing behind the tee box clapped, as well as the players who were close by on the putting green. Allison and I looked at each other with proud smiles, and then I looked over to my Mom and Dad, who were delighted to hear their granddaughter's name announced. Needless to say, my dad clapped a little longer than anyone else.

Liz then lined up her shot and stepped up and striped one long and high and right down the middle with a slight baby draw.

"That's the way to smoke it, Liz!" yelled my dad.

She turned and smiled and winked at my dad, and then she picked up her bag and headed down the fairway with the other players. Mom said they were going to stay close to the clubhouse and watch Liz from a distance on the first hole and wait for her to come back toward the club house on number six. Dad just didn't have the strength or endurance to walk the course, and it was a little chilly for him. Al and I said we'd see them in an hour or so. And then I grabbed Al's hand, and we walked out along the outskirts of the first fairway together to see our oldest play the sport she loved so much. I could tell it was going to be a great day.

Liz wound up having a solid first round, and a score of seventy would start her out in a tie for third place. Mom said she stuck an approach shot on the sixth hole to within a foot and putted that in for a birdie in her first round. As you can imagine, they were thrilled with the play their granddaughter had displayed on the course. They wound up watching a little of the seventh and then headed back to Bridges for lunch and a nap. We followed her for all but three holes and then had to get back to the house to prepare for the Clarkson women's hockey team to show up. Luckily, a coach gave us a ride to the clubhouse in a golf cart, because we were pretty far out on the course. It was a great Saturday morning, and we talked about how great Liz had played and what wonderful recovery shots she had made when she was tested every once in a while. Then the conversation quickly turned to preparing lunch for thirty people at our house in the next hour.

It was a little daunting to think about having thirty college hockey players and coaches over for lunch, but again, Al had it all well planned. It would be a repeat of last night, with trays of pasta and salad and bread and plenty of water and Gatorade. She also had cooked up a couple of trays of chicken breasts to boot. Thank goodness we had a stove in the garage too, because we had both going full bore, heating up all the food. I set up some banquet tables and chairs that I had borrowed in our living room for the players, and we had enough room for the coaches to all sit together with us in the dining room. Gracie shot me a text and said the team had finished the warm-up skate and was walking over to the house and would be there in ten minutes.

"All the tables and chairs and tablecloths are set up in the living room, Al. I have water and Gatorade in a couple of coolers out there too," I said as I walked into the kitchen.

Al was checking on the tins in the oven, and then she closed the oven door and put the oven mitts on the counter.

She turned and smiled at me and then walked over and gave me a gentle hug. "Thanks, Jack. It's nice to have you here working alongside me for this. I can't wait to see Gracie," she said.

It felt good to hold her for a while in my arms. I stroked her hair, and she turned her head up and looked into my eyes. "I love you, Al," I said warmly.

"I love you too, Jack."

We just stood in the kitchen for a while, and then, out of the corner of my eye, as I glanced out of the window, I saw the hockey team walking in our driveway and making their way to the back door.

"They're here," I said joyfully to Al.

We turned and waited for them to parade through the back door. The first one in was Gracie, who was all smiles and wearing her green-and-gold Clarkson warm-ups.

"Hi, Mom. Hi, Dad," said Gracie, a little more reserved then usual. I think she was a little careful of a big overreaction with all the other players and coaches nearby. But she had a huge smile and came in and gave us each a quick hug and kiss.

The coaches were the first ones behind her, and then there was a line of players that extended through door and well down the middle of the driveway. Al held onto Gracie a little longer than me, and I gave her a kiss on the forehead.

"We missed you, Gracie. We're so glad you're home," I said softly. And then I turned to extend a welcoming handshake to the first coach in through the door. Rosie was right in the middle of the action, and, of course, the star of the show.

"Come on in, everybody. Make yourselves at home. Lunch is all ready," said Al in a festive tone.

Al and I introduced ourselves to the coaches and led them into the dining room. And then the players came in and introduced themselves to us one at a time and filed into the house to find some room. Everyone gave Rosie the attention she craved, and Rosie ate it up and followed everyone into the other rooms and bounced around from player to player.

"Help yourself, everyone. The food is all ready on the table. It's buffet style, so just grab a plate and something to drink, and tables are set up in the living room," said Al as she showed everyone where the food was spread out in the kitchen. We let the players get their plates first and make their way to the living room. I had put the television on and found a college football game for them to watch while they ate, and that kept them entertained. Rosie stayed with the team and moved around the tables searching for a pat on the head here and there, as well as a handout.

The coaches fixed their plates and sat with us in the dining room. They were very appreciative that we had opened up our home to the team. We had some nice conversation about how fun it was traveling with twenty-five young ladies, and they even shared some stories about road trips to different campuses. They had three preseason games, and these matches were a great way to get a look at the new players and get ready for the season. The coaches were excited for the upcoming season and said the team looked in unbelievable form, which was a blessing so early in the year. They also said that practice was one thing, but playing another team on the road was another. They knew how tough it was to play in the most feared rink in college hockey, with the most intimidating fans. Preseason or not, to face the Big Red in Lynah was the ultimate challenge. Throughout the years, the men's team had consistently packed the house, but the women were coming on strong and gaining tons of momentum. They had been stringing together phenomenal seasons, and it showed dramatically in the stands over the last few years. Al had heard through one of her contacts at the athletic office that the place was on the verge of selling out, and that was a couple of days ago. She said it seemed as if the students were getting extremely anxious for the upcoming season and were ready to get things started. That meant one thing. It was going to be loud, and the kids were going to be charged up for the game.

"Al?" I said easily as I sat on the coffee table to the side of the couch. After the team took off, she had lain down to take a nap on the couch on the sun porch, and I had cleaned up the kitchen and dining room. That had been about three hours ago.

She just looked up at me with sleepy eyes and smiled. I sat there and returned the smile and brushed her hair with my hand. She looked exhausted but happy and at ease.

"It's time to get ready for the game," I said.

She nodded and then produced a big yawn. I told her Liz had called when she was sleeping and told me she had finished up her second round. She had shot a seventy-three, and that put her in fourth place by herself. She was tired after a full day of golf but in good spirits, and she said she knew what she had to do in the final round to attack the leader.

We each took a quick shower to liven up and then put on our coats and headed out the back door. We made our way to the suspension bridge behind our house and then onto the Cornell campus. We could feel the excitement on campus.

The noise got bigger and louder as we approached the rink, and then it got insane as we stepped inside the building. The Cornell band was in full swing and getting the crowd fired up. The music that they cranked out was, by far, the biggest weapon in Cornell's arsenal.

We made our way over to our seats, which were just inside the doors and situated high in the stands behind one of the goals. The visiting team's section was across the rink in the far corner, but I thought that would be too much for my parents to handle at this stage of the game. Besides, Dad and Mom were season-ticket holders and had had these seats for the last eight or nine years. As we got closer to our seats, I could see my mom and dad huddled together and bundled up for the coolness of the rink.

"Hello again, you two," I said as Al and I walked up to them.

My parents turned and smiled and got up to greet us. Mom was upbeat, as usual. Dad looked good, but he had a drawn-out look in his eyes. I'm sure this was a big day for him physically, and he wasn't used to so much action. But he gave me a strong grip of the hand, as always, and produced a smile that showed he was ready for the game. It felt strange that we were about to root for a team other than the Big Red, but it was a great feeling as we waited for our daughter to step onto the ice in her first collegiate hockey game. The four of us were thrilled, especially my dad.

Then, suddenly, the Clarkson team made their way onto the ice, and we stood up and clapped our hands in unison. Needless to say, we were the only ones in the section, and everyone else turned and stared at us. We saw the number-four jersey skate by with the name McNamara on the back, and we all pointed to her. Al and I held hands and smiled. We were proud of our daughter, and it was nice to see her suit up in front of a big crowd, even if it was against a team she had cheered for her entire youth.

Most games between these two teams, whether it was the men or ladies, have wound up being very physical, low-scoring games, and this one was no exception. It was a very gritty game, and we knew that was Gracie's style of play. With no score going into the third period, Gracie knocked a Cornell forward to the ice hard as she crossed the blue line, and the ref signaled a roughing penalty.

"Oh, that's a bullshit call! Let them play hockey!" my dad yelled out, supporting his granddaughter with my mom shaking her head in disbelief of his comments. But that was my dad. He said what he wanted, and when and where he was didn't mean that much to him. And he seemed really focused throughout the game, which Al and I both found quite amazing. His state of mind had gone from confusion or looking as if he was overwhelmed to exhilaration, but I was happy that he looked not only content, but totally into the game.

Clarkson wound up killing off the penalty, but Cornell scored with a little over two minutes to go in the game, giving them the lead. And with just under a minute to play, the Clarkson team called time-out to prepare for a faceoff in Cornell's zone. They pulled their goalie to get six skaters on the ice, and Gracie was one of the defenseman chosen for what would be the last shift of the game. After the puck was dropped, there was a big battle in the corner, and the puck was passed back to the defenseman, who crossed it over to Gracie. She then whipped a wrist shot at the net, and it seemed to hit off someone's shin pad and go into the net. The red light came on to signal that it was a goal, and all four of us stood up and clapped and cheered. Gracie skated fast to her teammates, the ceremonial group congratulation took place in front of the net, and then she skated over to the boards and hammered the glass with her glove and pointed at us. She knew exactly where we sat at the Cornell games. We waved down to her and clapped and yelled louder to show our support.

"That's my granddaughter!" my dad screamed out as he clapped. The rest of the crowd then understood our connection with the opposing team, and when it was announced that Grace MacNamara had scored the goal and she was from Ithaca, she got a few more cheers. The game ended in a tie, as there was no overtime in preseason games, and we stayed and talked about it for a while in the stands. We talked about Liz and Gracie and what an exciting day it had been. Dad looked completely tuckered out, but the excitement of the game and seeing Gracie play seemed to keep him going.

After a while, we made our way to the team bus, which was parked outside the rink, and I knew Gracie wanted to see us one more time and that it would make my dad's day to see her too. She was one of the first players to come out of the rink's lower doors, and we were right there to greet her.

"Great job, Gracie," I said as I moved in for a hug. Al then followed, and we huddled together. Then she let us go and went over to my parents. My mom gave her a hug, and then it was Dad's turn.

"Great game, Gracie. I loved it when you put that other player on her butt...and what a great goal. I'm so proud of you," he said as her held her.

"I'm so glad you were here, Grandpa. I miss you," she said back to him. I could tell they were both trying their best to keep control of their emotions. We were very close to our kids, but the bond they had with their grandparents was truly special. That was always a nice feeling for me.

We stood there and talked about the game for a while and then told Gracie about Liz's day at the Cornell course. She was the last player to get on the bus, and we stood and watched her board and then take a seat toward the rear, right by a window facing us. We waved to her and she waved back, and then the bus started up and pulled away. My dad stood quietly and stared at Gracie's window as the bus slowly pulled away to make its way up to Colgate University for their second game of the weekend. Gracie and my dad were waving until they no longer could see each other.

We said our good-byes, Mom and Dad made their way to their car, and we started our walk back home. It was a great day and a nice walk home on a crisp, clear night. It felt good to walk together and talk one on one as we strolled through campus to the suspension bridge. We held hands all the way home and talked about our girls.

We slept like babies that night and were up bright and early the next morning. We were at the course at eight o'clock for a shotgun start and followed Liz the whole round. She wound up shooting a sixty-nine, which, unfortunately, was only good for second place. She played lights out, but another player beat her by a stroke. Liz was so competitive that she was miffed that she didn't win, even if she did have a great tournament. That was the way she had always been. She had been competitive in every facet of her life since she was a little girl, and she always wanted to win anything and everything she ever entered. It didn't matter if it was a spelling bee or an art contest or a Division One golf tournament. She got that trait from one person and one person alone: her grandpa.

9

THANKSGIVING

O ver the next few weeks, Al and I seemed to settle into our normal routines. We both worked a lot of hours and even spent time in our offices on the weekends. We did see Liz and Gracie a few times after the big weekend at home, though. Liz had a golf tournament hosted by the University of Connecticut, and Al and I drove there and spent the weekend in Storrs. Liz had another great tournament and finished in the top ten. And, of course, she didn't feel that great coming in the top ten, as she wanted to be first. Al and I thought differently and were always proud of everything she did, on and off the course.

Al and I had a great weekend in Connecticut, and we spent a lot of time with Liz after her rounds and had dinner with the team one night too. We seemed to be on good terms and we put the girls ahead of our own feelings. We attended a few more of Gracie's hockey games as well. We drove up to Hamilton and saw her team face off against Colgate and also attended a home game at Clarkson when they played RPI.

Gracie had played her way into a starting role and was actually seeing a lot of time on the coveted power play.

It was nice to spend time with the girls and see them in action, but we needed to take a little bit of a break from the road, too. We spent a lot of time traveling to the events, and we had gotten a little tired of the trips after long work-weeks, coupled with sleeping in hotels and eating fast food. Our chemistry was still a little off, and we were not very intimate during these road trips. Allison looked tired to me most of the time. She looked as if something had been weighing heavy on her mind. There were plenty of times when I wanted to bring up Robert, but I guess I wanted to leave well enough alone. We did have some nice conversations here and there, but it seemed always just to fill the time. We wound up talking about our jobs or the girls, but we never really tackled any deep discussions about our emotions or feelings. This was the pattern that developed as we went along for the next couple of weeks. With the girls out of the house, Rosie seemed to be the one to provide a buffer between us and to hold us together just the same. The Saturday before Thanksgiving was a gorgeous day with a beautiful, beaming sunrise, and I leaned over to Allison and made a suggestion.

"Al…Al?" I asked as I tried to wake her gently. "How about I make us some breakfast and we take Rosie for a stroll around Beebe? Then maybe we can go take a drive and go have lunch somewhere," I suggested.

"I would like that," she said softly. She smiled, closed her eyes again, and rolled over for another fifteen minutes of sleep.

I laid there still for a few minutes, just staring at Allison. She looked so peaceful and happy with her eyes closed and her head resting on the pillow. Her hair was so radiant and wavy, and she always had these full, dark eyebrows and high cheekbones. I sat still and admired her easy smile as she slept for a little while longer. I thought of when we first met and how nervous I was to ask her to go out with me. She looked as beautiful this morning as the day I scraped up the courage to talk to her so long ago. I smiled to myself and felt it was going to be a good morning and great weekend. Even if we weren't exactly on the same page, we still had each other, and we still had our favorite walking area. We still had Beebe Lake. And as soon as I mentioned Beebe to Allison, it didn't take more than two seconds for Rosie to wake up and come over to the bed, filled with anticipation. So, after we showered and had some breakfast, we grabbed Rosie's leash, and out the back door we went.

Unlike Friday nights, Saturday mornings were a very quiet time in our neighborhood. I don't think the students lifted their heads until after twelve, and then it still seemed a slow-paced day until they did it all over again Saturday night. We headed down Thurston Avenue, crossed over just before the bridge, passed by Noyes Lodge, and went down the path toward the lake. I don't know whether it was all the running around with the girls' sports or the long hours at work, but Al and I were both in a peaceful state of mind this morning. When we passed the canoes stacked up on the left at the beginning of the trail, I took Rosie off her leash and let her meander ahead of us and sniff around the path. Al and I seemed to be making a little headway and connecting again, and we shared a laugh when Rosie came to a halt in the middle of the small wooden bridge and looked over her kingdom.

"Every time. It's just amazing," I said as we strolled toward her, and then she leaped ahead to lead the way again. We made our way up to the granite bridge and took a rest. We stood and looked out over the lake, and I placed my hand over Allison's.

"I love you, Al," I said as I looked at her and smiled.

She squeezed my hand and turned to me. "I love you too, Jack," she said.

I looked into her eyes and pushed her hair back from her brow. I leaned into her and put my arm around her waist and kissed her. Allison looked at me, and I could see she was content. Then she laughed lightly as a curious grin formed on her face.

"What's so funny?" I asked.

"Look down," she said.

As I looked down to my right, there was Rosie sitting right beside me, looking up for affection.

"I love her, but she is so jealous of me," said Allison as we both leaned over to give her acknowledgment.

We continued the walk and sat at our oval picnic table to rest a little before we continued along the other side of the lake. After about fifteen minutes of admiring the view, Rosie got up from underneath the table and let us know it was time to walk home.

When we got home, I let Rosie in first, and she ran right for her dish to get a big drink of water. Then she slowly walked over to her bed in the living room, and, after a quick circle, she plopped down to take her nap. Allison did a little laundry as I puttered in the yard and stacked up some firewood by the back door. As lunchtime approached, I went in to clean up and get ready for the ride.

I went into the living room, and Rosie was still sleeping in her bed. I knelt down, and she raised her head to say hello. I don't know how I hadn't noticed before, but her face had grown so white, and she looked old to me. I had always treated her as if she were a teenager, but all of a sudden, it hit me again. She was twelve years old. She was an old gal, and I should probably be taking it a bit easy with her. I began to think that the long walks around Beebe were probably not the best thing for her at this stage of the game.

I let her lie back down and called upstairs to Al, and then we took off to go have lunch. We wound up going south down Route 13 to Newfield and having lunch at a cute little place called Stella's Barn. This had been one of our favorite places for the last few years to have lunch when we went for a ride on the weekends. The food as well as the service was terrific, and owners were wonderful people. It was just a quaint and lovely country restaurant that made you feel welcome as soon as you stepped in the door. We had a great lunch and then went back to Ithaca and walked around the Commons and enjoyed the day outside. After an hour or so, we went back to the house. I told Al that I wanted to check on my parents. She thought that was a good idea, and she would also give her parents a call and see how they were making out down in North Carolina.

As I walked over to Bridges, I sensed that Al and I were doing a little better. I guess I was just nervous about mentioning Robert and risking putting us at odds again. She had alluded to the fact over the drink today that she had a lot going on at work and needed to spend some extra hours on the job. She seemed to be getting over my being late, and not helping with the Siena golf dinner and missing going with her to the doctor's office. I made it a point to put Allison's needs at the top of my list, as they should have been in the first place. I was just hoping that I would stick to my plan and wouldn't fumble the ball anymore.

As I walked through the large wooden antique doors at Bridges, my thoughts quickly shifted from Allison to my dad. I walked upstairs and then started down the hall to his room, and I noticed my mom standing outside his door. She had a concerned and worried look on her face and was staring straight ahead. Then she turned and noticed me. A smile broke out, and she walked toward me. I smiled back, and she came right to me, and we embraced in the hallway. She didn't cry, but I could sense she was exhausted.

"Mom, is everything okay?" I asked.

She didn't answer right away. It was an uncomfortable feeling.

"He had another bad night, Jack. I didn't want to call you and worry you. The doctor is in with him now, and he's settled down, but he was combative with the staff. And then they called me, and I came down late last night around eleven," she said as she patted my back and then released her grasp.

My heart sank, as I had been expecting the exact opposite report. Dad had seemed to be doing a little better, and he had had such a nice time with the girls. I was perplexed at how things could fluctuate and swing from one extreme to the other and how his behavior could change so rapidly, and without warning. It was a hard pill to swallow.

"He's doing fine now, and I've been in talking to him, and he appears very distant. But he has calmed down and was good with the doctor, and then the staff came in one at a time, and he was better...I just wish..." she continued to explain but couldn't finish. And then she came back to me and sobbed on my chest.

I could see it was hurtful to see her husband battling this disease and that it was extremely tough on her to try to help him through it. The doctor stayed in the room for a long time with my dad. I just sat with my mom in the living room, and we talked and looked out the window. She had been up all night and had slept on the couch in the living room or sat up in Dad's chair and rested as best she could most of the night, but she looked worn out. I tried to talk about other things with her to take her mind off my dad. I talked about the girls and their schools and their sporting events and our travels to see them. She settled down after a while, and then I suggested she go home and get some rest. So we walked downstairs and found her car, and I drove her home. I told her I would go back and check with the doctor and give her a call later that evening.

I walked back to Bridges and went upstairs and peeked inside my dad's room. He was asleep, so I closed the door gently and went and found the doctor. His office was down the hall, and he filled me in on everything and talked again about the different stages of this disease and where Dad was and what to expect from here. I found myself not asking questions or conversing with the doctor but remaining quiet as I thought of how to handle all of this moving forward. It just seemed to overwhelm me. He suggested that I go home and get some rest and give him a call tomorrow. I walked home slowly and tried to digest everything that was going on in my life. A woman walked by me with her dog and said hello, but I didn't respond to her. I guess I didn't notice anyone, as I was lost in thought, and I just walked quietly through the neighborhood and made my way home.

Allison was sitting in the living room, and Rosie was in her bed beside the fireplace. Al was on one end of the couch under a quilt and reading a book. When I walked into the room, she looked up at me, put the book down on the coffee table, took off her reading glasses, and placed them down on top of the book. I walked over and sat down next to her and told her about my parents and everything that was going on a few blocks away. I did most of the talking, and then, after a while, she told me about her call to North Carolina. She said her mom had fallen down and broken her wrist and was in a cast. It had happened yesterday, and she had been to the emergency room and then had a long day at the hospital. Her dad was still able to drive, and he had taken her back and forth from the hospital and had taken care of her the whole day. Still, Allison felt guilty about not being there to help her parents, and I felt like a heel taking up most of the conversation telling her about my parents' issues. We had had such a great morning and a great day strolling around the commons, but, unfortunately, it was ending on a somber note.

The next few days went by very quickly, as we both had full schedules at work and were busy getting ready for the girls to come home the day before Thanksgiving. I checked with the doctor Monday morning, and we had a long talk about Dad. It seemed the disease was slowly progressing, and he told me that his episodes would be more frequent and he wanted to brace Mom and me for the inevitable traits that would appear when we visited him.

Dad had gotten some different medication and had a calm week at Bridges, and I saw him every evening with Mom. His appetite wasn't great, but he was in good spirits, and we sat around and enjoyed a cup of coffee with a slice of Mom's pie that she had brought in for us. Mom was spending most of her time with Dad and would take breaks by going for a walk or going grocery shopping. When she was in the room, she sat right by my dad all the time and would hold his hand as they talked or watched television. When I stopped over in the evenings or during lunch, we would watch the news and talk about the girls. I could tell his memory was continuing to fade more and more, as he would forget a name or place during the conversations. But I tried to make him feel comfortable and often inserted some lighthearted humor into the situation and told him that I forgot things here and there too. I could see he was getting frustrated with himself, and the confusion was starting to show in his facial expressions. Still, we made the best of the time we spent together, and I always gave him a hug when I left for the evening.

Al had worked late most of the week, and she made a couple of trips to Wegmans to do the shopping for the Thanksgiving meal. We met up in the evenings, and I helped her unload and put the groceries away in the kitchen. She had talked to her parents a couple of times during the last two days and her mom was doing better, but I could tell she missed her parents and wished she were there to tend to them. I tried to keep the conversation about her parents and the girls and not talk too much about my work or my mom and dad.

The girls had made plans to travel together back home for the holiday. Gracie was going to catch a bus and leave bright and early Wednesday morning and make her way from Clarkson through the Adirondacks and then go down the Northway to Siena. She'd meet up with Liz by noon, and then they'd be home by four or five o'clock. We were glad they were traveling together and felt good that they would get to spend some quality time in the car together. Traveling through the Adirondacks can be pretty dicey in the winter months, so we were very content with Gracie taking the bus to Siena.

My mom and dad were going to have Thanksgiving with us, and Mom and I both felt that Dad was okay to be away from Bridges for a few hours and that seeing the girls would put a big smile on his face. At least that was the plan we came up with, and we kept our fingers crossed and hoped for the best. We also knew that if we told him it wasn't a good idea, he'd probably walk over by himself anyway.

Al and I both went to work Wednesday and would meet back at the house at two o'clock and prepare for the girls to come home. We were excited and looking forward to the family being together and having the kids in the house. We missed the noise and banter of the two girls and the excitement they created when they were home. It had gotten pretty quiet, and we were both ready for a little more action in our home.

"They should be here any minute," Al said with enthusiasm as she stood by the sink and looked out through the kitchen window into the driveway.

I was on time today—thank goodness—and helped Al prepare lasagna for our dinner tonight. I set the table, and we had music on, and everything was going smoothly, and we were full of excitement. I opened a bottle of Cabernet, and we each had a glass of wine. We even danced a little to Jack Johnson. It was funny that the girls seemed to bring out the best in us all the time.

"And here they are," I said as I saw Liz's old Jeep meander into the driveway and come to rest.

Al just looked and then turned and ran out the back door to greet them. I followed, with Rosie a close third, and met the girls as they stepped out of the vehicle. Rosie overtook me and greeted Gracie as soon as she opened the door. It seemed that the girls' arrival provided some jump in Rosie's steps. I was right behind her, and Al ran over and gave Liz a big hug on the other side.

"Hi, Rosie. Hi, Dad…Mom," exclaimed Gracie enthusiastically as she ruffled Rosie's hair and then came over and gave me a hug. It felt great to hold my daughter close, and I missed her and didn't want to let go.

"It's so good to have you girls home. We missed you both," I said as I looked at Gracie and then over to Liz and Al.

"I missed you too, Dad," replied Gracie. Then I switched places with Al and gave my oldest daughter a big hello.

"I'm glad you're home, Liz," I said as I squeezed her tight.

"I'm glad I'm home too, Daddy," she said as she gave me another squeeze. Liz hadn't called me Daddy since she was a little girl, and it made me feel good. They had grown up so fast, but I always seemed to look at them as if they were little girls. I guess it was a way of never letting go of great memories.

Liz went back over to Al and Gracie, and then they joined in a group hug, and I could tell that Allison loved it. "I'm so glad you girls are home," she said.

"Let's go inside, and you can tell us all about your trip and school. I made lasagna, and it should be ready. I'm sure you girls are hungry," she said.

Rosie led the way back inside, and we put out the dinner and sat around the table and talked and laughed for a long time. The girls told us all about school and their teams, and we talked loudly over the music in the background. It was great to have some commotion in the house again. I hadn't seen Allison this excited since Liz and Gracie had come home a month and a half ago. I put my hand on her leg and rubbed it and smiled to her. She put her hand on mine and smiled back. It was a great family moment for us.

We had a great dinner, and Al had made a chocolate pudding pie, which was the girls' favorite dessert. We sat around the table and listened to Liz and Gracie tell stories about kids at school and road trips with their teams and boys they thought were cute. It was wonderful just to listen to them and see the excitement in their eyes. Al and I were very happy that they both enjoyed their schools and were having a great time. They asked about my mom and dad and how they were doing, of course. I let them know they were doing great and would be here tomorrow, late morning, to spend the day with us. I didn't want to tell them too much about my dad because I didn't want to see them upset. Gracie wanted to walk over and see him after dinner, but I told her that he'd been going to sleep a little earlier lately and needed his rest for the big day tomorrow. She reluctantly complied, and we talked about mom and dad for a while and also about Al's parents. We let them know Grandma Peg had broken her wrist. The girls wanted to set up a trip to visit Al's parents during a school break, and that made Al burst with excitement. She always wanted to create a stronger bond between her parents and Liz and Gracie, but distance was in the way and we didn't have the luxury to visit as much as we wanted to.

Al and I cleaned up the kitchen and let the girls settle into the living room to watch some television with Rosie. It had been an exciting day for old Rosie, and she was lying in her bed as the two girls sat together on the couch and watched a New York Rangers hockey game. I walked into the living room to join them and noticed that they were whispering to each other, as if to keep a secret. But I didn't want to be nosy, so I just left it alone. Al and I watched a little of the game with them, and we could see they were exhausted from their busy day. They kissed us good-night and went upstairs to their rooms to get some sleep. It had been a great first day, and Al and I retired early too. We knew tomorrow was going to be a big day, and we wanted to make sure we had the energy to keep up with our offspring and not miss a beat.

The girls slept in the next day. Al and I got up early, and as she started preparations in the kitchen, I set the table again. I turned on the television and found the channel that showed the Macy's Thanksgiving Day Parade and turned up the volume. It was around ten thirty, so I thought it was a good time to let the girls know it was time to get around and come downstairs.

Just then I heard a car come into the driveway and knew my parents were here. I walked into the kitchen and stood with Al, and we looked out the window and watched them get out of the car. Mom got out the driver's side and walked over and opened Dad's door and extended her hand. As I looked at my Dad stand up, I noticed that he looked very feeble and a little disoriented. His face looked as though he hadn't slept much, and he stepped very gingerly out of the car. He had on his London Fog golf jacket and his red plaid Scottish cap. I felt Al's eyes on me as she saw him move toward the house with my mother holding his arm. I think she could feel the sadness that I felt inside.

"Listen, Jack. Your mom is taking good care of him. You have to come to terms with this thing, and we have to just enjoy everything the best we can. Plus, the girls will be down, and you don't want to upset them. Let's be happy, okay?" she said as she walked to the back door. Then we welcomed my parents.

"Hello there. Happy Thanksgiving," my mom said cheerfully as my dad smiled. Al let my mom in and gave my dad a hug.

"Hi, Mom, Dad. You guys are looking dapper, as always," I said.

I kissed my mom and shook my dad's hand. He certainly seemed more fragile, but he still had that bear grip. He nodded to me and said hello, but he didn't call me by my first name right off the bat. I took their coats and walked into the foyer by the front door and hung them up in the closet. Then I went back into the kitchen. Allison was getting some coffee cups for everyone and telling them about how excited the girls were to see them. I stood next to my dad and put my arm around him.

"How are you doing, Pops?" I asked.

"Not too bad for an old guy, son," he replied with a smile.

It put me at ease to hear him call me son. I felt better immediately. Then I heard a rumble on the stairs as the girls yelled and hopped all the way down.

"Grandpa! Grandma!" yelled Gracie as she ran into the kitchen and right into my dad's arms. Liz was right behind her and yelled out and gave my mom a big hug hello. The noise woke Rosie up in the living room, and she made her way into the kitchen wagging her tail in excitement.

"We missed you guys!" said Liz joyously.

"We missed you, too," replied my mom.

Gracie was hugging my dad, and he was holding her head close to his chest. Liz quickly moved over to join in.

"We missed you, Grandpa," said Liz as both girls looked up to him. He was fragile but tall and had them by a couple of inches.

"I missed you girls, too," he replied as he closed his eyes and squeezed and held them tight.

It was a real festive Thanksgiving in our house. Al cooked a great turkey dinner with all the trimmings, and Mom helped her out in the kitchen. We all sat around the big dining room table and had a lot of laughs. I think Al really appreciated my mom's help and company, and I know my mom liked coming to the house and taking my dad out for a family get together. Family time was always the best time in our house. There was nothing better than sitting around a big table and sharing a lot of food and laughs with the people you loved. Liz and Gracie were very animated with their stories, and they were also very loud. We had the music on in the kitchen, and they had to talk a little louder, and it added to the excitement of it all.

Al and I looked at each other during the meal and smiled. This was a big change from all the quiet dinners we shared in the evenings. It felt great. Dad didn't participate as much as in times past, but he was really enjoying himself. He was definitely a little more forgetful with names and places, and it was very noticeable, but he was in great humor. I think the girls really brought him up in spirits, especially when they mentioned their secret as we were having Al's famous dessert of chocolate pudding pie.

"Well, are you going to show them, Gracie? Or what?" said Liz as she looked over to her sister with a sinister grin.

Gracie seemed to be astonished by her sister's suggestion, and then she looked around at the table. Everyone's eyes were on her, waiting to see what Liz was talking about. Then Gracie came clean with her little secret. "Well, I wanted to tell you guys a couple of weeks ago, but I just didn't know how," she started as everyone kept looking at her.

"Well...we all had our helmets off during practice one day...and we were just goofing around on the ice...and then... actually, Katie didn't mean it...her stick just came up to my face and..." She stopped and reached up and pulled out one of her front teeth and smiled at everyone.

My mom, Al, and I were speechless, and Liz started to laugh real hard. But I think Grandpa almost fell off his chair because he was laughing so hard.

"That's my Gracie!" he yelled as he slammed his hand on the table. I think some milk came out of my nose, and even Al started to smile a little, as she was still dealing with the shock.

"You know, I always thought it would have been your sister to knock one out!" my dad bellowed, and we all started to laugh real hard.

Gracie was laughing hard and holding her tooth out and showing the gap in her smile, as she felt more relaxed now that it was out in the open. Apparently, after her tooth was knocked out, the team physician recommended she go to the dentist, and he had done such a wonderful job in giving her a well-matched false tooth that it didn't even show during her smiles. I still can't believe we didn't notice it when she came in the day before. The guy had done a great job, and he said that Gracie should talk to us and think about a permanent fix after the season. Needless to say, we were taken aback at first, but we went with the flow and just enjoyed the moment. Allison had a little tougher time dealing with her younger daughter missing her front tooth and just shook her head in disbelief here and there, as did my mom. They didn't share the same passion for sports that my dad and Liz and I did. We knew that this stuff was just part of the game.

It was a long day for the old folks, and we had a great time. And when it was time for Mom and Dad to go, we all walked them outside to their car. The girls held them all the way there and gave them each a kiss. Dad got himself settled in the car and put on his seatbelt. As we waved I could see Gracie make a special gesture to my dad. She pointed to her eye and circled her heart and then pointed to my dad. He smiled back to her, and I could easily make out what he said.

"I love you, too," he mouthed to Gracie, who came over to me and held me. All four of us stood in the driveway and waved as my parents backed out slowly and took off down Judd Falls Road.

We all were exhausted that evening. After all the food, the parade, football, and laughter, we just watched a movie for a little bit in the living room, and then Al and I left the girls on the couch and went upstairs to bed. Right before I said good-night to Al, I had a nice laugh to myself.

"What are you laughing about?" Al asked.

"Well, it's just that I never thought I'd have a daughter who looked like one of my childhood idols," I responded with a smile.

Al looked at me with a question in her eyes. "Oh yeah? What idol are you talking about?"

"Bobby Clarke, the captain of the Philadelphia Flyers," I replied. "You'd have to see a picture of him when he played to know what I'm talking about," I said.

Then I kissed Allison goodnight and turned over and shut off the light and went to sleep.

The next day the girls made their rounds and connected with some of their friends who were also home for the holidays. Again, it was nice to have a little more action in the house, and Allison definitely enjoyed a little more girl power. She seemed to have a lot more bounce in her step, and she enjoyed it even more when the girls brought some of their friends over to hang out. We wound up going to the Glenwood Pines for Pinesburgers on Friday night, and it brought back a lot of memories of when the girls played youth sports and of the many awards dinners that were held at this grand establish-ment. They were older now, but they still made their way to play pool and had fun at the bowling game in the bar area. There were always a lot of kids in this area, and Allison and I just watched and had a drink and enjoyed some stories of when they were kids.

The girls slept in on Saturday, and I wound up cooking pancakes for them around eleven o'clock. Al had always liked to bake, and she made some blueberry muffins. After breakfast, the girls took a batch over to Bridges to visit my dad. Mom was there when they arrived, and she called them into the room when she noticed them standing in Dad's doorway. Liz told me later that Grandpa looked as if he didn't recognize them at first, but when Grandma called their names, he produced a smile and a wave. They had a nice visit and watched some television with my mom and dad and wound up staying a couple of hours. Liz had told them that they would stop by and say good-bye on their way out of town on Sunday. That made my parents extremely happy, as well as Gracie, of course. The girls came back to the house for only a few minutes before Liz announced they were going to go down to Newman and see if anyone was hanging around, and then they would be off to one of their friends' houses in Lansing. Al and I knew they'd be buzzing around to see everyone, and we were only too happy to let them do that, knowing they would be coming back for dinner and another night at home.

The next morning we were all up bright and early. Al had done a ton of laundry for the girls, and I made them some sandwiches for the road from the leftover turkey. Mom had called me and said Dad was very tired this morning and to tell the girls that he needed the morning to rest. Liz understood and could read between the lines, but Gracie was another story. I just reiterated that it was best to let Dad have his sleep and told her I would call her during the week from Dad's room and would put him on the phone so they could chat. That seemed to appease her, so we loaded up the car with all their laundry, and Al gave them some money, as she always did, and got them ready to go back to school. As we were saying our good-byes, Liz asked where Rosie was, and it was funny that she wasn't outside. I went in and found her napping in the living room and woke her to go outside.

"Rosie, you good girl, weren't you going to say good-bye?" Liz said as Rosie moved carefully down the porch steps to the girls. They both got down on their knee and petted her and gave her a kiss. I think it's safe to say that everyone could see our beloved Rosie had gotten older and was starting to really slow down.

"Okay, girls, you have a long trip—especially you, Liz," I said.

So they gave their mom a big hug and said good-bye and gave me a kiss and piled into the Jeep. I held Al's hand as we waved, and she rested her head on my shoulder as the girls backed the truck up and pulled out of the driveway. Then Liz honked her horn, and they were on their way back to college.

It had been a wonderful Thanksgiving, and Allison and I were in great spirits. We had always agreed on one thing since becoming parents. There was nothing better than having the whole family together and spending time with one another. I knew she wished her parents were with us, but that was simply not to be. Not this weekend, anyway.

10

THE LETTER

I t doesn't happen often, but Al was up and around before me on Monday morning. We had had a great end
to our weekend and took Rosie for a short walk around
Cass Park on Sunday afternoon. It was a beautiful, brisk, and
sunny afternoon, a perfect time to go for a walk down by the
marina. It was amazing weather considering what time of the
year it was, so we took advantage of the day. Rosie didn't seem
to want to walk too far, so we kept it to a minimum and took
a seat at our favorite picnic table, which was positioned just
along the water's edge and shielded by a big overgrown pine
tree that had a huge, twisted branch that provided some nice
shade. Rosie curled up at our feet underneath the table with
a dish of water, and we had some lunch, which included some
sandwiches I had made and a bottle of French rosé, which we
had picked up on the way down to the park. We sat and shared
a blanket on our laps and enjoyed the sun and the wine and
soaked up the beauty around us.

From this table we could see the ninth hole of the Newman
Golf course across the lake, and we talked about the girls and

wondered how many times they must have played that course over the years. We sat and talked about Liz and Gracie and their sports and their friends and how they were getting more interested in boys at school. Each of them had friends who were boys as they grew up, but neither of them had had a serious romantic boyfriend. It sounded as if that was going to change over the next year, by the way they were talking at Thanksgiving. We enjoyed a great lunch, and, after reminiscing about the kids for a while, we packed up and went back home. I brought in some firewood and sparked a fire in the living room, and we sat and read for the remainder of the evening. We retired early and went upstairs and made love, which put a wonderful finishing touch on a beautiful day. As I said, Al doesn't usually beat me out of bed on workday mornings, but she was out of the shower and fully dressed when I was just turning over to check the clock on the end table.

"Wake up, sleepyhead. It's time to get to work," Allison said playfully. She seemed to be relishing the moment of being the first one out the door this morning.

I sat up in bed and stretched a bit as Al was finishing dressing and putting on a nice black-and-white silk scarf to match her outfit. I just sat and admired her as she stood in front of her dresser mirror fixing the scarf just right, and then she grabbed her purse and was ready to go. At that moment, her cell phone, which was on the end table, buzzed as a text came in. I picked it up to hand it to her and noticed it was a message from Robert. My mood instantly swung in the other direction as feelings of jealousy and mistrust came over me.

"What's this guy texting you for, Allison?" I said in an accusatory tone.

She looked back at me and took a few seconds to reply, as she seemed to digest that I was insinuating something. "I've been helping him at work, Jack. He's been going through a bad breakup and needed some advice and some guidance," she replied, hoping to make sense to me.

Unfortunately, I wasn't in the best frame of mind to comprehend such a rational response. "I just hope it isn't anything more than helping him with work," I muttered. And, looking back, I was sorry I said it. It was a totally immature overreaction.

"What the hell is that supposed to mean, Jack? You know you have a lot of nerve to say that to me, especially after last night. Don't you trust me?" she said, shaking her head and grabbing the phone from me.

"Well, I just remember you had a crush on him at one time. And I drove up to your office to take you out to lunch one afternoon, and I saw you and Robert together, and he gave you a kiss. And I talked to Peter the other day, and he said he ran into you and Robert having lunch together at Agava. I mean, what's going on here? Are you having an affair with him?" I asked in a huff.

Al shook her head and closed her purse and turned and looked in the mirror and then back to me. "You know, Jack, at this stage, if you don't trust me, then I don't even know what we're doing together," she said, half brokenhearted and half pissed off.

"I can't believe you have the nerve to say this after all these years and after what we shared last night. Why didn't you bring this up before now? You know I've always put you and your parents first all the time. I always put everyone before me. I've got things going on too, you know. But you never seem to have time for me so I can share what I'm going through. Anyway, I have no time for this nonsense. I have a busy day and need to get to work," she said, and she stormed out of the room and down the stairs.

I just sat in bed as I heard her car start and then pull out of the driveway. I sat and wondered how a perfect weekend could be followed by such a crappy Monday morning.

It was a very unproductive day for me at the office. All I did was sit and stare at my computer till early afternoon and think about Allison. I felt bad about giving her grief about Robert's text and accusing her of possibly having an affair, but I had to get it off my chest. My timing was awful, though, and I should have approached her about Robert sooner. In all honesty, the same day I saw them embrace would have been the best time. I wouldn't have carried it around with me, and I would have found out right away if Al was having an affair with him.

I sat in my office, confused, and tried to figure out my next move. Maggie and the guys could tell I wasn't myself and tried to talk to me, but I just said I wasn't feeling great and had a bit of a headache. Maggie came back to my office around two and suggested I go home and relax, and she would rebook my remaining appointments. I let her know that was a good idea and left for the day. I think Maggie sensed there was something a little bigger going on than just a slight headache.

Instead of going home, I thought it best to take a drive. I drove out to Myers Park, which was a state park in Lansing, just about five miles outside of town. It was a beautiful park that sat right along the east side of Cayuga Lake, and Al and I had taken the girls there dozens of times to enjoy the beach. We had also been to a few outdoor parties on different occasions that people held in their pavilions. I thought it would be a nice spot to sit for a while and try to clear my head.

I parked the car, walked out to the black-and-white checked lighthouse that sat on the southern tip of the park just outside the marina, and just stood there and looked across the lake. The water was extremely calm and appeared as if it weren't even moving at all, and the park was extremely quiet. I just stood there and tried to find an answer to my problem, but I couldn't come up with one. I thought I should have called Allison in the morning, but I also wanted to give her some space.

I wound up finding a bench over by the marina and just sat and thought and stared across the lake for long time. Besides an old-timer walking his dog, I was the only one in the whole park. As the sun began to set, I decided to take off and go get a beer before I went home, so I stopped at Rogues' Harbor in Lansing. Al and I had stopped there many a time for a drink, as we passed through Lansing quite often on our way back and forth to hockey tournaments in Auburn and Skaneateles. As I walked in through the doors and took a seat at the bar, a strange feeling came over me. I had never sat there without Al. I felt melancholy and ordered a beer and decided I would just have the one and make my way home to patch things up with Allison. I didn't know the young lady behind the bar, and she just gave me my draft and left me to myself. I didn't take the time to finish the beer, as I got anxious to get back to the house. So I put a couple of bucks on the counter and said good-bye and started back home.

I turned into the driveway, and the first thing I noticed was that Al's car wasn't there. She must be working late again— and I hope it's just work, I thought as I shook my head in disbelief. I parked the car and unlocked the back door and walked inside. By this time, Rosie was usually right there and wagging her tail like crazy. She was always alerted by the sound of the gravel and would be right there as soon as I opened the door. Not today, though. I shut the door behind me and turned, and she came slowly walking into the kitchen to greet me. I guess the years were quickly catching up to her and she was doing the best she could do. I gave her a pet and scratch under the chin, and then I noticed the note on the kitchen counter with a pen next to it. I felt uneasy as I walked over and picked it up and read it.

> Jack,
>
> I have so much to say that I don't know where to start. I guess I'll just start with this morning. It really hurt that you should accuse me of cheating on you. I think by now you should be able to trust me along those lines, and I shouldn't ever have to defend myself. It hurt even more that you should give me so much grief after we had such a wonderful day and evening together. It made me feel even worse knowing that you were thinking this way when we made love last night.
>
> As for Robert, he has been going through a terrible breakup, and the reason he kissed me on the cheek outside my building was to say

thank you and good-bye. He accepted a position at NYU and is transitioning to the city. He wanted to bring his boys closer to their mother and thought that would help in their relationship. He had been totally depressed and wanted to go to lunch and talk, and I agreed. And that was all we did, Jack—talk. He was having a hard time, and it was hurting him, his kids, and his work, so I thought it best if I stepped in and tried to help him.

He's been down in the city these past couple of weeks, and the message he sent me this morning was that he had been having lunch and talking to his wife, Carol, a lot, and that they've decided to give their marriage a second chance. He just wanted to let me know about it and tell me that he's eternally grateful for listening to him and helping him and his sons.

Putting Robert aside, I also have been missing my parents. We never get to see them that much anymore. I love your mom and dad, and I've loved having them around with the girls, but I miss my folks too. It seems that you are always consumed with your parents and aren't willing to give mine the same time. I've tried to listen and help as much as possible with your dad, but my mom needs help too.

I have a lot going on at work too, and other things that I need to talk to you about, but right now I just need a break. I've decided to go to North Carolina for a couple of weeks

and help my mom and give my dad a break and chill out for a while. I was hoping to hear from you this morning, but since I didn't, I decided to leave around noon and hopefully pull in to my parent's house before midnight. Jack, I guess I just need some space now and will call you later this week. I'll be fine and will let Liz and Gracie know I'm taking some time to be with my parents. When I come back, I need to talk to you about something, and hopefully you'll have an open ear for me.
Allison

After I read the letter, I just stood and stared out the kitchen window. I felt terrible and shook my head and uttered just one word.

"Shit."

11

MY GIRL ROSIE

It was a quiet, worrisome, and reflective evening in my house Monday night. I fixed a fire in the living room and poured myself some brandy and sat in my chair and read the letter over and over. I sat and looked at the fire and thought about my relationship with Allison. I thought about my mom and dad. I thought about the girls and how they were doing so well and getting older and would soon be ready to make their mark in the world. I sat and thought about everyone, but it seemed I didn't have anyone. I started to think about possibly losing my best friend in the world, Allison. I thought about how the girls would be out on their own after they finished college. I thought about my dad and how his situation seemed to be getting worse and how my mom looked so tired every time I saw her.

I got up from my chair and put another piece of wood on the fire and stoked the coals. I stared at the family pictures on the mantle, and it brought a smile to my face and made me feel lonely at the same time. I missed everyone and started to get mad at myself and wished Al were home with me. But she wasn't, and I didn't know what she was thinking, and that was the most uncomfortable feeling of all. Did she still love me? Did she still want to be with me? I was hoping she still loved me and would be home soon. I picked up one of the family pictures that showed the girls when they were probably nine and ten and in their youth hockey uniforms. Al and I were with them, and we were all laughing with big smiles. We were always all together, and I missed those days, I thought as I put the picture back on the mantle.

I sat back down in my recliner and reached down to my left side to pet Rosie, who had been lying by my chair the whole night with me.

"At least I have you, girl. You're always here when I need you, aren't you?" I said to her as she rested quietly by my side. And that certainly was the truth. Rosie was always there to make me feel better when I was feeling down. She looked up to me after a while, and again I noticed the change in her in her appearance as well as her demeanor. Her face was certainly showing her age, and she looked very, very tired. I sat and wondered where the time had gone, and my mind drifted to memories of the past again. I sipped my brandy and sat in my chair till about midnight, and then I went upstairs to bed. It was a lonely walk up the stairs, and it felt even worse sleeping by myself. I tossed and turned most of the night, and by the time Tuesday morning rolled around, I was exhausted and felt mentally drained.

Maggie seemed to pick up quickly that something might be wrong, and we had a chat alone in my office at lunchtime. I told her about the letter and about Robert. She sat and listened to my story, and she gave me her advice. She understood that life could get pretty crazy and confusing at times and told me to hang in there and that next time I talk with Allison, I should really concentrate on doing one thing and one thing only: listen to what she's saying and what she might need from me. Maggie said the girls were in good hands at school and my dad was in good hands with my mom and the staff at Bridges. She advised me to concentrate on Allison right now, and things would fall into place again. By the time we were done talking, I thanked Maggie, and she gave me a hug and told me to keep my chin up. When she left my office, I thought about how lucky I was to work with such a great person. I also started to feel like a hypocrite, because Maggie was giving me the same attention that Allison had given Robert. I still felt it best to give Al a little time to be with her parents and not give her a call just yet. And if she wanted to call me first, then I'd know she was ready to talk again. And so, for the next couple of days, I buried myself in my work and tried to keep as busy as possible.

It was Thursday afternoon, and I still hadn't heard from Allison. I decided I would give her a call from home after work. I stopped by Bridges, and Dad was sleeping and my mom was out walking. They said the doctor could be reached in the morning and that my dad was doing okay, but he had been getting a little more reserved and irritable and he was becoming more and more combative with the staff. I told them I appreciated their help and support and that I would reach out to my mom and come back another time.

As I left Bridges, I called my mom and got her on her cell phone. She said she needed to go for a long walk and sounded very stressed out. I told her to try to relax and have a good walk and that I was on my way home and would stop and see them later. I pulled out of Bridges and made my way home.

Rosie was still in her bed in the living room and barely looked up when I went over to her to give her a pat. After a little encouragement, she got up and followed me into the kitchen, and I gave her a fresh bowl of water and some food. Then I picked up my cell from the dining room table and dialed Allison's' cell number.

"Hello, Al," I said into the phone as I started to walk in a circle around the kitchen.

"Hi, Jack," she replied.

"Al, I just want to say I miss you. And I love you."

Then there was a short pause.

"I love you too, Jack. It's nice to hear your voice. I'm glad you called." As soon as Allison told me she loved me, I felt a whole lot better all of a sudden. She began to tell me why she had left and what was going on down in Carolina with her mom and dad and what she was doing to help them. I remembered what Maggie had told me. She had said to just listen and hear what Al was saying and how I could be there for her. And that was what I did. I let Al talk. She told me she was overwhelmed with things in our house and that I had let her down a few times when she really needed me. She understood I needed to be there for my dad, and she wanted to be there for him too. But she needed me for support every once in a while as well. I told her I was sorry that I had let her down and that I would try to be more attentive and understanding of her needs, and I told her again that I loved her and that she was the most important thing in the world to me.

She told me she loved me again, and we started to talk about her parents. Her mom was getting her cast off next week, and she wanted to be there to take her to the hospital because her dad was getting uncomfortable with driving in the city traffic. Her mom was in good spirits and her dad was in relatively good shape and didn't require the assistance that my dad needed, but she felt at ease because she was there spending time with them and helping them out. She told me how she had been doing much of her work on her laptop by video conferencing and e-mail. She said she stayed caught up, and we even had a laugh about how much technology had changed since we were kids. We talked about Liz and about Gracie. We talked about everything, and I tried hard to let her do most of the talking and me do most of the listening. And you know something? We had a great conversation.

But after about twenty minutes, she said something that made me feel uncomfortable and awkward inside. "Listen, Jack. I love you and miss you. I want you to know that. I really do. But when I get home next week, I need to sit down with you and talk to you about something, and I want to talk to you face to face. I don't want to talk over the phone. Okay?"

This caught me off guard, and I really didn't know how to reply all of a sudden. It kind of took the wind out of my sails. "Sure, Al, of course" was what I said to her. And then I told her that I loved her again, and she said she loved me too, and we said good night.

I stood in the kitchen for a while and tried to think about what Allison would want to talk to me about when she came back home. Not one good thing ran through my head, and I felt insecure all over again. I stood holding the phone in the kitchen and felt melancholy again. I walked into the living room and checked on Rosie. She was fast asleep in her bed.

I went back into the kitchen and put on my barn coat and started out to Bridges.

As I reached the end of my driveway, I decided to extend my walk to clear my head. I headed down the block and went out onto the suspension bridge that crossed the gorge behind my house. I walked out to the middle and then stood by the rail and looked out into the gorge, which was alive with turbulent, fast-moving water making its way down to Cayuga Lake. It was violent but peaceful. I had stood there many a time since we'd been living in Ithaca. It always seemed to be at nighttime. I stood in the middle of the bridge and looked out across the gorge and down to the city of Ithaca the way Rosie stood in the middle of her wooden bridge at Beebe Lake. I thought about Allison and our relationship and wondered whether we would make it. Was I thinking too much again? I don't know. Was she going to come home and break up with me? I was hoping not. I had tried to listen this time.

I stood there and stared and watched the water run over the slate and crash down through the gorge's path. I tried not to think anymore. I just watched the water. I felt better as I let the water put me at ease, and I decided to walk some more. I crossed the bridge and walked up the railroad-tie steps onto the Cornell campus. I was now facing the Johnson Museum and stopped to look at the everlasting light display, which I could see from our house. Al and I had spent a lot of hours in there. We'd take the girls there to show them all the great art and get them away from the golf course and the hockey rink. I remembered having a laugh with Al, as we both knew they'd rather be driving a golf ball or shooting a puck than look at famous portraits. At that moment, I smiled lightly and turned left to head down the road to Thurston Avenue. I walked across the towering bridge that brought everyone onto the north side of campus. It was busy with students who had their backpacks and were probably making their way to the library or favorite place to study. I crossed over the bridge and went down the street and crossed over Thurston to make my way to see Dad and Mom.

I arrived at Bridges and took the stairway to Dad's room. As I walked down the hall, I could see Dad's door closed, and I noticed Mom sitting on a sofa in the large living room. She had a cup in her hand and was staring out through the large window to her right. She turned and saw me and gave me a warm smile. She didn't need to tell me how Dad was doing. I saw it in her eyes.

"Hello, Jack," she said as she looked up to me with misty eyes.

"Hi, Mom," I replied as I sat beside her and kissed her on the head.

Over the next hour, she told me how Dad was starting to struggle more and more with everything, from remembering names to remembering places, and he was getting more and more confused. She said he looked at her at one point today and struggled to remember her name. He did after a moment, but it broke her heart. The staff was doing all they could to make them as comfortable as possible, and the doctor had spent some time with him a couple of times today. She said that Dad was very tired today and slept more than usual. She seemed to think that he was more comfortable sleeping and that it was his way to avoid the embarrassment of being confused with simple things. The doctor had changed his medication again to adjust to his current behavioral patterns and was very nurturing to him. He had just left about an hour ago and would check on him in the morning.

I sat and had a cup of tea with Mom, and we talked quietly. We talked about the past with Dad and how he had been so strong and outgoing, but that just made it worse for her. I offered to walk her home, but she wanted to stay there longer and be there when he woke up. I kissed her on the cheek and told her I'd call her tomorrow. On my way home, I felt more torn than I'd ever felt in my whole life.

I woke up the next morning with my mind in complete disarray. As you can imagine, I hadn't slept very well. All I did was toss and turn and turn the television on and off every hour or two. I tried to read, but I just couldn't focus on the story line. It rained most of the night, and pretty hard at times. There was tin sheathing that covered the small roof over the back door just outside my bedroom window. The rain pinged against it all night long, and after a while, it developed a rhythm that put me to sleep. I'm guessing that it was about four in the morning when I finally dozed off. I woke up around seven, without the use of the alarm clock, and sat up in bed for a while. It was hard to get motivated, and it felt good just to sit and think under the covers. After watching numerous weather reports during the night, I knew it was supposed to be real cold this morning, and the rain was going to shift to snow. I didn't feel the need to rush into the morning but thought it best to get going and get to my office and stay busy to keep my mind off of things.

I walked downstairs and went into the living room, and Rosie was still on her bed. She hadn't come up to bed at nighttime for the last couple of days, as tackling the stairs was too much for her. She looked up at me and then put her head back down on the bed. She looked so tired. I stood and looked at her and wondered how she had changed so much so quickly. Just a few months ago, she had seemed to be running and jumping and chasing the girls. Old age had just snuck up on her, and it showed in her demeanor and in her face. It was all white and wrinkled, and she appeared exhausted. I started to feel guilty about playing too much with her and running and walking her too long. After all, she was twelve years old. She shouldn't be able to walk or run around the lake or chase Liz and Gracie in the yard for an hour. But she did it. She always did it. I guess I just wasn't paying attention to her age.

"Rosie, come on. Let's go outside," I said easily to her.

She opened her eyes again but still didn't get up.

"Come on, girl. Let's go outside, and then you can rest all day long. Come on," I said again as I tried to coax her into getting up.

She stirred and got up feebly and walked across the living room to make her way into the kitchen. It looked as if it was taking all the strength she had to make it to the back door. I opened the door for her and then opened the storm door. She moved very slowly down the back steps and walked out into the yard. I thought the air would do her some good and rejuvenate her, so I walked back into the kitchen. I made a bowl of cereal and then opened the blinds to the kitchen windows. The cold rain had turned to snow, and I thought of how much Rosie loved the snow and how she used to chase the girls around in the yard after a big snowstorm.

I sat at the dining room table and ate my cereal and thought about my day. After a couple of minutes, I walked into the kitchen and put my bowl in the sink and looked out through the window to see if Rosie was done with her business. I couldn't see her, and I walked outside and called for her to come to the back steps. She didn't come, and I walked out to the corner of the yard and called her and looked around. The sun wasn't all the way up, and the snow was coming down in big wet flakes. I walked into the middle of the yard and searched into the trees that outlined our yard, but I still didn't see her. Then I looked over to my right, and there she was, lying on the ground by the white wooden bench that sat beneath the old maple tree. I walked over to her and knelt by her and stroked her head. She was still breathing, but very lightly. Her tongue was hanging out, and she was slightly panting, and her eyes were open. Her hindquarters were in a small pool of rainwater, and she was covered with big wet snowflakes. It looked as if she was embarrassed and wanted to hide from me.

"Rosie," I said gently as I brushed the snow off of her and felt her chest. I felt sad, but I also knew I had to get her to the veterinarian right away. I ran into the kitchen and grabbed my keys and then ran to her and picked her up. I put her in the front seat of my car and took off for the animal clinic, which was on Route 13, about three miles outside of town. I drove as fast as I could, and I talked to her the whole way. I kept rubbing her back and talking to her to make her feel as comfortable as possible. I kept telling her to hang in there, but she was breathing very slowly and not moving at all. I pulled into the parking lot of the clinic, ran to her side, and picked her up and ran in the front door. The office was just opening, and the girl at the front desk looked surprised as I ran in with Rosie in my arms.

"Where's the doctor! Where's Dr. Barnes! I need help! She's barely breathing!" I yelled as I held my dog and ran into the adjoining rooms in search for the doctor. Just then I saw the doctor as I made my way down the hallway in a frantic state. Dr. Barnes had been our family veterinarian since Rosie was a puppy. He was an amazing doctor as well as a good friend. He was in the back room and just taking off his coat.

He looked at me and realized the graveness of the situation. He ushered me into another room. I put Rosie on a table, and he started to check her out right away. As he brushed her off and smoothed the fur away from her belly, we both became quiet, and my mouth hung open. Her whole stomach was red. The doctor immediately stopped and rubbed his brow and sighed and put the stethoscope to her again. He checked her eyes and then looked at her stomach and felt around with his hand. Rosie winced in pain and started to whine as her mouth closed and legs slightly twitched.

The doctor took the stethoscope earplugs out and rubbed Rosie and looked at me and put his hand on my shoulder. "She's had an abdominal aneurism, Jack, and it's opened up, and she has internal bleeding. Unfortunately, these clots can go undetected, and then they become weak and rupture. She's in serious pain and suffering bad right now," he said with a serious look on his face.

He took off his glasses, and then he rubbed her back, and she winced again. "I'm sorry, Jack. We need to put her down," he continued.

I looked at him in disbelief and then back to Rosie. I put my face close to hers and felt her nose and lightly petted her head.

"There's got to be something you can do, isn't there, Phil? Can you give her some medicine? Can you give her something to keep her alive for a while?" I asked in desperation.

He was quiet and looked at me petting my dog.

"You don't understand. She's all…she's…" I couldn't finish my sentence. My eyes welled up as I held my face close to Rosie's, and I looked up to the doctor.

He could see the plea for help in my eyes. "Jack, she's in pain and suffering, and we need to do what's best here. I know you don't want to hear that, but even if I gave her something, she'd still wouldn't make it through the next day or so, and she'd be suffering as well. I'm sorry," he said, and then he paused.

"She's had a good life, Jack. You gave her a real nice life with Allison and the girls. It's just one of those things. It's just her time." He turned and went to the counter. The nurse came in, and they prepared the needle to put Rosie down.

I stroked Rosie's head and paw and touched her belly as Dr. Barnes and his assistant prepared for the procedure behind me.

"You were always such a good dog, Rosie. You were my buddy. I want you to know that. You are such a special dog. You don't worry; I'll be right here. The girls and Al love you too. They'll miss you. I'll miss you, Rosie. You are my special lady," I whispered as the doctor came over.

The nurse helped hold Rosie in place, and she gave me a sympathetic smile.

It was the worst feeling of my life. I watched as Rosie's eyes slowly closed, and then she was gone. I scratched my head and put my hand to my mouth and tried not to cry. I just stared at her lying there. The doctor and nurse both came over to me and put a hand on each of my shoulders to show their respect and condolences. They led me out of the room and gave me some water, and I sat there in the waiting room with tears in my eyes. After a few minutes, the nurse brought over some papers and Rosie's collar and gave them to me. She said she was sorry, and I noticed her eyes had welled up too. I think she could tell how much I loved Rosie.

I walked out of the building and got in my car and started home. I tried to regain my composure on the drive home, but it was very hard for me. As I got halfway home, I noticed Rosie's collar in the passenger seat beside me. It felt awful as I thought of how many hundreds of times she had sat in that seat as we went for drives and how she had been totally content just to look out the window and be with me. And now she was gone. At that moment, I felt like the loneliest man in the world. The girls and Al were not at home, and I felt as if I had no one. I thought of how special Rosie was to all of us. I pulled into the driveway and turned the car off and just stared straight ahead at the garage doors and sat there for a while. We had lost an important part of our family, and I had lost my faithful companion.

12

THE CROSSROAD

I sent a text to Maggie and let her know Rosie had passed away and that I wouldn't be in the office on Friday and told her to shift all appointments to another time. She replied with some kinds words and told me to call her if I needed anything else.

I wound up going back to my house and sitting and thinking in the living room. It felt very odd not to have Rosie there. I stared at the corner of the room to the side of the fireplace, where Rosie had her bed. It still had a couple of her favorite chew toys on it, and that just made me more heartbroken. I thought about when I had first brought her home. I thought about the look on Allison's face when I let her in the back door and she came trotting up to her and then licked her and started to snoop around the kitchen. I remembered Allison's smile and how she almost dropped her cup of coffee in surprise and how she gave me a big hug. I thought about the look on Liz's and Gracie's faces when she ran into the living room and shuffled right up to them as they were lounging on the couch on a Saturday morning. I thought about all the times she had chased the kids and their friends around the yard. I thought about the camping trips and the muddy paw prints on the rugs. I remembered how a skunk had sprayed her one morning, and when she came in the house, everyone ran upstairs because of the smell. I had to give her multiple baths of tomato juice and soap. Most of all, I thought about our walks together around Beebe Lake. I thought about how she had loved it more than I had. I just sat in my chair and thought about Rosie and looked out through the window at the snow. The house was quiet without Al and the girls, but now it was deadly silent. It was a terrible silence that hurt my stomach and made me queasy. I decided to go for a walk to ease my mind.

I went down the block and turned up Thurston Avenue and walked toward the campus. I crossed over the street and walked past Noyes Lodge and walked down the path that brought me to Beebe Lake. As I walked, the snow was coming down fat and wet and building up on my barn coat. As I sat down on the small granite bench, I brushed off my hair and my coat and rested and stared across the lake. A few Canadian geese were out in the middle of the lake, and they appeared to be huddling together to shelter themselves from the cold. I could hear the water going over the falls to my right, and I could see the ice starting to form on the top. There always seemed to be a couple of big dead trees at the top of the falls that helped the ice take shape and start the process of winter. It was very still around the lake except for the geese, but it was a dismal quiet.

This little bench seemed to provide a kind of comfort for me during tough times. I sat and thought more about my dad. I thought about Al and the girls. And most of all,

I thought about Rosie. I sat and tried to keep bad thoughts at bay. It was very hard, and my mind seemed to go back and forth quickly between my worries. I got up and decided to walk some more and made my way down the path. The gravel path was wet and soggy from the night's rain, and it was getting covered with the heavy snow that layered the drenched walkway. I walked onto Rosie's wooden bridge and stood in the middle and looked out at the lake just as she would have done at this point. I started to get overwhelmed as tears came to my eyes.

"She was just a dog, damn it! She was just a dog!" I yelled out loud as I slapped the side of my leg.

Just then I heard some barking, and a small black Labrador came running up to me on the bridge. He caught me by surprise as I wiped my eyes and looked down at him.

"Digger! Digger, come here!" a woman's voice yelled out.

I bent down and gave the dog a pat and found myself amused at his appearance. I was certainly in disarray, but his friendliness made me feel better, even though he had caught me off guard. His paws were completely muddy, and his nose and mouth were covered with dirt and grass. He was a young Lab, and his skin was big and droopy as it covered his lanky legs. He was wagging his tail back and forth quickly and was just a big black bundle of happiness with a collar.

"I'm sorry, young man. I thought I was the only one out here with my dog today. I didn't think anyone else would take his or her dog for a walk around the lake in the snow," said the older woman as she walked up to the bridge and snapped a leash on the dog's collar.

"He certainly looks like he loves the snow," I said, trying to muster a smile.

"Oh, he loves it, all right. He loves making a mess of himself any chance he can. His name is Digger. He digs up everything with his big paws and his nose. I probably have a hundred little ditches in my yard thanks to him. But he's the sweetest thing you'll ever meet, and he loves people," she replied as she told the dog to sit at her side. He stood there wagging his tail as he sat with a big smile, as if to tell me he was the biggest and best digger in Ithaca and everyone should know all about him. He was a youthful dog and had eyes that let you know if there was a big hole to dig, he could certainly get the job done and he was always available.

Then it came to me. This was Marion, the lady who had the female golden retriever I'd seen a few times around the lake.

"Sorry, Marion. I didn't recognize you at first. I thought you had a golden?" I asked as I gave her dog another pat on the head.

"I do. Libby's at home resting right now. I just picked up this little scamp a few weeks ago from the SPCA to keep her company," she replied.

"Where's your dog? Is he running around here?" she asked as she looked around me and over to the brush.

"No, I don't have her anymore. She passed away, actually. Her name was Rosie. She died this morning," I said glumly.

"I'm sorry. I see you're holding her leash, and I thought you had let her off to run around. I'm sorry," she said.

I looked at my left hand; I hadn't even realized I had her leash. I shook my head in disbelief, as I must have grabbed it in habit on the way out the door.

"Thank you," I replied softly, and I began to get a little choked up.

She could tell I was kind of broken up about Rosie. "You know, people think that they're just dogs. Just animals. Some people, anyhow. As you know, they're not. They become part of your family. They give you love, and you give it right back. And they're so loyal. Just treat them nice, and they want to do everything for you and with you," she said as she looked down at Digger.

I looked down at her dog and tried to produce a smile. It was hard to do, but I couldn't help but produce a slight grin at this young dog.

"Well, young man, I'd better be getting on my way. I'll leave you to your thoughts. I'm sorry about Rosie," she said compassionately.

"Thank you," I replied softly as I leaned over and petted Digger. He appreciated my hand and gave me a few big licks and tail wags, and some dirt fell off his nose. His skin shook around as he moved his body and wagged his tail. He looked like someone's little brother who had to wear a sweater that was three times too big for him.

"Well, try to enjoy the rest of your day, Jack. I got to get home to the other one and check on her. And hang in there. Life can be hard sometimes. I know how it feels to lose someone special like Rosie. It's hard at first, but things have a way of turning around as time goes by, and you'll learn to be at peace with it. Well, hope to see you out here again," she said as she signaled to Digger that it was time to leave, and then they started down the path.

As I watched the woman and her dog walk down the path, my mind started to wander, and I thought of a sign I had once seen in an old coffee shop. It said that pets weren't your whole life, but they certainly made your life whole. Whoever had made that sign certainly had it right.

I stood on the wooden bridge for a few moments more and looked out over the lake. The older woman had made me feel better just by talking about it. I took a deep breath and closed my eyes and tried to be at peace with everything. Then I continued down the path to the stone bridge. I stood in the middle and leaned against the wall and absorbed the view. Every time Al and I walked the lake, we would stop here and take a break together and enjoy the view. Now it was just me, and it felt strange. I continued around and walked past the oval wooden picnic tables. I didn't want to sit there alone. I thought it would be a complete waste of the most romantic spot in the world. I would sit there again only when Allison was with me. I walked around the rest of the lake and thought about how ironic it was that today should be so beautiful and I should feel so melancholy. I walked through the woods and past the falls and out onto Thurston Avenue. I held Rosie's leash all the way home.

I hung up her leash on the wall hook in the kitchen and picked up the phone to call Allison. When I told her, she started to cry and got upset and told me she was real sorry because she knew that I had a real special bond with Rosie. We had a long talk, and it made me feel at ease to hear her voice again. We talked about what a wonderful pet Rosie had been to all of us and all the great times we had had with her. She said her mom's wrist was healing great and that she was getting the cast off tomorrow. Al would be leaving real early Tuesday morning and would be at the house by ten or eleven that night. I told her I would call the girls and let them know about Rosie. I knew it would be a tough call, but I felt it best to get it done and let them know as soon as possible.

"Al, I miss you."

"I miss you, too, Jack...and I miss the girls," she replied. We talked for a little longer and then said we loved each other and said good-bye.

I put the phone on the kitchen counter and stared through the window. I looked at the bench in the yard. I could still see the imprint in the ground that Rosie had made there only a few hours ago.

I called the girls and let them know about Rosie, and they both took it pretty hard. I got Gracie just after a morning skate, and I got a hold of Liz studying in the library. Needless to say, it didn't take long for each of them to cry over the phone. I tried to be as positive as a parent can be during these times. I didn't want to have them grief stricken, as they were going through finals. I kept telling them it was just one of those things and that she had had a great life with us, and we'd all have some great memories for the rest of our lives. I talked to each of them for about thirty minutes, and at the end of each call, I think they felt a little better. As a parent, I guess we're always trying to keep our kids' emotions in check and protect them from pain, but sometimes there's just nowhere to hide from it. In this case I did the best I could do and told them that I looked forward to seeing them at Christmas in a few weeks.

I kept busy around the house for the next couple of days and cleaned it up as much as possible and straightened up the garage and loaded some firewood inside the back door. I took some long walks down at Stewart Park on Saturday and Sunday afternoons and got some exercise. We had only gotten a couple of inches of snow, so the paths were pretty clear for walking down there.

As busy and active as I stayed on the weekend, Monday morning seemed to come pretty quick, and I was up and out the door by seven o'clock. Maggie and Stacey came in around eight thirty, and Teddy and Rocky showed up shortly before nine. Everyone stopped by my office and offered their condolences for Rosie, and Maggie gave me a big hug. All of us had a cup of coffee together in the snack room, and we all shared stories about our pets and pets that had passed away. The conversation and amusing stories seemed to help keep my emotions in check. This was certainly not the first time that I had felt very fortunate to work with such a good group of people. As we finished our coffee, Maggie let us know about all the appointments we had today and told us she had prepared all the files and folders and put them on our desks. And with that said, we all got back to work and dug in for the day.

It seemed we were all booked throughout the day and had clients coming and going all day long. We worked our tails off, and it felt good to keep busy and talk to people. It kept my mind off of everything else that had been on my mind for the last few days. At about four o'clock, Maggie came back to my office and told me that Helen was on the line and that she had called on Friday too. Helen was always a little evasive on the phone and didn't give Maggie much information as to what she needed from me, so Maggie couldn't relay any real pertinent information. It bugged her a bit, because Maggie was very efficient and detail oriented and wanted to do a nice job. I gave her a wink and picked up line two.

"Hello, Helen. How are you?" I said cheerfully into the receiver.

"I'm fine, Jack. I'm really calling to see how you're doing. I had called on Friday and heard your dog died, and I wanted to check in on you."

"I'm doing okay, Helen. It was a real tough day Friday. She was such a great dog and a big part of our family. It's definitely pretty hard not seeing her around the house," I said. That statement brought back some more feelings, but I kept them in check and tried to stay in a positive frame of mind.

"Well, I guess it's going to take some time. But stay busy at work and keep your chin up, and I'm sure you'll start to feel better. And just stay around your friends and talk about it a lot, and it will help you too. And that's another reason I called, Jack. I want to invite you to dinner tonight. I want to introduce you to someone. I think it could be another great client. She's an older woman who just lost her husband, and she has a lot of money and a huge estate to settle. I think she could be a huge client for you," she said enthusiastically.

"What time and where do you want to meet?" I asked.

"I'm having the dinner at my house, and Rachel said she could be here at six o'clock. I think you'll like her, too. She's a very funny and outgoing lady."

I thought about it for a moment, and I was sure Helen could tell that I was on the fence. Then I came to the conclusion that it would be good to stay busy and talk with people. The house was straightened up, and Al wasn't coming home till tomorrow night. I guess I felt it was good timing.

"Sure, Helen. I appreciate the invite and the opportunity. I'll see you at your house at six," I replied.

For the next few hours, I prepared for my appointments tomorrow. Maggie stayed late and helped me run the reports I needed, and we both walked out of the office together around ten minutes before six.

"Thanks for all your help with everything, Maggie. I'm off to Helen's to meet a prospective client. I'll let you know how it went in the morning. Keep your fingers crossed for me," I said as I walked over to my car.

"You're welcome, Jack. And good luck tonight. See you in the morning."

Helen lived in a huge mansion on Highland Road that was equidistant between our house and my mom's house. I don't know if it was technically a mansion, but it certainly was the biggest house, by far, in Cayuga Heights. The first thing you noticed was the overwhelming stone pillars that stood at the entrance of the driveway, and they each had large colonial lights on the top that put visitors in their place as soon as they started up the circular cobblestone drive to the front door. The driveway had lights that had an old English feel to them, and they were up and down each side and positioned about ten feet apart from each other, sticking up proudly from the ground. The grounds were perfectly landscaped, and every time I've driven by the place on a weekend, I could see two or three gardeners working in the yard all throughout the year. There was an immaculate array of trees and bushes that were protected by tall wrought iron fencing that encompassed the entire compound. The home had a way about it that would make even the most prominent businessman feel small and less fortunate.

I pulled up to the front doors and turned off the ignition and made my way to the front steps, which were engulfed with massive clay pots containing English boxwoods of every height and perfectly carved barberry bushes that had a pristine air about them. The mammoth double wooden doors each had a perfectly combed pine wreath with an exquisite red bow that let you know where she stood in the pecking order of life. I had been there a few times in the past, usually just to drop off checks or pick up stock certificates that she needed to deposit into her account, but had stayed only long enough to have a cup of tea or talk for a few minutes in her parlor. Today had an altogether different feel about it, and I was curious and anxious about the evening, as my mind had had a chance to drift to my personal issues on the drive over to her house.

Be that as it may, I took a deep breath and rang the doorbell. Even the doorbell sounded important as it made huge, echoing gongs that seemed to shake my insides. I heard faint footsteps, and both mammoth doors opened slowly and a huge hallway chandelier came into full view. An older, white-haired man with fuzzy eyebrows that sat above his oval, metal-framed eyeglasses greeted me. His hair was combed straight back and ordered to stay in place.

"Hello, I'm Jack MacNamara, and I'm here to see Helen," I said, both taken aback and humored my reception as well as the old man's appearance.

"Good evening, Mr. MacNamara. Ms. White is expecting you. Please come in," said the butler as he stepped aside to let me in and closed the doors behind me. He then led me into the living room, and, as I walked behind him, I chuckled lowly to myself as I noticed that his perfectly creased outfit did not move at all, and as he walked carefully through the room, his hands, which were covered with white gloves, remained still and had a mannequin look about them.

As we walked into the room, Helen was standing by the bar, holding a glass of wine. After the butler announced me and left the room, I was in awe of how she looked. She had on a stunning black evening dress that fit perfectly, and the string of white pearls she was displaying made for the perfect accent to the dark dress. She had on high heels, and her hands and left wrist displayed some gold pieces that would produce envy from most any high-society type. Her hair was dark brown and cropped and gave her a sassy but sophisticated style. Her eyes were big and brown, and her smile was flawless. Helen was a few years older than I, but she looked amazing, and she gave me a look that let me know she was well aware of her exterior features. She smiled, and I walked toward her and extended my hand.

"Hello, Jack. So glad you're here," she said as our hands met.

"Thanks for inviting me, Helen. I really appreciate your keeping me in mind for prospective clients and being such an advocate. And I just want to say that you look stunning. I'm glad I left my tie on," I replied as I tried to insert some humor and let her know I was a gentleman as well.

"Of course, Jack. And thank you for the compliment. You look great with or without a tie, I'm sure. And I always will keep you in mind if I meet an affluent person who needs a talented and good-looking advisor. I always think of you," she said with a wink, and then she turned and called in the butler to fix me a drink.

"A glass of wine, Jack? Or maybe something stronger?" she offered.

"I'll have a glass of wine. Whatever you're drinking is fine, Helen. Is your friend here yet?" I asked as I looked around the room and to each doorway. I began to feel slightly uncomfortable.

"Well, Jack, I didn't want to call you so late at the office, but Rachel called about an hour ago and had to cancel. She had something come up and said she was sorry, but she'd be more than happy to get together with you for lunch this week or meet at your office. I thought you and I could have dinner anyway. I didn't think you'd mind, since we had everything all set up anyway. I hope that's okay?" she said sheepishly but with the savvy of a worldly aristocrat.

I immediately felt that I had been put in an awkward position, and I took a moment to try to respond to her. Her smile was more seductive than professional, and I should have bowed out gracefully at that point. But I didn't feel the need to be rude, and I said to myself that I would have a drink, talk some business, eat dinner, and, hopefully, be on my way home in an hour or so. That was my plan, anyway. Sometimes my words didn't convey my true thoughts, and that was my own flaw that I'd been dealing with my whole life.

"Sure, Helen. I'd be happy to stay for dinner. Thank you. And maybe you can tell me a little more about Rachel and how I can help," I suggested as I accepted the glass of wine from the wrinkle-free servant and watched him walk away, without emotion, into the next room.

"He doesn't say much, but he's a very loyal and efficient worker," she said in an amused tone as she shook her head. Then she took hold of my arm and led me around her home. The house had multiple floors, but we stayed on the first floor and still didn't see everything it had to offer as far as priceless artwork and collectible books and sculptures. I remember thinking that her accounts with me were huge but were probably a miniscule part of her net worth. Each of these pieces of art was probably worth a small fortune.

As we walked around the house, she held on to my arm, and she would point with the other hand and explain how she had come about each piece. My jaw dropped when she started to talk about the prices she had paid. Sotheby's and Christie's came up multiple times. As I sipped the wine, I was overwhelmed by the cost of the first floor's collection and felt quite dizzy and out of my league in her presence. Helen had always seemed like quite the flirt, but I thought that was how she was with everyone. I didn't think it was just me. I thought she liked to come on to all men with her flirtatious ways and then cast them aside. It appeared to me to be just a game for her or some sort of trivial amusement. At least I told myself that as I tried to rationalize the situation.

It was working just fine until we walked arm and arm into a small room all the way in the back of the house that was surrounded by huge picture windows, and right in the middle of the room was a table set for two with a large candle glowing in the darkness. The only other light that I could see was the crescent of the moon. It was noticeable through the windows, which seemed to stretch from the table to the ceiling and gave impeccable views of her manicured grounds.

"Isn't it a beautiful night, Jack? And I'm so glad you're here," she said as she looked to the table and then to me.

Any other guy on this planet would kill to be in my position, I thought. A sexy and charismatic woman whose wealth was in another stratosphere, and it was me she had picked for a romantic candlelit dinner in her mansion. My mind seemed to clutter fast as confusing thoughts rushed in at the same time. At this point, I knew I was in way over my head and should have left when I had the opportunity. But I hadn't, and it was my own doing. So again I started to plan my escape as she led me into the room and we walked over to the table.

Then she showed me a fountain containing a Greek statue in the middle of her backyard. After a moment in which she provided a description of the fountain, she released my arm and sauntered toward the other room to summon the butler. Needless to say, my eyes reluctantly followed her all the way to the doorway. The guilt then started to creep back into my body, and I took another sip of wine and was hoping the food would be quickly on its way and that it would all be over soon.

Helen announced to the servant that we were ready for dinner and to bring the bottle of wine to the table. When she turned and smiled, it was hard not to be attracted to her, but I kept telling myself it was a mistake. I'd always prided myself on demonstrating the utmost professionalism and ethics, but her sultry smile and seductive mannerisms seem to cloud my judgment.

"I hope you like roast duck, Jack. It should go perfectly with this Cabernet," she said smoothly as she walked back to the table.

"Of course. Sounds great. Thank you," I replied as we both sat down.

I tried to turn the conversation toward her fund-raising efforts and the alumni events she attended, trying to make the time go by as fast as possible. As we ate our dinner, it was hard not to feel drawn to her. I had so many mixed emotions running through my brain at the same time that I lost my train of thought a couple of times during conversation. I thought about

Al and how much I missed her. I began to think about our last couple of phone conversations and tried to understand and figure out what she wanted to talk about when she got back home. I wondered if I had pushed her too far and if she wanted to break up with me. I really didn't know what to think, but it hurt to think she would want to separate just because I was spending a lot of time with my parents in their time of need.

It was an odd feeling to have Allison on my mind and look at this attractive woman across from me who seemed to be interested in me. As she talked, my mind focused on how much I loved Allison, and I started to think about her and the girls. I remained quiet as I thought of my family and listened to Helen, but my eyes seemed to roam from her beautiful facial features and alluring smile to her neckline and pearl necklace and how it lay perfectly across the top of her low-cut dress. I would catch myself and then turn toward the window and stare out into the moonlit night.

"I'm sorry, Jack. I'm doing all the talking. Tell me more about what's going on with you. How are you and Allison getting along?" she asked, and then she took another sip of wine keeping her eyes focused on me.

"To be honest, Helen, Al has been down in North Carolina with her parents for the last week or so. We've been a little at odds lately, and she needed some time with her parents...and I guess some space from me too. I've been spending a lot of time helping my mom and dad, and I've been busy at work and with the girls. And I guess life just got in the way a little, and I haven't been paying too much attention to her," I said as I swirled my wine glass gently and looked out the window to my right and then back at Helen.

Just then her servant came in and cleared our plates and left just our glasses and the bottle of wine on the table and exited the room.

"You know, Jack, I hope Allison knows what a catch she has in her hands. You're a handsome man, and you have a great practice and a lot of good clients who appreciate your work and time. You give a lot to the community and always have for years. I just hope she appreciates all you do. I know I do," she said as she reached her hand across the table and put it gently on top of mine. She left it there for a few moments and then pulled it slowly away.

"Thank you, Helen. I appreciate you and your business as well. Thanks for letting me open up...I guess I'm not very good at that...just had a lot on my mind with everything," I replied as my mind started to drift to thinking about Allison.

"Jack, I just want to say I care about you. I like you, and I always have," she said as she reached her hand back to mine, and, like a fool, I didn't move mine.

"Let me show you something," she said as she stood up and offered her hand. She walked me over to the window behind her, which was facing the backyard. She held my hand, and I felt nervous but excited at the same time. We were side by side, and she was holding my hand as we looked out the window into the night.

"Isn't it perfect, Jack? The night. The moon. Just spending time and enjoying a nice dinner and being with a good friend. Sometimes a change is good for everyone. Sometimes there's someone else who is a better fit for you right in front of your eyes, and all you have to do is reach out," she said as she looked at the moon and then to me.

I turned to face her. She was elegant and attractive, and it was awkward and exciting and confusing at the same time.

"Jack, would you kiss me?" she said softly.

My heart immediately dropped, as I was caught off guard at her request. I thought for a moment and then held both her hands and looked into her eyes. She was stunning and alluring and very close to me. I stood quietly for a moment, and then my cell phone buzzed loudly in my pocket. It seemed to break the trance I was in, and I apologized to Helen and told her with everything going on, I had to check my phone for emergencies. It was a text that read "Good night, young man. Time to go home."

A huge feeling of guilt immediately came over me, and I shook my head slowly in disbelief. I felt so foolish and so rotten. I didn't recognize the number, but I didn't have to in this case. I knew I was doing the wrong thing, and it was time to put a stop to my immature and juvenile behavior before things really went too far to turn back. The feelings I had seemed to be the exact opposite of the moral fiber and integrity I had prided myself on throughout the years. I guess I was just feeling awkward and vulnerable, but I knew it was time to get the hell out of there.

"I'm sorry, Helen. I'm really, really flattered that you think of me in that way. But I'm married, and I'm in love with Allison. I know we're going through a rough patch right now, but I love her, and I always have and I always will. She's the world to me," I said as I pulled up one of her hands and kissed it and smiled at her.

"I'm sorry. I have to go now, Helen."

She just smiled slightly and nodded, and a look of sadness came over her face. And then she closed and opened her eyes, which had gotten a little misty. "I know" was all she said.

I left her side and made my way to the front door to let myself out of the house. I could feel her eyes on me as I walked away, but I didn't look back. As soon as I stepped outside and closed the door behind me and smelled the fresh air, I felt better immediately.

13

MY LOVE RETURNS

I sat up in bed most of Monday night trying to think of who could have sent me the text at Helen's house. It was a California area code, and I couldn't think of any friends or clients or anyone who would have done it. I thought it could have been a mistake. Every once in a while, I would get a call or text from a number I didn't recognize, and it would turn out to be some student from Cornell dialing or texting the wrong person. I convinced myself that it must have been one of these out-of-town students texting a friend.

My thoughts then turned to Allison. I felt like an idiot for putting myself in such a position. I was angry with myself, and the guilt seemed to swamp my brain and not let go. I thought again about when I first met Al and how she caught my eye and how hard I tried to get her attention that first night and how I felt when we fell in love. She was my soul mate, and no matter what was going on right now between us, she certainly didn't deserve that type of behavior. I promised myself I wouldn't be in that type of situation ever again and tried to come to peace with the whole thing.

Then I thought about my dad again, and I thought it would be best to see him during the afternoon tomorrow so I could give full attention to Allison in the evening. I started to feel more at ease knowing I had a game plan, and just as I reached to turn off the light, I stopped and lowered my arm. I stared at Rosie's bed sitting empty near my dresser. I lay still for a few moments and stared at her bed and then out the window into the darkness. Then I turned the light off and tried to sleep. After about an hour or so, I was able to get some rest.

I arrived at the office before eight and buried myself in my work till lunchtime. Maggie had me very well organized for my appointments, and things seem to move along like clockwork. I told her I hadn't gotten to meet the prospective client last night and that if someone named Rachel called, to try to book her for next week. I left it at that and didn't mention that I had stayed for dinner at Helen's house.

As five o'clock approached, I was pretty well spent. I was doing reviews back to back and returning phone calls in between the appointments. I gave my mom a call and told her I'd stop by Bridges on the way home, and off I went to see how my dad was doing. I was hoping he was having a good day.

As I was pulling into the Bridges parking lot, I noticed my mom sitting outside the doors. I got out of the car and walked up to her, wondering why she was outside. She was bundled up in her coat, hat, and gloves and sitting very still.

"Hi, Mom. You okay?" I asked. "Why are you out here?"

She looked at me, and I could see how tired her eyes were and wondered how much sleep she had been able to get, as she seemed to give my dad every ounce of her energy.

"I'm fine, Jack. I just needed some air, and I knew you were on your way. Your dad is sleeping now. He wasn't when you called. He's been sleeping a lot lately. More than I've ever seen him sleep, even when he was at home," she said.

"Would you like to go for a walk, Jack?" she asked.

"Of course, Mom," I replied.

She took hold of my arm, and we walked down the steps and along the slate path and out onto the sidewalk. It was a calm but cold night, and there was no snow in the air. I walked with my mom along the fence that outlined the property, and she held on to my arm the whole time. I noticed that they had gotten the grounds ready for Christmas, and the place looked beautiful. There were huge wreaths with red bows under the grandiose windows, and they had put up a Christmas tree in the living room that lit up the whole block with all its different-colored lights, which seemed to sparkle and give you a warm feeling. The place looked very welcoming, and the Christmas ornaments just made it look even more graceful. Mom told me that all the residents had helped put bulbs on the tree and that even Dad had come out of his room to take part in the festivities. He didn't stay long or talk much, but he did participate and have fun with the other residents.

She let me know how conscious he was about not being able to remember things and that it was really hurtful to him. He just wanted to be by himself in his room, as he had a tremendous feeling of insecurity, but she had managed to coax him out against his will, and he had had a nice time. A lot of the staff and other residents would drop in to see him lately, but he had begun to address them without using their names, as he had done in the past. Mom also said that his hand was consistently shaking, and that also bothered him. She told me that he seemed to be getting tired of the way his body and mind were treating him.

"And he's so goddamned proud," she said with a slight gasp.

I let her hold my arm, and we walked through the neighborhood and looked at all the houses that were getting into the Christmas spirit. Every house was a different shape and style, and they all had their personal ways of saying hello to the holiday. There were lights that were big and bold, and there were lights that were all white and looked pristine as they sat on trees and shrubs with precision. There were snowmen on front porches and wreaths with different-colored bows. There was a little bit of everything honoring the holidays, and it showed a lot of individuality and togetherness.

We walked and talked about Christmastime when I was little and how my dad had had so much fun with it. We shared a laugh as we remembered that he always had a big glass of red wine and would offer a prize to the person in our family who could hang an ornament on the highest spot on the tree. It was a prize that he won every year until my brother and I grew as tall as he was. We talked about all the surprises and chaos and how he added a little something to his coffee on Christmas morning as the shredding of all the wrapped presents was in full swing. We talked about all the different kinds of gifts and sporting equipment we got and how everyone would play all morning long. We talked about how Mom made this huge breakfast of eggs and bacon and toast and how we sat and laughed around the table. It felt nice to think about those times, but it also felt sad as we came back to the entrance of Bridges and stopped at the front gate.

We stood there for a while and talked more, and Mom asked about Allison. I let her know that she had gone to see her parents for a little while and that she was returning that night. Mom was sharp as a tack, and she knew that there was a little more to the story. I opened up, and we talked awhile about what was happening, and she offered her advice.

"Jack, don't be so quick to judge Allison. You have a real nice woman there, and you just need to go home and talk with her tonight. Don't worry about your dad or the girls right now. Just go sit with her and talk with her, and don't look too much into the other stuff. Absence can make the heart grow fonder, and you two will be fine. Trust me," she said as she pulled my face down and gave me a kiss.

"Now you go home and let me go check on your dad. And don't worry about him so much. He's tougher than you think," she said with a smile.

And so I gave her a hug and watched her walk up the steps and in through the doors, and then I got in my car and went home.

It was ten o'clock when I heard Al's Subaru come into our driveway and park by the garage. I had been anxiously waiting for her, and I went outside quickly to meet her as soon as she stepped out of the car. I could see her smiling through the front windshield at me, and I quickly went around to her side as she stepped out and shut the car door.

"I'm so glad you're home, Al. I missed you so much, and I'm glad you're here," I said as I grabbed her and held her tight.

"It's good to be back, Jack. I missed you too. And I missed our home," she replied as she rested her head on my shoulder. I hugged her for a while and put my mouth and nose against her head. She felt wonderful, and it was great to have my wife and my soul mate in my arms again.

"I love you, Al. I want you to know that. I mean really *know* it," I said as she pulled her head off my shoulder and held her face close to mine.

"I love you too, Jack," she said softly.

Then I kissed her and held her close. "Come on, Al. Let's get you inside so you can relax. I have a glass of wine waiting," I said as I held her waist, and then we walked to the door together.

Once inside, we sat and talked at the dining room table. We sat and we talked about everything. We talked about Rosie, and she told me how sorry she was that she had died. We both knew how much she meant to our family. We talked about her parents and how her mom was making out, and she let me know that the cast had been removed and the bone had healed in a perfect manner. Her dad was doing okay, but his driving was becoming more and more of a liability and was something that needed to be figured out. He was very adamant and offended if anyone suggested that he give up his driving privileges. Al inserted some humor into the situation with her stories about her parents and how different it was to stay in her childhood house as an adult and see all the funny and quirky little habits her parents had picked up as they had gotten older. We also talked about getting our whole family down to North Carolina for Easter and having a nice family get-together. That made Al feel good, and she grabbed and held my hand on the table when I suggested it.

I filled her in on my parents and the latest with my dad, and she wanted to go see them tomorrow. She said she'd cook some dinner and let my mom know, and we could bring it over and have a nice meal together. She knew my dad was struggling, but she still wanted to go see him and spend time with him. We talked about the girls and how they would be home soon for Christmas, and that made us most excited. To have the house full and vibrant again was something we both looked forward to with great anticipation.

There was only one thing that was weighing on my mind. I hadn't wanted to bring it up right away, but now that we had talked for a while, it seemed to be a good time. "Al, you mentioned that you needed to talk to me about something, and you wanted to wait till you were home," I said in a questioning tone as I looked at her with slight concern.

She put her glass on the table and took a breath and looked out the dining room window for a moment, and then she turned to me. "Jack, there is not an easy way to say this, so I'll just say it. I have breast cancer," she said as tears formed in her eyes.

I just looked at her, and my heart sank into my stomach. I was in shock, and my mouth fell open, and I didn't know what to say or do. I got up and picked her up out of her chair and held her. She rested her head on my chest. I rubbed her back and stroked her hair, and she just softly sobbed on me.

I felt as if I had been kicked in the gut. I can only imagine how she was feeling. As I rubbed her and kissed her head, a massive feeling of guilt came over me. I felt so ashamed. I had been wondering for over a week what she had wanted to talk about face to face. I thought she possibly wanted to separate and move in different directions. But she wanted to sit and talk about the bad news she had received from the doctor, and she didn't want to tell me over the phone. She wanted to talk to me and be next to me when she let me know about her diagnosis. That was the way Al had always been. She always seemed to put everyone else's feelings above her own. She did it with me, the girls, my parents, her parents, friends, and colleagues. She did it with everybody.

I felt like a selfish fool as she opened her heart and told me what she had heard at her doctor's appointment. We sat back down together at the table for a while, and I held her hand as she went through all the details and what the doctor had told her to expect. Apparently, she had had a second appointment with Dr. Liebenthal after her mammogram. She didn't tell me about either appointment, and she went by herself because I had been working late and then going over to see my dad at Bridges. She thought it would be best for her just to go by herself and deal with it alone. And that was when the doctor confirmed the multiple tumors in her breasts and reviewed the mammogram and the procedure to remove them.

She had wanted to go and be with her parents and tell them about it, and sit with her mom and dad in person as she told them of the diagnosis as well. It was sheer coincidence that her mom had fallen and broken her wrist, so she got down there even earlier than she expected to, but she was going anyway. She said it felt good to be near her mom and dad and talk about it and stay busy and help them out too. She said being with them helped her out, and talking and walking with her mom relaxed her and put her at ease, as she wanted to be with another woman. She wanted to be with her mom and spend some time talking about her condition, but she also wanted to see how her mom and dad were doing in their golden years. Her mother had told her that it was nice to have her around the house and that two people living alone can get in each other's way a lot of the time. She told me how they both laughed out loud in a store when they discussed their men and their quirky ways. Al even managed a slight smile as she thought of her time in North Carolina with her parents and remembered a lot of little things that made her laugh. I was in awe of her strength and the way she seemed to find humor in everything, knowing that she had this terrible disease.

On the other hand, my mind was racing as I listened to her, and we talked more about her situation. The procedure was going to be in just under two weeks—a few days before Christmas. She said she didn't want to tell the girls over the phone, and she didn't want them to concentrate on anything other than school and finals. She would tell them after they came home, and she felt more comfortable telling all of us in person. Either way, she knew they'd have a real tough time with it, and she wanted them close to her when she broke the news.

Al and I stayed up for a while talking about everything, and we wound up finally going upstairs to bed at two in the morning. By the time we got in bed, Allison looked totally exhausted, both mentally and physically. I was still extremely restless as I digested the news, but I wanted her to know that I would be right by her side every step of the way.

"Al, I just want you to know something. I just want you to know that I will be with you through this whole thing. I'll be right alongside you. And you're going to beat this damn thing,

Al. You hear me? You're going to beat this thing, and every-thing is going to be okay," I said.

She smiled at me and gave me a kiss goodnight.

"And Al, I love you more than anything in the world. I love you, and I always have."

"I love you too," she said as she caressed my face. Then she said goodnight, and it only took her about two minutes to be solidly asleep. I watched her most of the night and thought about how much I loved her. I didn't sleep at all that night. I just lay awake and thought about my best friend, who was sleeping beside me.

The next morning, I quietly got out of bed. I didn't want to disturb Al, who was still sleeping soundly, so I went downstairs and started the coffee pot. She had slept all night long and hadn't moved at all, and it looked as if she could be in bed for another couple of hours. So I stayed downstairs and had cof-fee and waited for her to awaken. I called Maggie and told her I would be in after lunch today, and she said she would shift an appointment that I had around eleven o'clock to the after-noon and take care of anything else that came up.

It was about ten o'clock when I started to hear footsteps upstairs, so I grabbed a cup of coffee for Al and walked it up to her. She had gotten back in bed, and she was sitting up with a big smile on her face. She said she felt great and hadn't had such a great night's sleep in a while. She was also very excited to see I had brought her up some coffee. I walked over and gave her the cup followed by a gentle kiss.

We sat and talked a little, and she said she wanted to keep as busy as possible to keep her mind off of the operation and that I should do the same. She was going to take a couple of hours and get a little organized at home and then go into work in the afternoon. Her resiliency and fortitude were quite amazing. She told me that she didn't want to talk about the cancer anymore today and that she wanted to go to work and come back and bring some dinner over to Dad and Mom. If they were up for it, she could put something in the Crock-Pot before she left for work so that it would be ready when we met up later at the house. So I popped in the shower and got ready for work. Seeing her in good spirits made me feel good. It gave me hope. I knew if anyone could beat this horrible thing called cancer, that person needed to have unbelievable strength and courage and a huge heart. If anyone could beat it, that person would have to have all this and God on his or her side. That person would have to be made of tough stuff. That person would have to be someone just like Allison.

Both of us kept busy at work as best we could and tried to stay as positive as possible. We stayed in touch with the girls. They were doing great in school, and their tests had been going extremely well. We felt guilty about not divulging Al's condition, but she was adamant that it was the best way to handle the situation.

We spent a lot of time going for walks around the neighborhood after work. Cayuga Heights was very pretty at nighttime, and it kept us in good spirits to see all the houses decorated for the holidays. We visited my dad and mom on our walks, and Al made dinner a few times to give my dad some home cooking and give my mom a break. Dad was struggling more and more with his memory loss, and his hand shaking was pretty bad. Sometimes he would recognize me right away, and sometimes he would look at me like a stranger for a few seconds before he realized it was me. I could see he was doing the best he could do, and Mom was right by his side at all times. Sometimes I would stay with Dad, and Mom would walk with Al around the neighborhood to get some fresh air and get out of the room for a while.

One night, while they were out walking, Al filled her in on her condition, and my mom talked with her for a long time. Al later told me how appreciative she was and how easy it was to talk to my mom. They wound up walking a lot together when we visited, and I think this really helped Al as she got closer and closer to her surgery.

I stayed with my dad, and we talked about golf and baseball and hockey on his good days. I did most of the talking, and most of the time, he just seemed to nod back at me. I took advantage of those moments we shared together. We talked mostly about Gracie and Liz, and he just kept telling me what a great job Al and I had done raising them, and he was proud of the way they had turned out. He would also tell me how proud he was of me. I don't care if you're a young kid or older person; a son or daughter can never hear those words too much. He would lose his train of thought here and there and have to regain his focus, but I would help him with a name or place and keep the conversation smooth so he wouldn't feel uncomfortable or embarrassed.

Dad wasn't eating great and was losing a little weight, which was noticeable since he was a big man, but Mom kept on him to eat as much as possible and would bring him a lot of homemade cookies and muffins to entice him. My dad always had a major sweet tooth, so it was easy to get him to eat if you put a plate of fudge brownies in front of him with a cold glass of milk. Al would also bring him some homemade cookies along with the dinners she prepared, so he got pretty spoiled between the both of them. Needless to say, the food was wonderful at Bridges as well, so Dad had a pretty good thing going as far as his meals.

The girls arrived home one snowy afternoon, and they were all smiles as they stepped out of Liz's Jeep in the driveway. Al and I were right there to greet them and help bring all their stuff into the house, which was mostly dirty laundry that looked as if it had been building up for a few weeks. It was great to have them home, though. The house was much more lively, and that was what we needed. That was what Al wanted.

I had put up a lot of lights on the outside of the house and decorated the porch with a wreath and an old sled and some dwarf pines, and Al had had a ton of fun putting up decorations up inside the house. I could see the girls' eyes light up when they walked into the house and noticed all the decorations, and Al had made some chocolate cookies that were resting on the stove, so the house smelled good too. It smelled and looked like the holidays, thanks to Allison.

I had left Rosie's beds out, so the girls got a little sad when they saw the empty beds with her toys. But they said they were happy I didn't put them away.

Al had a tray of ziti in the oven, and in no time at all, we were all sitting around the table. Al and I listened as the girls told us stories about school and how exhausting it was to study for finals and how glad they were to be on break for a while. We all had a lot of fun at Gracie's expense as she removed her tooth multiple times while she ate, and she seemed to get a lot of food stuck in the gap and had to put her fork down to carefully pick out the macaroni that was wedged in the opening. She actually seemed to like having the gap in her smile and said that it was now part of her new personality.

We wound up sitting around the table most of the night listening to the girls and their stories, and Al and I would make eye contact every once in a while and hold hands as we watched our girls. The girls wound up going to bed around midnight, and Al and I sat together in the living room for a while in front of the fire. Tomorrow was a big day for us. We were going to Moore's Tree Farm out in Lansing to cut down a tree and decorate it in the afternoon. It was a family tradition, and the girls loved it. Unfortunately, after we brought the tree home, we were going to tell the girls that their mom had cancer, and we knew it was going to be a hard pill for them to swallow. But we also had faith that they would be able to handle it.

We must have wandered around the tree farm for an hour before the girls picked out a nice fat Fraser fir tree and then sawed it down and put it on a cart and dragged it up to the front lot, where they would shake and bundle it for you. It was part of the fun and excitement to watch the girls as they strolled around to try to pick out the perfect tree. We followed and laughed as they bickered about each other's choices until they came to an agreement after twenty or twenty-five prospective sightings. After we got home, we unloaded the tree, and the girls helped me set it up by our front living-room window.

We played Christmas music in the house, and we all decorated the tree together. There were a ton of ornaments, but our favorites were the ones the girls had made as children in elementary school. They always seemed to produce a memory or a big chuckle at the fine craftsmanship the girls showed when they were in first, second, or third grade.

After the tree was done, we put out some lunch meat and made sandwiches and had a nice lunch. Afterward, Al announced that we should all go into the living room and talk for a while. The girls looked at each other in bewilderment, as Allison had made her request with a rather straight and serious face, and then we all moved into the living room. Al sat next to Liz and Gracie on the couch, I sat in the love seat, and she began to tell them about what she had going on. It was a very emotional conversation, to say the least, and all of us were crying at one point or another. Gracie, being the younger one, seemed to take it the hardest, and that always meant that Liz had to stay strong. Liz said she was angry that her mother hadn't told her about it sooner, but she understood why and soon got over it. They both gave their mom a lot of hugs and almost immediately began to say really positive and supportive things that made Al and me feel extremely proud. I sat back and let Liz and Gracie talk to their mom and watched two girls giving their mom a ton of love and support right away. I was ecstatic that it didn't take them too long to wipe their tears away and begin to show encouragement and come out with positive stories about others they had heard of who had survived this ugly disease. I was very happy it was finally all out in the open.

I felt it would be good to let the girls talk alone, so I walked into the kitchen. I leaned against the counter and thought about the coming week. As I rubbed my brow, something caught my eye on the refrigerator. It was a magnet that Liz had made when she was little that had a picture of Allison on it and said, World's Best Mother. I nodded to myself as I thought there could be no statement more accurate, and again I felt blessed that the girls should have a mother like Allison. Then I started to get nervous and worried all over again. My wife was going into the hospital in two days to try to rid her body of cancer.

Al and I went in to work for the next couple of days and tried to stay as busy as possible. We thought that too much downtime wouldn't be good for anyone, and she certainly didn't want to just sit around the house and talk about her cancer, as she felt that would make the girls even more upset. So we worked, and the girls made their rounds and visited their friends who were home from school, and then they usually came back in the afternoons. They visited my dad and mom at Bridges a few times and even took my mom out for breakfast one morning down at the State Street Diner while Dad took his nap.

Gracie and Liz both noticed the changes in my dad, but they handled it quite well and sat and talked with him about their schools and golf and hockey. They noticed his hand tremors and could tell his memory loss was much more severe, but they were determined not to let their emotions get the better of them. Even Gracie remained poised as she sat and held Grandpa's hand under the table, and she smiled at him as she let him know about some of her tougher opponents on the ice. Every time she mentioned how she had knocked a player to the ice he would smile, and then she would return the smile. Of course, she took out her tooth to emphasize her toughness, and that would almost get him laughing out of his chair.

When each visit came to a close, they would hug my parents and give them each a kiss. They hugged their grandpa as if it were the last time they would see him. It was always a little longer every time. It usually brought a tear to the old man's eye, and he tried his hardest to hide it. Unfortunately, he could never hide the fact that he loved his granddaughters. Mostly, he loved them for the love they showed him.

On the evening before Al was to go to the hospital, the girls said they wanted to cook dinner. They wanted to make a special dinner for their mom and give her a nice little break before she had her surgery the following morning. Liz announced that they would make pork chops and mashed potatoes and stuffing and a green bean casserole. She nominated Gracie as her first assistant to help in the kitchen and set the table. Gracie was only too happy to take a small role, because she was clueless about cooking and didn't mind doing the grunt work and leaving her sister to the master chef role.

I was home early, and it was both impressive and amusing to see the girls at work in the kitchen and dining room. They had some country music going, and Gracie had done the table up real nice and was quite proud of her effort, even though her big sister stated that she had spent most of her time on her cell phone and not helping her out. Liz looked a little perplexed at times as she checked her dishes and opened the oven from time to time. But I didn't interfere and just sat at the dining room table with an everlasting grin as I watched my girls try to navigate all the different seasonings and synchronization that went into dinner preparation. Needless to say, they looked like fish out of water, but they gave it the old college try. It was fun to watch Liz bark orders at Gracie when she needed something done and Liz didn't think she moved fast enough. It was fun for me, that is, but not so much for her younger sister.

Al was all smiles as she came in through the back door, and she was relishing the fact that her daughters were cooking for her and she had the night off. She took off her coat and had a seat at the table with me and enjoyed the remainder of the show.

Everything looked fabulous. The girls used their mom's best dishes to show off their creations, and we eagerly watched as they set the table with pure culinary precision. They both looked like proud peacocks as they sat down and joined us at the table. Al lifted a glass and made a toast to their efforts, and then we set off together to enjoy the luxurious feast that lay before us.

Unfortunately, the truth came all too quickly, as we realized that we shouldn't have judged a book by its cover. As it turned out, Liz had left the boneless pork chops in the oven a little too long, and they were a tad well done. Gracie said that she didn't want to take another bite because she didn't want to lose another tooth. She then offered to take them back to Clarkson because the team was short of hockey pucks, and that statement quickly produced a piercing stare from her sister, who was sitting directly across from her. It was a good thing Gracie wasn't in range, or I'm sure Liz would've given her more than a dirty look.

All of us must have put a forkful of mashed potatoes in our mouths at the same time, because we all looked at each other in unison. It was Liz who said she didn't remember adding glue to the recipe and didn't want to take another bite for fear of not being able to open her jaws again. She shook her head in dismay, and Al tried to make her feel better by saying everything was very tasty. But we all knew the truth.

The final straw fell to the floor when Gracie likened the green bean casserole to an algae experiment she had had this semester in biology class. Luckily, her sister went from being upset to screeching with laughter, and we all joined in the fun. Al gave Liz a big hug for her first effort in the kitchen, and we sat around for a while and made some more analogies about Liz's unique and suspect cuisine.

After Gracie made one final comment, telling Liz she was no Julia Child, I took matters into my own hands and said I was ordering pizza. It was quite a unanimous decision, and we cleared off the table and deposited the food into its rightful location, the garbage can, and waited with extreme anxiousness for the pizza to come so we could each get the awful taste out of our mouths. When the pizza arrived, we sat around and had a great time and laughed hysterically, and it was quite a wonderful evening. And that was exactly what Al needed—a fun night with her family that was full of big belly laughs.

The next morning came all too quickly, and the house had a somber and melancholy feel to it. Al didn't want the girls coming to the hospital with us, and she gave them a list of chores that included laundry and room cleaning to keep them busy for the day. The girls gave their mom a lot of words of encouragement and hugged her good-bye and said they would see her later that afternoon. Liz had specifically told Gracie not to cry, and her little sister kept her promise. She didn't cry in front of her mom, but as we left through the back door and passed the window to the kitchen, I could see her sobbing in her big sister's arms. I was glad Al didn't peek in through the window.

We were at the hospital by a quarter to seven and sat together behind the closed door of a small room, waiting to meet with the physician who was going to perform the surgery. It was a quiet ride up the hill, and Allison just seemed to want to look through her window and relax and not talk too much. I held her hand and let her be with her thoughts. I was trying my best not to display how worried I was, but she knew me all too well.

We felt a lot better when the doctor showed up exactly on time and described the operation. He told Allison what to expect and carefully went through the steps of the procedure. He put an x-ray up on the wall and showed us where the cancerous spots were in her breasts and described where he would be making his incisions and the exact order in which he would make them. She had multiple areas of cancer in her breasts that needed to be removed, and it was going to take a lot of time and precision to remove them. But the doctor told her that he had performed similar operations and had plenty of experience under his belt, and he told her to relax and that she was in good hands. He also mentioned that it would be very difficult to remove all the cancer at one time, but he had experience in dealing with these types of situations and had had much success in the past. He also said that there was a slight chance that the tumors had increased in size, and he was hoping there had been no rapid advance of the cancer since the last diagnosis.

I could tell Allison was very comfortable with him but was anxious to get this operation over with and get back to her own home. After the review with the doctor, a nurse came to take Allison to undress and prepare for her operation.

"Mr. and Mrs. McNamara, I want you to know you are in very good hands with this doctor. I've done a lot of these procedures with him, and he is excellent," she said as she looked at us both with caring eyes and a competent and trusting smile.

"It's going to be all right, Al. Everything is going to go smoothly, and I'll be right here for you when you get out," I said as I gently held her close and stroked her hair and kissed her forehead and told her I loved her.

"I love you too, Jack. But listen. This is a long procedure, and it'll be a few hours, and I know how you are in hospitals. I can see you pacing around and wanting to come back here, and I think it's best if you just leave for a few hours and come back around noon. That way the doctor and nurses can concentrate on what they have to do. Can you do that for me?" she said as she looked up to me.

"Yes, of course, Al," I said. I gave her one more kiss and squeezed both of her hands and gave her to the nurse. It was hard to see my wife walk down the hall with the nurse, and I felt queasy and lightheaded. Al had been right when she said I didn't do well in hospitals, and I remembered when I almost passed out as I watched Liz being born. The doctor had to walk me to a chair.

I watched her turn the corner with the nurse and stood there and hoped with all of my might that she would come back to me cancer free and that everything would be okay.

I felt it best to leave the girls by themselves for the morning and let them keep busy and do their chores as their mom had delegated. I drove past the house and parked at the lodge and walked down to Beebe Lake. It was a mild winter morning, and it started to snow lightly as I walked around the lake. I didn't want to sit at the granite bench today, so I continued past it and walked over Rosie's bridge. As I came to the big stone bridge, where I usually went to the right after crossing over, I turned left and walked down the narrow trail that brought me to a wooden bench that overlooked a small waterfall. There wasn't a soul in sight, and I sat and listened to the rush of the water and watched the snowflakes drift down into the pool of foamy water circling on the bottom of the small gorge. Ice had formed on the edge of the falls and at the bottom of the gorge, and it began to simulate my own thought patterns. My mind seemed to be partly frozen, like the ice, and unable to do anything to help my wife. And the other half of my brain was like the fast-moving water, as I had so many thoughts rushing through my head that I couldn't think straight. I felt paralyzed and helpless as I thought of Allison.

And then I started to get angry and overwhelmed as I sat and watched the falls. I just sat and sat and sat, and my thoughts got worse and worse and more morose than ever. I decided it would be best to not be still, so I started out for a walk around the lake. The snow had begun to accumulate, and there were no other footprints on the path. The lake was the quietest I had ever noticed. I felt lost and just kept walking around the lake, and I stopped every once in a while to stare at the water or watch the falls. I must have walked around the lake at least three or four times, and each time I began a new loop, my footprints were covered from the snow.

I wound up back where I had started. I sat down at the bench and tried to calm myself down and put some positive thoughts in my head. I kept thinking about how the doctor had stressed that this was a very difficult procedure and he hoped the cancer had not spread even more. I thought about how many times through the years I had come across people who had loved ones succumb to this horrible disease or lose their breasts because the areas were overcome by the tumors.

My mind began to race again, and I got up and walked in the opposite direction of the lake. I walked along a winding dirt path that led me onto a narrow road. After about a half mile, I wound up standing in front of a small green-and-white chapel, which stood proudly on a corner plot of land overlooking a stream that fed Beebe Lake. I was breathing hard and felt winded, and I stood there looking at the large wooden doors of the chapel as the snow fell on me. I stood for a few moments and then walked up the brick steps of the chapel and pulled open the large door and stepped inside. My heart seemed to slow down as I looked around at all the stained-glass windows and wooden pews and Bibles meticulously placed in wooden holders behind each bench. There was no one around. I continued down the aisle and sat in the closest pew, and I continued to look around and found myself staring at the little red-glass candles that were lit in front of the chapel.

I closed my eyes and began to calm down, and then I got down on my knees and thought for a while and said a prayer for Allison. I kept my thoughts and prayers silent for a while and then began to talk out loud.

"Please, God, listen to me. I haven't asked for much through the years, and I know I'm far from perfect. I know you know the mistakes I've made in my life, but I've tried to be a good person. I'm asking you to help my wife. I'm asking for your mercy and for you to help her. She gives her heart and soul to help others, and now I need you to help her. Please help her...she's my best friend. Do you hear me? She's everything to me, and she's my best friend, and I need her," I said out loud in a desperate tone of voice, looking to the front of the chapel.

I received no sign and just sat with my head down. I heard soft footsteps and turned. A minister had walked in and come up from behind me. He stood at my side and looked at me and smiled. I felt he realized my desperation by the look of my eyes. He began to tell me about the chapel and talked about how old it was and about the congregation and how everyone had helped with restorations. He began to tell me about its history and about a time when a flood had wiped out most of the chapel. They thought they'd have to knock it down because it was so disheveled and needed so many repairs. But the community all helped and pitched in together and, little by little, the small church came back to life. It had weathered snowstorms and damaged roofs and a flood and major windstorms that had blown most of the wooden shingles off the exterior walls. He told me they just kept repairing it and never gave up. He said giving up just wasn't an option to the congregation and surrounding community.

"Through it all, we always realized one thing and one thing alone, and it's very similar in life. When times are tough and your world appears bleak and there seems to be no light at the end of the tunnel, you have to have faith. That was the one thing that the congregation realized, so they never gave up. They always had faith," he said as he put his hand on my shoulder. He squeezed my shoulder and looked at me and smiled. Then he turned and walked away.

I sat for a while and thought about his words, and then I seemed to come to peace with my thoughts and the overwhelming feeling seemed to all of a sudden disappear. It was clear to me what I had to do. I had to pull myself up by my bootstraps and get back to the hospital and be strong for my wife and family. So I made my way back to the car and drove back to the hospital.

I felt stronger as I went in through the hospital doors and went straight to the waiting room and asked about Allison. They told me she was still in the operating room, and then they said that as soon as the doctor was finished, they would come and get me. It was about eleven o'clock, and the doctor had said it would be noon before he completed the surgery. So I paced the floor of the waiting area and tried to have some composure as I looked out the windows and thought about Allison. I did my best to only let positive thoughts enter my mind as I watched the snow drift down and collect on the cars in the parking lot. I kept looking up to the nursing station and, after an hour or so, I saw the doctor talking to one of the nurses. It looked as if he was giving her instructions.

I walked over to him quickly. He saw me coming and handed his clipboard to the nurse, and she turned and walked back toward the operating room. He took off his glasses as I came up to him, and he could see how anxious I was for the results.

"How is she, Doctor? How is she?" I quickly asked, looking for a facial expression to give me a sign before he spoke.

"Mr. McNamara, Allison is doing unbelievably well. This was a very difficult procedure, but I believe I got all the malignant tumors out, and I was able to save both breasts. It had spread a little more since she was last examined, but I was able to remove everything. She is a very lucky woman, and she did quite well during the surgery. She does have a lot of scarring that is visible, but she should heal well. She's still under the anesthesia and asleep. She needs to rest awhile today, and she can go home in two days.

"Again, she is very, very lucky. We were successful in removing everything today, but she is still susceptible to further cancer down the road due to her body makeup. So we must continue to monitor and stay on top of her situation. You must help her as well and be there for anything she might need during her recovery stage. This is a very traumatic and emotional time. She was one of the fortunate ones," he said with a stern face as he put his hand on my arm.

I looked at him and then up to the ceiling and back to him. "Thank you, Doctor. Thank you," I replied sincerely as my eyes started to water.

He nodded, and we shook hands. He told me that I would be able to see her in another hour or so, and the nurse would come and walk me back to her. I turned and walked away with a smile on my face, and, all of a sudden, I felt so blessed. As I was walking, Liz and Gracie were coming into the waiting room and saw me. They ran over to me, and we all embraced.

"How is she, Dad? How is Mom?" asked Liz, and both she and Gracie looked for me to give them the only answer they would stand for.

"She's doing fine, girls. She's doing just fine. Everything went well. The doctor said he removed all the cancer in both her breasts, and she's doing fine. Right now she's sleeping, and we can go see her in about an hour. She's going to be okay…she's going to be okay," I replied. I kissed both of them on the head, and we stood and held on to each other in the waiting room.

There were people moving quickly all around us, and coming in and going out of the waiting room, and doctors and nurses were walking past us to talk to others in the area. We didn't move for a while. All three of us just stood in the middle of the room and held one another.

Allison looked so calm and peaceful, and her eyes looked extremely tired as the nurse walked us into her room. She smiled as all three of us gently moved to her side.

"Hi, Al," I said as I caressed her hair.

"Hi, Mom," continued Gracie in a soft voice with Liz to her right.

Allison had both arms draped to her side and was still covered up pretty well, and she was very still in her bed.

"Hi, guys. I'm okay. I'm just tired," she replied.

I kissed her forehead and held her hand, and the girls each held her other hand, and we were all really gentle with her.

The doctor came in and said he was glad the whole family was in the room, and he talked to all of us.

Allison was very glad to hear firsthand about how well the procedure had gone, and her smile got real wide when the doctor told her she was currently cancer free. He then reiterated that she needed to have frequent checkups and that the whole family needed to pitch in with her recovery at home. The girls were very quick to nod and said they would help out with everything at home and take care of their mom. Allison squeezed my hand tight when they said they would make all the meals and do all the laundry.

The doctor told Allison how lucky she was and said that she was a very fortunate woman and that she must have some unbelievable inner strength. Then he said good-bye to us and informed us that Al still needed to rest and not to stay too long. Liz whispered some words into her mom's ear and kissed her. Then she took Gracie by the arm and said they'd be back later to check on her. I stayed around for another hour and sat in a chair and let Al fall asleep. And after a short while of watching her peacefully sleeping, I left for home.

When I pulled into our driveway, I noticed there was a car that I didn't recognize parked behind Liz's Jeep. It was a dark-green Mini Cooper. I couldn't think of whom it might have belonged to, so I walked past the car and up the back steps and into the house. I could hear a lot of laughing coming from the living room, so I followed the voices and moved past our dining room and foyer and came into the living room.

Immediately a perplexed look came to my face. Gracie and Liz were kneeling down in the middle of the floor, and Gracie was holding on to a sock that had a small puppy tugging on the other end of it. It was a tiny little golden retriever with a kelly-green collar. Gracie was tugging, and the little puppy was pulling as hard as she could in the other direction. Both girls were laughing hysterically at the fortitude and tenacity of this little yellow spitfire. There was an older woman seated in the chair on the other side of the room, and she looked at me as I looked at her in a state of confusion.

"Hello, Jack," she said in a friendly tone.

I looked at her for a moment and then recognized her as the woman I had been seeing walking around Beebe Lake with her dogs. She had the female golden, Libby, and the last time I had seen her, she had had Digger.

"Marion?" I replied.

She nodded her head and then looked toward the girls playing with the puppy.

"Okay, what's going on?" I said as I looked at all three of them, scratching my head in bewilderment.

Then Marion began her story. "Well, I got a call from your wife, Jack. She called me from North Carolina. Apparently, she got my number from one of my neighbors who works in her department at Cornell. She told me about Rosie and had heard about my Libby and how she had just had her litter. She knew how upset you were about Rosie, and she wanted to see if I had any more puppies available. Of course, I knew how upset you were when I saw you down at the lake. But Libby hadn't had her litter yet, and I didn't even want to bring it up at the time. Well, it turned out that I only had one more left that wasn't spoken for, so I promised her this one. I named her Sophie, and your wife seemed to like the name, too. And so here we are. She's yours now," said Marion as she raised her eyebrows and a big grin came to her face.

I was taken aback with what she had just said, and my mouth fell open. I thought about it for a while as I watched the girls play with the puppy, and then they looked up to me for my reaction. I slowly knelt down to the floor. The puppy dropped her end of the sock and made her way to my hands. She was beyond cute and had a coat of hair so soft that it begged you to keep petting her. She sat still for me and smiled at me, looking for affection. I noticed her little silver tag on her collar. I read it, and I realized that I would never find anyone in the world like Allison. On one side of the tag, it had her name, Sophie. On the other side it read, "Merry Christmas Jack. Love, Allison." As I read it out loud, the puppy seemed to look at me and let me know that she was all mine. Then she scampered back to the girls again and grabbed the sock, and the tug-of-war started all over again.

"Your wife is some special lady," Marion said as she felt my emotion after I read the tag.

"Yes…I know," I said softly as I nodded my head in disbelief.

I left the girls with Sophie and went back to the hospital in the late afternoon. I picked up some cookies and a sandwich from Ithaca Bakery, just in case she didn't like what they had for dinner. I told her how amazed I was in her efforts to give me the best Christmas present ever, and she knew I would love the new addition to the family. She loved that I had brought her some local treats, and we sat and ate the sandwiches and cookies and talked about everything, from the girls to our parents. Then we shared a big laugh about our newest addition.

The girls and I were back and forth to the hospital for the next couple of days, and when I brought Al home on Christmas Eve morning, the house was more alive than when she had left it, and she said it felt great to hear the noise and see the little puppy run in and out of all the rooms of the house.

Allison slept a lot the first day back, and we played quietly with Sophie in the living room—as quietly as you can play with a puppy, anyway. Liz wanted to give it another go and cook dinner that night, but she was outvoted. Gracie and I ordered Chinese food, and to this day we stand by our decision. In her defense, Al had given Liz some help in the kitchen and showed her how to make some nice pasta dishes such as lasagna and baked ziti, and Liz did, in fact, make some great dinners during the Christmas break.

We had a real quiet evening, and Allison retired early and slept soundly during the night. The girls and I sat up and watched *It's a Wonderful Life* together in front of the fire and kept entertained as Sophie meandered around her new surroundings. She had had a long day as well, and we all looked at one another when she made her way to Rosie's bed to the side of the fireplace and went to sleep. All of us smiled at one another and I didn't say anything, but I thought of Rosie. And as I watched her all cuddled up with her little tail curled around her body up to her chin, I was glad I had left the bed there, in its rightful place for its new owner.

The girls were exhausted and wound up going to bed pretty early on Christmas eve. Al slept through the night. I stayed downstairs on puppy duty, and Sophie seemed to sleep only in fifteen-minute intervals. We had found Rosie's old crate from when she was a puppy in the garage and set it up in the living room. Sophie seemed to get the idea that her crate was going to be her new home and wandered in and out of it during the night, and it was fun to see her drag her favorite sock around as she left and entered her den.

I stayed up most of the night and caught some shuteye in my easy chair, and when Sophie was sleeping, I went and checked on Allison. When she woke up early Christmas morning, she was quite sore, but she wanted to come downstairs and sit with me. I helped her out of bed, and we walked gingerly down the stairs and sat on the couch together and watched Sophie sleep. I made some coffee, and we sat quietly in the living room and enjoyed our tree and watched the yule log burn away on television as the music played softly in the background. I opened the doors to the sun porch that adjoined our living room, removed the blanket that covered the wrapped presents we had picked up for the girls, and placed them under the tree.

The crinkling of wrapping paper seemed to awaken Sophie, and she came out of her crate to explore the situation and see what all the fuss was about. She started to pull at the presents, and, before we knew it, she was tearing all the wrapping paper off the gifts in a frantic state and bringing the ripped pieces into her crate.

I thought it best to go upstairs and wake up the girls before Sophie had unveiled all their gifts for them without their approval. The girls woke up slowly, but they quickly moved downstairs when they heard the high-pitched barking that Sophie produced. And they were all smiles as they went over to the tree and knelt down and watched their new puppy wrestle with the colored wrapping paper and shake it frantically around the living room floor. The most laughter came when Sophie came face to face with one of Liz's gifts. I had gotten her a small Saint Bernard stuffed animal that resembled her school mascot, and Sophie immediately took offense to the new arrival. Liz placed the stuffy directly in front of her, and Sophie gave it her meanest look. Her head and front paws were on the ground, and her hind end was up in the air with her tail wagging back and forth, letting the stuffed animal know who was boss in this house. We laughed till our sides hurt as Sophie ran circles around the Saint Bernard. After about ten minutes, we thought it best to let her win the battle and bring peace to the house. So we hid the stuffed animal underneath a blanket on the couch.

The little dog made our Christmas morning quite eventful, and after the girls finished opening their presents, I made them a nice bacon-and-egg breakfast and we lounged around the rest of the morning. I walked Al up to the bedroom, where she took her medicine and got some much-needed rest. I could tell she was very tender and sore. The medicine helped with the pain but also made her very sleepy.

Mom and Dad showed up at the house around lunchtime, and when I announced their arrival, Liz and Gracie ran out into the driveway to say Merry Christmas and give them a hug and escort them inside. Mom had said that she didn't know if Dad was up to the visit but would play it by ear, and if he was having a good morning, they would make it over for a little while. Needless to say, everyone was happy to see Grandpa step out of the car, especially the girls. Mom wanted to help Allison out with dinner and had prepared a loin of pork with all the trimmings and vegetables, as well as some loaves of banana bread, which was another of the girls' favorite treats.

I could see Grandpa's hand shaking from the kitchen window, and his steps were very short. It was hard for me to see him struggle up the steps, as he needed the girls on either arm. Liz and Gracie had mentally accepted my dad's physical and mental health, and they just enjoyed having him around and were very mature about the whole situation as time went by.

The girls positioned themselves to either side of their grandpa at the dinner table, and they held his hand from time to time and leaned against him and rubbed his back or shoulder to try to produce a smile. He seemed far away at some points of conversation and didn't say too much, but the girls seemed to drag some words and laughter out of him from time to time. Sophie made her way under the table and found my dad's shoelaces, and he started off being annoyed. But then he had a lot of fun playing with the puppy and trying to keep her at bay, and he actually looked and acted a little like his old self at that moment.

After dinner, my mom went outside to her car and brought in a couple of presents for the girls. Gracie received a hockey stick that was signed by Bobby Clarke and a poster of him and his infamous smile as the captain of the Philadelphia Flyers during a hockey game in the seventies. Mom had gotten the idea from my story, and she used her connections at the Cornell Athletics Office to track the hall of famer down and get him to sign the stick and ship it to us. And, of course, Gracie loved it. Liz was given a framed picture of Jack Nicholas that showed his piercing stare, and the Golden Bear himself had signed it. My mom had spotted it at an auction online. My dad had always said that Liz had the same stare as Jack and that she looked equally as intimidating on the golf course. Liz also got a poster of Tiger Woods, who was her real idol. Tiger was wearing one of his red shirts that he always wore on Sundays and giving one of his famous fist pumps as he showed his ferocity after sinking a huge putt that annihilated a competitor. After the girls gave my parents hugs and kisses for their gifts, they ran upstairs and came back down with some presents of their own to give to my parents.

When they came back downstairs, each of them was holding two framed pictures. Gracie had put together a collage of pictures from her youth that had Grandma and Grandpa at her side. Most of them showed her during her youth hockey days and her birthdays. There was a smaller picture that she gave to Grandpa for his room. It was a picture of her and my dad standing side by side. She was in her Ithaca hockey uniform. He had his arm around her, and both of them had huge smiles. Gracie was about four years old in this picture, and what stood out most about it was that she was missing all her front teeth. They hadn't been knocked out, though; they had fallen out, and she was waiting for the new set to appear. Of course, my dad had a big laugh when he held it, and then Gracie smiled back at him and added to the situation by taking out her false tooth.

Liz gave my parents a picture that showed her in her youth at many different stages with my parents. Most of the pictures showed her during golf tournaments, and a lot were with my mom and dad down at Newman. The second framed picture was for Grandpa's room as well. It was one with Liz and my dad, and she had the first putter he had given her to see if she was interested in golf. He had hacksawed one of his putters in half and taped a grip on the end and given her a couple of golf balls. Mom had snapped a picture of them both practicing together on the putting green at Newman, and she was only as high as his knee. Grandpa stared at this picture for a while and then nodded to Liz. Then he looked back at the picture once more as if he was searching for the time and moment it took place. At that point, Liz and Gracie went over to him and hugged him as he sat at the table. He put the picture down and put his arms around his granddaughters and it looked like he didn't want to let go. That brought a tear to my mom's eye, and Al and I just sat back and savored the moment.

The girls gave Al and me a picture for Christmas as well. It showed the whole family and Rosie out in our yard during a barbeque, and it looked as if it was from about ten years ago. I loved it as soon as I opened it, and it took me only about a minute to find the perfect place for it. I put it right on top of the mantel above the fireplace in the living room. Everybody loved the choice.

By late afternoon, the girls were sprawled out on the couch in the living room and sleeping away. Mom and Dad had taken off shortly after we had a little dessert and coffee; they both needed to go take a nap due to the excitement of the big day. The only one with a lot of energy was Sophie, who had been scrambling around underneath the tree and exploring the insides of all the open boxes.

I walked Allison upstairs and into the bedroom and shut the door behind me. She looked worn out and was ready to tuck down for a snooze. As I shut the bedroom door behind me, I noticed the door to our third floor was open, and the upstairs lights were on. Al had made this area into two guest rooms, and there was a bathroom up there too. We used these rooms when the girls had sleepovers and needed more space.

As I walked into one of the bedrooms, it had looked as if a raccoon had gotten trapped in the room and couldn't find his way out. There were photo albums and pictures scattered all over the bed and floor, and it looked as if the girls had taken some pictures off the wall and stolen the frames. I later found out that they had stayed up all night looking for pictures with their grandparents and needed some frames to cap off their efforts. I was amused and baffled at the same time, and I smiled to myself. Leave it to college kids who have no money to use their creativity and ingenuity to come up with the perfect Christmas presents. They say a picture is worth a thousand words. Well, that old cliché was certainly true in the McNamara house this Christmas.

14

THE MENTOR

The girls kept a low profile after Christmas, and for the remainder of their break, they spent a lot of time around the house and visiting my parents at Bridges. Al had the week off after Christmas, as was customary at Cornell, and she took an extra week to recover and spend some time with the kids. Sophie needed a lot of attention, so it turned out to be good timing, with everyone around the house to pitch in with potty training and to get her used to sleeping in her crate at night.

The day before the girls were scheduled to go back to school, I picked up Rosie's ashes at the veterinarian's office and brought them back home. I placed them on the mantle and wound up staring at them the whole morning, and it just didn't seem right to me. I gathered up the troops, including Sophie, and we all went for a walk to Beebe Lake. Liz and Gracie took turns carrying Sophie and giving her a break to walk here and there, and I held Al's hand as we made our way down Thurston Avenue and crossed the street and went down to the start of the lake. It was a beautiful and sunny late morning, and also very quiet, and the lake was quite tranquil except for the slight rumbling of water moving over the falls. We started down the path, and the girls gave Sophie some freedom, since there was no one around, and let her off her leash.

As soon as the small wooden bridge came into view, Sophie took off in a sprint, and all of us laughed at how quick she was for such a little thing. Al and I just looked on as the girls chased her down the path, but Sophie was a good twenty yards in front of them and had plenty of gas in her tank. Sophie made it to the bridge. It seemed to pique her curiosity, and she started to sniff around the wooden planks. Liz and Gracie stopped just before the bridge, and when Al and I caught up to them, we all just stood and watched our new addition in amazement. Sophie had sat down in Rosie's old spot and was looking out over the lake, as if she were following the instructions of her predecessor. Al and the girls had seen Rosie take this position on the bridge, but I had seen her do it every time we walked the lake together.

We walked slowly onto the bridge and stood together and looked out over the lake with Sophie sitting in front of us. I took out Rosie's ashes and knelt down by Sophie and sprinkled them into the water. As I knelt down, I said a silent prayer and looked up to the sky and smiled and then rubbed Sophie's head. Al put her hand on my shoulder, and I stood up and hugged her. The girls joined in, and we all embraced one another on the bridge.

"Now I feel better. She's home," I said to everyone as I looked down at the water and watched as the ashes slowly disappeared and became part of the lake. Then I picked up

Sophie. We all walked along the path, and I held my little companion in my arms all the way home.

There were only a couple more days in January, and between the temperature and the snow, it felt every bit the middle of winter. The girls had a great break and enjoyed hanging around the house and playing with Sophie, and we even got in some skiing in their last couple of days. It snowed pretty hard their final week, and we all went over to Greek Peak and spent the day on the slopes. Actually, just the girls and I skied, as Al had no interest in downhill skiing and always preferred to sit inside by the fire and read a book. She enjoyed cross-country skiing, and we usually went over to the Cornell golf course on the weekends during the winter to get some exercise. But she was still a bit tender, and we thought it best to give it a few more weeks, as we knew the snow would continue for a while.

Liz and Gracie also spent a lot of time with my parents. Al made cookies for them to take over to my mom and dad, which seemed to make their way around to the other rooms. The other residents were quite thankful and loved seeing the girls stop by with the treats. Mom had put the girls' pictures on Dad's wall and on his dresser, and it spruced up his room. Mom said it wasn't unusual to find Dad staring at the pictures for long periods of time, trying to recall all the different moments. Mom said she came in one morning, and Dad was sitting up in his chair and crying and holding one of the pictures. She just stood in the doorway and watched him. She said it broke her heart to see him so sad, and she wished he weren't battling this deadly disease so he could spend some more quality time with his family, especially his granddaughters.

It had been snowing through the night, and by the time I got to work, we had collected about seven or eight inches. This was Al's first day back to Cornell, and I thought I'd give her a ride and spend a little more time with her in the car before I headed to my office. She had been getting a little stir crazy and was ready to get back to the grind, and she was in good spirits as I drove through campus and dropped her off in front of her building.

Sophie was now potty trained and was comfortable with sleeping in her crate at night, which we had moved to our bedroom. She was super easy at nighttime, and as soon as we motioned to tuck into our bed for the night, she would walk into her sleeping quarters and lie down on her comfy bed with her special little pillow—the pillow being Liz's torn-up sock that she had fallen in love with since she first played tug-of-war with the girls.

The second special item that made her sleeping arrangements more comfortable was propped against the inside corner of her crate. Apparently, when Liz was in the shower one morning, Sophie wandered into her room and snatched the stuffed Saint Bernard off her bed and chewed the dickens out of it. By the time Liz had gotten back into the room, the stuffy had only one eye, and the insides of her arms were all over the room. Liz said she stood in her doorway with her mouth open, and Sophie strutted right by her and took the stuffed toy into her crate. From that point on, at bedtime, Sophie liked to stare at the defeated stuffed animal and relish her victory for a few minutes, and it seemed to lull her to sleep.

We also gated the top of the stairs and let her roam around the second floor to get used to her surroundings. That was just one of the little dog's quirks, and on another day, Gracie discovered her other unusual trait. Sophie had become a huge golf fan, and there were at least three different occasions when one of the girls came into the living room and found the dog staring at the television, completely mesmerized by a golf match. Gracie said that one time Sophie didn't even acknowledge them as they came back into the living room from making sandwiches and sat down on the couch.

Since Al was heading back to work, we had to set up an arrangement for the daytime. We put up a gate in the kitchen and made sure Sophie had plenty of water and a few toys. Since my job was a little more flexible, I could check on her at lunchtime every day, and, weather permitting, let her outside to run around a little bit till I got home at night to give her a good stretch of the legs.

At about two in the afternoon, when I was daydreaming at my desk and looking out the window and watching the snow pile up outside, Maggie came quickly down the hall to my office with a terrible look on her face.

"Jack, it's your mom on line one. It's about your dad," she said as she came in my door. I could tell by the concerned and worried look in her eyes that it was urgent. I picked up the phone immediately.

"Mom, It's Jack. Is something going on with Dad?" I said into the receiver.

"Jack, Jack, I'm glad you're there. Your dad had a stroke or heart attack...they're not sure right now...could you come here, please?" she replied in a frenzied tone of voice.

"Where are you, Mom? He's alive, right?" I answered quickly.

"Yes, he's alive...he's with the doctor now...they're still working on him...I don't know...it was terrible, Jack...I was just coming into his room at Bridges to have lunch with him, and he was sitting there watching television, and then he looked at me, and he had this strange look on his face...he just grabbed his chest and fell over, and I ran to him and grabbed him before he hit the floor and called for help. He couldn't talk, Jack...I called for help, and the nurse and staff came in, and the ambulance came...Jack, it was terrible...he couldn't say anything, and..." she said as she was sobbing into the phone.

"Mom, Mom, sshhh, sshhh...don't worry, he'll be all right...where are you...at the hospital?" I asked, trying to calm her down and get my coat on at the same time.

"Yes...the emergency room...please hurry up, Jack," she said frantically.

I hung the phone up and ran down the hall and yelled to Maggie that my dad had had a stroke and I was on my way to the hospital. I drove as fast as I could to Route 13 and headed down the hill and then sped up the other side of the lake to the hospital. I was worried and panic stricken the whole way. As I reached the hospital, I knew I couldn't be in this shape as I met my mother, so I calmed myself down and went quickly in through the emergency doors. As I scoured the waiting room, I saw her standing in the far corner of the room with a tissue pressed against her cheek. I called to her as I made my way quickly to her side. She immediately embraced me, and I could feel her body trembling with fear.

"Mom, is he okay? Is he alive…did the doctor say anything?" I asked right away.

"He was just out here, Jack. Yes, he's alive…he said he had a…he said he's…" she started but couldn't finish. Then she took a deep breath and composed herself and looked up at me.

"It was a stroke, Jack…he's had a stroke. The doctor said he had stabilized his heart, and he's breathing steady…but it was a bad stroke, much worse than the one years ago, and he needed to go back in and monitor him right now and would be back out again shortly."

As soon as Mom had gotten those words out, she seemed to calm down just a bit, but she wanted to hold on to me. I just rubbed her back and tried to talk softly to her to calm her down. After a few minutes, we sat down together, and she explained everything that had happened as we waited for the doctor to come back out. I was just hoping he would reappear with some sort of positive news, but it certainly didn't seem that it would be possible. All in all, I was just glad he was alive.

Dad had had a pretty severe stroke, and he had suffered tremendous nerve damage on the right side of his body. His vision was affected. He could talk, but it was very slow and he struggled with every sentence. He stayed in the hospital for almost a full week after the stroke, and Mom and I were with him for most of each day. I took the week off from work and brought Mom back and forth to the hospital, and we sat with him in his room and mostly watched television and talked with him. The doctor was there twice a day and talked with all of us and had already set up a rehabilitation schedule that would start in a few days. He tried to give Dad a lot of words of encouragement. The doctor's words seem to fall on deaf ears, though, and Dad showed little interest as the doctor was explaining all the different exercises that would get him back in shape.

A speech pathologist had been coming to the room for the last two days and Dad did the drills with the woman, but he looked as if he wanted no part of the process of learning to talk all over again. It was hard to see my dad lose his memory gradually as he felt prey to Alzheimer's, and it was worse watching him in a frustrated state as he tried to pronounce simple sounds or syllables. He shook his head a lot and pounded the side of his bed and dropped a few choice curse words, which would lead to the doctor telling him not to use vulgar language. Of course, Mom and I knew that telling my dad not to curse was like trying to tell him what to eat or what to wear. My dad said what he wanted to say, ate what he wanted to eat, and wore whatever clothes pleased him, and there was no changing that at this stage of the game.

To her credit, the speech pathologist was a real trooper, and she stayed with my dad and actually spent extra time with him despite his attitude and coarse demeanor. Mom and I tried to give him extra encouragement after the exercise drills to keep him positive, but he seemed to be running out of steam and would look at us in an embarrassed sort of way, as if to tell us he was sorry we had to see him in this state. It hurt me inside as I looked into his apologetic eyes, and he looked back as if to tell me he had given life all he possibly could and he just couldn't strike back this time to defend himself. Mom and I spent as much time as we could in the room with him, and we would only leave when he motioned that he needed some sleep.

Late in the afternoon on his last day in the hospital, Dad was doing a little better with his speech and had started his physical rehabilitation, which he would continue after he went back to Bridges. He still looked frail and wasn't eating very well, and the nurses had to keep after him to make sure he ate as much as possible during his stay at the hospital. He seemed to be in a fight that he realized he couldn't win, and he was becoming more and more demoralized each and every day. After the staff had left the room, I told Mom to go get some fresh air, that I wanted to talk to Dad alone. I stood to the side of his bed and grabbed his hand. He looked up to me, and then he closed his eyes as I spoke to him.

"Dad, I just want to say that I know how tough this is for you. I can only imagine how you feel right now. I just want you to know how lucky I've been to have you as a father. You were always there for me. You did everything for me, and I always felt very lucky to have you as my dad," I said softly as I looked down to him.

He squeezed my hand back, and I could still feel his strength as my eyes fixated on his arms, which had once been massive and muscular but now were damaged and wrapped with tape and tubes. He smiled back at me and then opened his eyes and tried his best to reply, as challenging as it was to him. He spoke to me slowly, and it was daunting for him to say each word.

"I...was...always...proud...to...have...you...as...my...son," he replied, and then he took a deep breath. His words made me feel so good inside that I just smiled and leaned over and kissed him on his forehead.

"I love you, Dad, and I always will," I told him as I held his hand. He took a moment and rolled his head to the side, and then he rolled it back again to face me. His eyes had welled up as much as mine.

"I…love…you…too…Jack."

Dad's last night in the hospital was peaceful. He slept well, and Mom and I went back to my house around ten o'clock, telling Dad that we would see him around seven the next morning. Mom had stayed at our house the last two days, and I think it was good for her to sit and talk with Allison in the evenings. She had a glass of wine ready for my mom as we walked in the door in the evenings, and we sat up for an hour together and talked for a while to try to unwind from the day at the hospital. I was the first one to go upstairs, as I thought the two ladies would enjoy some time to talk alone. Al had recovered physically from her surgery, but she was still emotionally fragile about her ordeal. I noticed that sometimes she got upset as she looked at herself in the mirror in the morning and lifted her nightshirt to check out the scars that remained from the incisions on her breasts. I tried to tell her that they were barely noticeable and that we were the only ones who would ever see them, but she got upset whenever she looked at them. I think that having some time to talk to my mom about the scars made her feel better about herself, and I think she just needed reassurance from another woman.

The girls had taken Dad's news pretty badly, and they both wanted to go there as soon as they could to be with him. Unfortunately, Gracie was out in Colorado playing in a hockey tournament, and then Denver had gotten about two and a half feet of snow over the weekend and closed the airports for almost two days. The team couldn't travel back until the day that Dad was scheduled to return to Bridges. Gracie had instructed Liz to wait for her to get back to Potsdam, and then they would come back to Ithaca together to see their grandpa. Both girls were very shaken to hear about their grandpa having a stroke, but I tried to reassure them that he was doing okay and was coming along fine, to calm them down.

Liz would've been home sooner, but she was threatened by Gracie not to go without her, so she stayed put at Siena. It was very hard for both of them to be so far away, but they called two or three times every day to check on the status of their grandpa. I couldn't put them on the phone with him, but I passed along their well wishes, and it always put a smile on his face.

Unfortunately, it would soon turn to sadness, as he again would fall victim to realizing his current physical and mental state. Gracie seemed to always take things the hardest, and this proved to be true again during her first game against the University of Denver. She had gotten the news about my dad the day before the game and was very distraught and told the coach that she didn't want to play. Gracie had become an integral part of the defense, and there would be a pretty big void if she didn't suit up. The coach also said it might be better for her to skate instead of sitting around and worrying about her grandfather. Unfortunately, it didn't turn out as the coach expected. Gracie got three penalties in the first period alone.

Two of them were for roughing, and one was for crosschecking. And at the start of the second period, she took it one step farther, and after she received her fourth penalty, for fighting, the coach was forced to sit her for the rest of the game. Actually, she realized that Gracie wasn't in a good frame of mind, so she thought it best to have her sit out the rest of the tournament. As it turned out, Gracie wasn't at all put out by having to sit and watch the team. She thought it was best for everybody, and she felt she had more important things to think about. She was worried about her grandpa and hoping to God that he would be okay when she saw him.

I passed along the girls' thoughts to my dad each time they called and told him that they said they loved him, but I didn't tell him about their coming to town to see him. I really didn't know how he'd take it, but I had a feeling it wouldn't be good, and I found out the next morning when we picked him up at the hospital and got him settled in his room at Bridges. It was lunchtime, and he had just finished with the speech pathologist and wasn't scheduled to do his physical therapy till the afternoon. That was when I told him that his granddaughters were on their way to Ithaca to come see him.

"Dad, listen to me. Liz and Gracie wanted to come and see you…actually…they're on their way and will be here tonight just after dinnertime," I said easily.

He sat up in bed. He gave me a stern stare and grimaced, and I knew right then and there that it was not something he wanted to hear.

"I…don't…want…them…to…see…me…this way!" he snarled as he tried to piece together his ultimate thought. He didn't say anything else for a few minutes, and mom and I sat by his side and tried to figure out what to say next. The room was quiet, and we sat there in silence until my dad spoke again.

"It's…hard enough…to have…you…see me…this way. I… don't want…them to see my like this," he said as he shook his head and looked about the most frustrated I've ever seen him.

"I'm tired," he said. He closed his eyes and moved his hand slightly to indicate that he didn't want us in the room and that he didn't want any lunch and just wanted to go to sleep. Mom kissed him on the forehead, and we left him alone. We sat in the living room and tried to figure out how to handle the rest of the day.

As it played out, Liz drove from Latham all the way up to Potsdam and met Gracie as soon as she stepped off the team bus. Then they headed back through Watertown and came down Route 81 to Syracuse and Cortland and made their way to Ithaca. Liz had driven about nine hours by the time they both showed up and walked through the big wooden front doors of Bridges. We were sitting up with Dad as they came in through his doorway, and they both looked exhausted but were happy to finally be with their grandfather.

I looked at them and smiled, and then I looked to see how my dad was responding to their entrance. He produced a slight smile and immediately got misty eyed as they walked to greet him. They both bent over and hugged him lightly from each side and kissed him. It's safe to say that all of us in the room were on the verge of tears, and although my dad had said he didn't want his granddaughters to see him in this shape, he certainly didn't show it. It was quite the opposite. He did the best he could to return the hugs and kisses, and Mom and I just stood back and watched them in their embrace. It created one of the most beautiful memories for us, and it took place during one of the saddest times for our family.

I took Mom back to the house around seven o'clock that night. The girls stayed with their grandfather, and it was two in the morning when I heard the bells on back door announce their arrival home. When we had all been at Bridges, Liz and Gracie sat and talked to my dad, and at first he just nodded in his response because he was uncomfortable letting them see how he struggled to get his words out. Liz and Gracie quickly put him at ease and let him know that it was okay to sound that way and told him that the rehabilitation and physical therapy would rectify everything over time. It made me proud to see how mature they acted during a difficult time, and it made me feel good to be the father of two girls who had such a wonderful relationship with my dad and mom. Gracie had brought a Clarkson hockey jersey that was signed by the team and gave it to my dad with a note from all the players wishing him a speedy recovery. Liz brought a Siena golf hat that was signed by all her teammates, and he quickly put it on his head, which brought a smile to everyone.

Al had walked over and brought some cookies with her that everyone enjoyed. But Dad's appetite was just not the same, and everyone in the room noticed he barely touched any food during the whole visit. It was also a little uncomfortable when Allison showed up because Dad didn't seem to recognize her right away and had a very puzzled look on his face as she stood in the doorway. The girls quickly let him know that it was all right and that they were forgetful sometimes too. But we all could tell he was agitated, as well as confused, by his facial expressions.

Still, we sat with him and enjoyed Al's cookies and listened to Gracie and Liz as they told stories about their college life away from home. It wasn't customary, but due to the circumstances, the staff let Liz and Gracie stay with Dad in his room well past visiting hours. They said he dozed off a lot, and they just sat and watched television till he woke up. They were happy to just be there with him.

When the girls showed up back our house, Allison went downstairs and met them in the kitchen, and they stayed up for a while talking and having some snacks at the dining room table. Al told me later that day that even though the girls behaved like troopers in front of their grandfather, they were both visually distraught when they walked in the door early in the morning. Allison said that they were very upset at how he looked and how he sounded, and they had noticed the bruising on his arms from the intravenous tubes at the hospital. Al said that Gracie kept on saying how unfair it was to have such a wonderful grandpa and questioned why he should be the one to have such a terrible disease, and a heart condition as well. Al tried the best she could to calm Gracie down, but it was always her big sister's shoulder that would help her through tough times.

Al stayed up with the girls for an hour or so before she let them know it was best if everyone went to bed and got some rest. The girls would only be able to stay till the tomorrow afternoon and then would have to get back to school. Tomorrow was Sunday; each of them had early classes on Monday morning, and Gracie had to be at hockey practice. Of course, Gracie didn't want to go back to school. She wanted to stay with her grandfather and help him in any way she could. But we knew that wasn't possible, and Al and I let them both know that he was in good hands with the doctors and staff at Bridges and that we were close by to see him at a moment's notice if need be. Besides, my mom would be there every day to tend to everything and anything he needed to make him comfortable.

Liz and Gracie woke up bright and early Sunday morning and walked over to Bridges to check on my Dad. They wound up spending the whole day with him and showering him with kisses and rubs and trying to get him to eat a little better. Both Liz and Gracie had sad looks on their faces as my mom let them know they should be getting on the road and that they had a long drive in front of them. Liz had found out that one of her teammates had a friend from Potsdam visiting for the weekend and arranged for Gracie to go with her back to Clarkson once they arrived at Siena. That saved Liz some driving and gave the other girl someone to share the ride with back through the Adirondacks at nighttime. So they each kissed my dad more than once and hugged him, and he let them know how special they were to him one more time.

"I...love you...Liz...Gracie...I...I...will always...be with you...always," he said as he held their hands and his eyes slightly watered. Then he let them go and watched as his granddaughters slowly left his room. Gracie came back and gave him one more kiss and then ran to catch her sister.

The girls had gotten back to school safely, and Al and I fell into our routines at home and stayed busy at work. Mom said that she could handle everything with my dad and that we needed to concentrate on our careers and let her take care of my father.

She did the best she could to stay on him with his rehabilitation and his eating, but he seemed to not show the interest or energy to go through all the exercises that helped with his speech and arm and leg movements. It didn't help that his appetite had disappeared, either, and he just didn't seem to be able to put anything solid in his stomach. He lost a lot of weight over the next few weeks and was not doing well mentally, as he began to get more and more confused when asked simple questions. Mom said that as soon as he said good-bye to Liz and Gracie, he didn't seem to want to live anymore. He seemed as if he was tired of fighting to stay alive and was at peace with himself knowing that he had seen his granddaughters one last time and that he told them he loved them and would always be with them.

It was eleven at night when my cell phone rang and woke both Al and me up from a sound sleep. I tentatively picked up the phone from my nightstand and answered it as Al looked at me.

"Jack?" my mom said in a sullen tone.

"Mom…are you okay…is everything all right?" I replied.

There was a silence on the other end of the line for a few moments. I could feel my mom trying to gain some composure in her voice. I closed my eyes as a bad feeling came over me.

"Jack," she started again but didn't finish this time either.

"Jack...Jack, your dad passed away," said my mom softly into the phone. I put my hand to my head and closed my eyes as I listened to my mom tell me how Dad had a suffered another heart attack and how everything had been so quick and awful and that an ambulance came as quickly as possible, but there was nothing they could do for him. His heart had simply given out, and she had been with him the whole time, and the staff had been right there to help, but nothing could be done to revive him.

My mom was very calm as she told me about my dad. She kept telling me he was in a better place and that he had been suffering too much and was tired of living his life with so many mental and physical complications. I could sense it was difficult for her to explain it to me and I felt that she was at ease with everything, but I knew that deep down, it tore her to pieces watching her lifelong love and companion suffer in his golden years. I knew she would rather see him in his final resting place than watch him slowly dwindle away. She told me she had kissed him not long before his heart failed and told him she loved him. She said that the reason she was so at peace with everything was that he had replied to her with the response she had been hoping for most of all.

"I...love...you too...Kate" were his last words.

15

D ad was laid to rest in the cemetery that sits across from the Country Club of Ithaca on Pleasant Grove Road. My older brother and sister had flown in from Los Angeles and Chicago and stayed with my mom for a few days. They had been in and out of town a few times since my parents moved to Ithaca, but they didn't have the same relationship with my parents that I did. My brother and sister had visited Dad while he was in Bridges, and Dad loved seeing his other kids, but he seemed to always long for his granddaughters. They were his beacons of hope, just as my mom was the apple of his eye. And since my siblings lived so far away, we didn't get to see them or their families too often. So it was nice to have them there, especially for my mother. I guess it was just the progression of life that sometimes puts family members in different parts of the world as they try to make their way. Since mom and dad moved to Ithaca, we naturally developed special ties through out the years.

Funeral services and calling hours took place down at Bangs Funeral Home, a well-respected establishment that had been serving the people of Ithaca for years. A lot of Mom's and Dad's friends showed up to pay their respects and talk about the times they had shared with my dad, and they all seemed to remember him in his prime. I enjoyed the stories with some of his friends, and they made me think back on the times we spent together in my youth. I thought of the countless hours he spent taking me to different sport practices and games and how much he taught me about life along the way. He was a hard man but a caring man with a big heart, and toward the end, he seemed to live vicariously through Liz and Gracie.

As I talked to some of his golfing buddies during the calling hours, they shared a lot of stories of his gamesmanship on the golf course, and the stories brought a lot of laughter to the men. Liz and Gracie stood to the side of the small gatherings and stayed pretty close to my mom and Al and my brother and sister. When the service was over and we walked down the front steps of the funeral home, we came face to face with the hearse that would take my dad to his final resting place.

Liz and Gracie held up pretty well during the services, but I did overhear Gracie saying she didn't like people laughing at her grandpa's funeral. She said she was glad it would just be us at the cemetery. She just wanted our immediate family there. Al and I had raised two strong young ladies who were extremely tenacious and tough on the rink and golf course, but one could easily see that their passion showed up equally for the love they felt for their family, especially their granddad.

Dad was given a military funeral because of his service in the Korean War, and because my mom wanted it done. She felt he deserved a proper and very respectful burial because of his commitment to his country. Father O'Hair from

St. Ignatius provided the eulogy and did a fine job, and even Liz and Gracie appreciated all the kind words that were said about their grandfather. After the salute, Mom was given a folded-up American flag by one of the soldiers, and Al hugged her as she started to cry. We all said some prayers, and Liz and Gracie each placed a rose on Dad's coffin, and then they walked to the car in tears.

I shared a moment with my brother and sister. We embraced, and my sister cried on my shoulder. Then my brother and sister walked Mom and Al back to the car. The priest put his hand on my shoulder and offered his condolences as he passed by me. I stood alone with my Dad and wanted to remain with him a little longer by myself. It started to feel so final to me that I began to get upset. To this point I had kept myself composed and had not broken down at all. But the emotion seemed to overcome me, and I couldn't keep it in and had to give my dad one final message.

"Dad, I want you to know how much you meant to me. I guess I can't say it enough. I just felt so lucky having you as my dad and really appreciated all the time you spent with me and all the love you gave me. I'll be watching over Mom for you. I know you would want that. She won't be alone. Al and I have already talked about Mom moving in with us. Actually, Liz and Gracie demanded it. And I also want to let you know how much you meant to your granddaughters. You did so much for them, and they appreciated every minute of it. They miss you a lot already. You were very special to them, Dad, and they'll always remember you. I want you to know that. We all miss you terribly," I said to him.

I had to pause before I completed my thoughts. I took a couple of deep breaths and wiped the tears from my eyes.

"I love you Dad," I said as I kissed my fingers and touched his coffin, and then I turned and walked away from his gravesite.

It was a quiet and somber time as all of us sat around the dining room table. Al had put out some fixings for sandwiches and made some homemade chicken soup. Mom and my siblings tried to keep everyone in good spirits and tried to bring the girls away from their melancholy moods. It was actually Sophie who did the trick when she scampered over to Liz with the beat-up Saint Bernard stuffy in her mouth. After the girls managed a slight grin and chuckle, they began to make themselves sandwiches, and Mom started up a conversation to try to put an end to the silence. She asked Gracie about the upcoming playoff series against Cornell. Gracie and Liz had both been in town since Monday, and it was now Thursday. Gracie's team was set to arrive tonight to get ready for the ECAC playoffs against the Big Red tomorrow night at Lynah Rink. Gracie's coach had let her come back to town early for her grandfather's funeral, but she expected her to play in the game on Friday, as she was an integral part of Clarkson's defensive lineup.

"I'm not going to play, Grandma. I just don't want to play anymore. I don't feel like playing," said Gracie in a dismal tone as she put her sandwich down on her plate and hung her head.

My mom nodded to her and then gave her an answer that set the tone for rest of the girls' lives. She said exactly what needed to be said.

"That's okay, Gracie. It's your choice, and you should do what you want to do. But let me ask you this. What do you think your grandfather would want you to do if he were here?"

Gracie picked up her head and thought for a moment about her decision. Then she nodded in agreement to her grandmother. Liz rubbed Gracie's back, and everybody seemed to feel better all of a sudden. My mom had let everyone know that now was not the time to hang our heads and hide. We all must carry on with our lives.

My mom then left the girls with one more thought. "Girls, you want to remember one thing. Your grandfather loved you more than anything. And I know you loved him. But he would want you to have a great life and do the best you could possibly do with the talent that you possess. Gracie, you give them hell out there on the rink. And Liz, you pummel them on the golf course. And remember your granddad will always be with you. He'll always be with all of us."

Al grabbed my hand underneath the table, and I smiled at her. And my brother put his arm around my sister's shoulder and pulled her close to him. Then I looked at my mom and winked at her, and we all ate our lunch as Sophie grabbed at our shoestrings under the table.

It was a packed house at Lynah, and Gracie was ready for the showdown. When they announced the teams' lineups, the usual jeers and boos were heard across the rink for the opposing team. As the two teams stood on their respective blue lines and faced each other, a special announcement came over the speaker. The Cornell coach had requested a moment of silence in honor of the passing of the grandfather of one of the Clarkson players. My dad had been a big supporter of Cornell hockey and Ithaca youth hockey for years and had also been a season ticket holder to the men's and women's Cornell hockey games. As they announced the player's and her grandfather's names, Gracie stared straight ahead and showed no emotion. At the end of the silence, she raised her stick to the crowd to show her appreciation of their support.

It wound up being the usual dogfight between the two teams, and Gracie played her heart out every minute she was on the ice. She was a big girl and demonstrated her toughness and strength every time she went into the corners to battle for the puck with one of the Cornell players. It was a scoreless game going into the final minute of play, and Gracie was on the ice.

Now, she certainly wasn't an offensive-minded player, but for whatever reason, she stepped up and picked off a pass at midice and headed toward the Cornell goal on a breakaway. As she crossed the blue line, a Cornell player lunged and tripped her to the ice, and the puck squirted away. A penalty shot was immediately signaled by the referee, much to the dismay of the Lynah faithful, and both teams cleared the ice, leaving just Gracie and the Cornell goalie to do battle.

Gracie stood alone at center ice and waited for the signal to start to the net. As the referee swung his arm down, Gracie sprinted with the puck toward the net. It happened so quickly, but after a slight head fake left and a quick move to the right, she slid the puck along the ice between the pads of the goaltender for the first and only goal of the night. She then pounded on the glass behind the net, and the entire Clarkson team came out to greet her and formed a huge celebration along the glass. After multiple pats on the helmet from all the other players, they all skated back to the bench.

And after the remaining seconds of the game ticked off the clock and the buzzer went off, the Clarkson players skated triumphantly to congratulate their goaltender with gloves and sticks waving, and then they made their way toward rink door. Gracie looked up to us in the stands and raised her glove and shook it firmly in our direction. I know deep down she was wishing that her grandfather were with us in the stands, but she knew he was there in spirit.

Gracie wound up getting the first star of the game and came out to a standing ovation from both the Cornell hockey team and all the fans in attendance. It was a classy move by the team and the fans, and one that she'll remember for the rest of her life. She raised her stick and moved in a circle, addressing the entire crowd, and then skated off the ice. A young girl of about five years old was standing at the gate with her mom clapping as Gracie walked by. Gracie patted her on the head and gave her stick to the little girl and then walked back into the locker room.

She came out of the locker room to do an interview with a local sports reporter and answered the usual postgame questions. The reporter, looking to draw some emotion out of Gracie and get more of a story, snuck in one final question to try to catch her off guard. "Wouldn't it have been great if your grandfather were here tonight?" she asked and quickly put the microphone back to Gracie.

"He was," Gracie replied, and then she walked back into the locker room with a smile on her face, much to the dismay of the reporter.

Unfortunately, that was the only game Clarkson would win, as Cornell won the next two and advanced to the next round. But still, it was a night for all of us to remember. Yes, it was definitely a defining moment for Gracie and special night for our family.

Springtime arrived and brought plenty of sunshine to Ithaca. It was now golf season, and we were down in Annapolis following Liz in a golf tournament hosted by the Navy team. This was a staple on the Siena Golf schedule and one of Liz's favorite golf events. She loved playing here and the course suited her very well, and they always had a super competitive and top-notch field. By the start of the final round, Liz found herself in the last grouping and tied for the lead with one of the Navy players. Liz had been wearing her grandfather's red plaid golf cap the whole weekend. She had worn this in her previous two tournaments, and it was now part of her golf attire during her Siena events.

Al and I watched as she stood on the first tee practicing her swing, and then she extended her hand to the Navy player.

"Nice hat. Where did you get it?" the player remarked in a sarcastic way.

Liz squeezed her hand hard and looked at her with stern and cutting eyes. "It's my grandfather's," she said strongly as she stepped away from the girl and placed a tee in the ground.

"Where is he?" the girl followed with a smirk.

"Right here," Liz said as she pointed to her heart. And then, after her name was announced, she pumped a long tee shot right down the middle of the fairway and came back to the girl.

"Your turn. Watch out for the water on the right side. And the rough is pretty deep on the left," she said, smiling, and then stepped to the side to let the girl hit. Needless to say, the girl drove one out of bounds on the right and had to hit again to place one in the fairway.

When all was said and done, Liz had won medalist honors to take first place, and with a commanding six-stroke win over the field. The girl who had started the day tied with her wound up shooting a ninety and didn't even make it in the top twenty-five players. Siena had a great showing and had three players in the top ten, so it was safe to say the coach was very pleased with his team. He would later come over to Al and me and laughingly tell us what Liz had remarked to him before the round started.

"I can't wait to kick the crap out of that Navy brat" was what Liz had told him.

Al and I laughed about it all the way home. We both knew where she got her rosy disposition and genteel attitude from and whom we could thank for it.

It had been two years since my dad passed, and it was a beautiful and bright and sunny summer day in Ithaca. Both the girls were home for the summer and had been spending a lot of time down at Newman playing golf. Liz was going into her senior year at Siena and had been named captain for the upcoming season. Mom had given Liz my dad's golf clubs, and she kept them displayed in the corner of her dorm room. They went quite well with the poster of Tiger and the framed picture of Jack Nicklaus. The red plaid golf cap from Royal Troon hung on her dresser mirror in her room at home, just above a picture that sat on her dresser, a framed photograph of Liz and her grandfather on the putting green at Newman.

Clarkson had made it to the ECAC finals but lost to Cornell once more, and Gracie swore to me that it would be different next year. Her coach had called a couple of days ago and let her know that she would be one of the three captains in the upcoming year. In addition, the coach let her know that the league had announced a new award recognizing the player who demonstrated leadership, courage, and sportsmanship in battling and overcoming personal adversity for the year in relation to loved ones suffering from cancer or life-threatening diseases. At the opening ceremonies of the first home game, Gracie would be the recipient of the first annual Ben MacNamara Memorial Award.

Gracie also displayed some items reminding her of my dad in her dorm room. She had the Bobby Clarke poster on her wall and the signed hockey stick just above it. In her room at home, she had the signed Clarkson jersey on her wall that she had given her grandpa. My mom thought it best for her to have it and felt that my dad would have wanted her to have it as well. On her dresser she had a Cornell hockey puck that was signed by the team and given to her the night they had a moment of silence for my dad. On top of the puck was her front tooth. She had gotten accustomed to not putting in the tooth and preferred to walk around with a gap in her smile. Her sister started calling her Bobby, in reference to Bobby Clarke.

The ironic thing is, she actually liked it and produced a huge smile when Liz addressed her with the new nickname.

It was Friday, and I was looking forward to getting home and spending some time with Allison and Sophie. They had just called and said they wanted to go for a walk and enjoy the rest of a perfect day. Al had been cancer free for almost two years and was doing great. She had also recently been promoted to dean of the Biophysical Engineering School, and the change had served her well.

Sophie had grown up to be a wonderful dog, and, just like Rosie, she loved her walks around Beebe Lake. Mom had agreed to stay with us on the weekends, but she still wanted to have her own home, so we took what we could get. The girls liked having her here on the weekends, and honestly, they wound up having dinner at their grandmother's at least twice a week anyway. I thought about my dad all the time and missed him every day. It's funny, but whenever I watched my girls playing sports, thoughts of him came into my mind. And with each golf shot Liz made or whenever I saw Gracie check someone during a game, I thought of my dad and smiled, knowing all too well that he was up in heaven and smiling down on his granddaughters.

It was just me and Maggie left in the office, as everyone else had taken half a day to enjoy the weather. I shut off my computer and made my way to the front and said good-bye to Maggie.

"Well, I'm off Maggie. Have a great weekend," I said as I smiled at her and pushed open the door.

"Good night, young man," she replied.

I stopped immediately in my tracks and turned to face her.

"It was you? You shot me the text that night? How did you know? And wasn't that a California phone number?" I asked, puzzled to find out it was my assistant who saved me from possibly making the worst decision of my life.

"Let's just say it was woman's intuition, Jack. I think I know Helen pretty well, and I knew you seemed to be in a vulnerable state of mind. I also knew that you had a great lady at home who loved you and a great family who needed you. I didn't want to see you do anything you would regret, either. I had a friend come in from Los Angeles and stay with me for a few days, and I borrowed her phone to send the text. I didn't want you to know it was me and didn't want to get involved in your personal affairs. But I didn't want you to make a big mistake, either."

"Thank you, Maggie," I said sincerely.

"Don't you know I always have your back by now, Jack?" she asked as she winked at me.

"Yes, I most definitely do. Have a good weekend, Maggie," I said and turned and walked out.

As I passed an old Subaru in the parking lot, I stopped and chuckled to myself as I read the worn bumper sticker on the fender. "Ithaca. Ten square miles surrounded by reality." It certainly feels that way at times, I thought. It certainly felt like the most special place in the world to my family.

I had made it a ritual to visit my Dad's gravesite every Friday after work, if I was in town, to pay my respects. So I left the office parking lot and made a right on Hanshaw Road and then another right on Pleasant Grove Road. I drove in through the iron gates of the cemetery and made my way to his site, which was situated in the far back right of the cemetery. Dad's gravesite sat directly under a forked pine tree, and the limbs actually hung over the tombstone. Mom had picked out the site for Dad, and she would later tell me the reason. Dad had always kidded her through the years that when he passed, he would like to have a "nice, shady spot" as his final resting place. So Mom thought it was an appropriate and serene place to lay her husband down to rest. She had also purchased the site right next to his so they could remain together for eternity.

I stopped the car and got out and walked over to his tombstone. I immediately smiled, as I could tell that Liz and Gracie had been there recently. There were fresh green-and-gold carnations on one side of his grave, and a single fresh red rose neatly lay on the other side. The girls would stop by every so often and deposit the carnations in honor of their granddad, representing their school colors. My mom, on the other hand, had told me that she had been stopping by every week since Dad passed to place a single red rose at his gravesite, representing the one and only love she had had in her whole life.

I didn't speak out loud this time but just said a silent prayer to him and told him I missed him. I stood there for a while and enjoyed the calmness of the cemetery. The only sounds I heard were a few small birds in the trees that outlined the plots to the right of Dad's grave. I then focused on Dad's tombstone again. Liz and Gracie had wanted to make the epitaph for Dad's stone, so I let them put the words together that would forever grace his final resting place. Once they finished what they wanted to put on the stone, they read the words to me as I sat in the living room one evening. I thought they were perfect: "A great teacher, a wonderful husband and father, and the best grandfather of all. Love, Liz and Gracie."

I always enjoyed reading that every time I visited my dad, and I could picture him smiling down at his granddaughters, full of love, when they came and visited him too.

As soon as I walked in through the back door, Sophie was sitting just inside with a leash in her mouth, waiting for me.

"She's been sitting there for fifteen minutes waiting for you," Allison said comically. She was standing over by the kitchen window, and the sun was shining on her hair.

I thought again of how lucky I was to have such a beautiful companion for life, and I went over to her and told her how wonderful she looked and kissed her.

"You really are and always have been a beautiful woman, Allison."

She smiled warmly at me and gave me another kiss. "How about taking your two ladies for a walk in the sunshine," she said as she grabbed my hand.

And so we set out down the block to our favorite destination.

As we walked down Thurston Avenue, Al and I reminisced about all the wonderful times we had had since we pulled into town close to eighteen years ago. We were so happy that the girls had grown so fond of Ithaca, and it made us feel good inside that we had chosen to relocate here. Every once in a while, I would hear someone make mention of how bad the winters were in Ithaca, and in upstate New York in general, and maybe they were right. Maybe you do have to be a little crazy to raise a family in a place that sees close to seventy inches of snow every winter.

But I also know that adversity builds character, and that's what stands out in Ithaca. Ithaca definitely has a lot of character, and I think that's why people stay and live here. Oh sure, we get cabin fever every once in a while, especially when the Cornell sports teams are on break and there are no games to see on the weekends, but I believe it's all about the attitude and perspective of the people who live here. They understand how great we really have it in this small town in the Finger Lakes. I've heard people mention that Paris is the most beautiful city in the rain. Well, I believe Ithaca is the most beautiful when it's wintertime and the snow has embraced our town and provided a backdrop that most artists can only imagine in their dreams.

But to most residents, it's a wonderful place to be in any season, and there's plenty to do here all year long. We found out very early that if you live in Ithaca, you had better learn to ski or skate. Our family hit the slopes and the ice rink shortly after we rolled into town, and we still enjoy both forms of exercise and entertainment. We ski and play hockey in the wintertime, and we swim and play golf and hike all summer long. Anytime I hear someone talking about how long and arduous the winters must be in Ithaca, I challenge him or her to find a more beautiful and picturesque place in the world for a family. Please show me another town that has the setting we enjoy every day in Ithaca. We have gorges, waterfalls, lakes, parks, and so much more right at our fingertips every time we step outside. Over the last few years, I've read a few articles that have labeled Ithaca as a perfect place to retire, due to the natural beauty and all the cultural activities at our fingertips, as well as the cost of living. I'm so glad we were able to find it out early enough in our lives and that we were able to raise a family here. You have to live here to appreciate all that the town has to offer its residents. You have to be an Ithacan to really understand how good we have it here.

As we walked across the street with Sophie in tow and headed down toward Beebe Lake, I reminded Allison of what she had said to me a few years ago. She told me that this was where we fell in love twice. We fell in love with each other at Cornell, and then we moved here and fell in love with the town. Our family fell in love with Ithaca.

The End

Made in the USA
Charleston, SC
13 March 2017